HAPPY
ARE
THE
OPPRESSED

ANDREW M.
GREELEY

JOVE BOOKS, NEW YORK

HAPPY ARE THE OPPRESSED

A Jove Book / published by arrangement with
the author

The Putnam Berkley World Wide Web site address is
http://www.berkley.com

ISBN: 0-515-11921-0

A JOVE BOOK®
Jove Books are published by The Berkley Publishing Group,
200 Madison Avenue, New York, New York 10016.
JOVE and the "J" design are trademarks
belonging to Jove Publications, Inc.

PRINTED IN THE UNITED STATES OF AMERICA

Fove quod est frigidum
Warm whatever may be cold
For John Costello, S. J.

The Cardin family is a creation of my imagination. So too is the Cardin House on Prairie Avenue and an article in *Chicago History* by Eileen Flynn about the family curse. My thanks to Marvin Rosner, M.D., and Dale Kauffman, M.D. In God's world—as opposed to my own fictional world— Northwestern Hospital does not have a special pavilion for treating hypothermia victims. Nor does it have a helicopter pad.

I learned much about Prairie Avenue from *Chicago Homes: Facts and Fables* by Jack Simmerling and Wayne Wolf. Mary Alice Molloy in the *Prairie Avenue Servants* told me much about the lives of both the masters and the servants on that avenue and set my fantasy to work in imagining Clare Marie Raftery. The staff of the Prairie Avenue House Museums, especially Michael Soet, the tour center manager, and Carole Merrill, the docent who guided me around, were very helpful to me in my efforts. Ms. Merrill found me out as soon as I walked into the Glessner Coach House on Eighteenth Street: "You're writing a novel about Prairie Avenue, aren't you, Father Greeley?" Margaret Daley, who also lives on Prairie Avenue now, told me what I was missing if I didn't visit it.

I'm grateful to all of them.

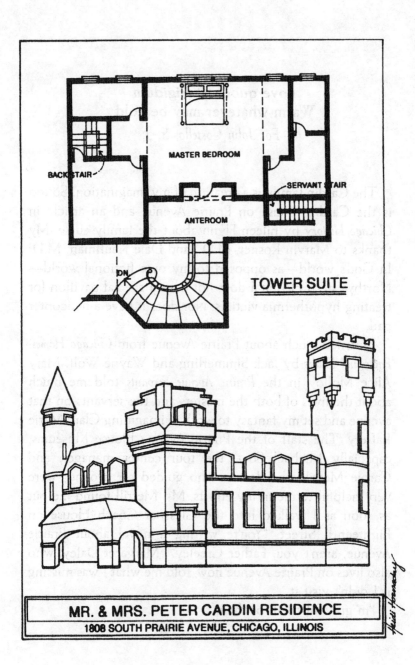

MR. & MRS. PETER CARDIN RESIDENCE
1808 SOUTH PRAIRIE AVENUE, CHICAGO, ILLINOIS

CHAPTER 1

"YOUR GRACE," THE handsome and wondrously underclad woman on my right said, "I'd like to make a general confession."

"Ah?"

"I am going to die."

"Indeed . . . might I ask what is the nature of your illness?"

"I am going to be murdered, Your Grace . . . before the end of the year."

I readjusted my pectoral cross (a silver St. Brigid cross made by my cousin Catherine Curran, the only one of its sort worn by any bishop in the Catholic world).

"Surely this fate can be avoided."

"It cannot be avoided. I wish only to die in God's favor."

Then, because it is my job as a priest to say such things even in the most unusual circumstances, I added, "You must remember, Ms. Cardin, that God loves each of us with a parent's tenderness and a lover's passion."

"I must confess all my sins so that God will not turn His back on me."

"Now?" I said with some dismay, losing for a moment the cool for which Bishop Blackie is (arguably unjustly) famous.

We were sitting at the speakers' table in the Grand Ballroom of the Drake Hotel, something less than an appropriate site for the outmoded Catholic practice of raking up all the alleged sins of one's life.

"Of course not," she said calmly and without a smile—she never smiled as far as I had observed. "I am asking for a recommendation of an appropriate priest. . . ."

"Surely among all the Jesuits here . . ."

"They are too lenient. I wish to prepare seriously for the end of my life. I need to hear no sermons about helping the poor."

Her voice was low and cool, utterly self-possessed. I shivered slightly. Despite her revealing white dress with its narrow belt of Christmas red and green around her slim waist—high skirt with a higher slit, low back, bare shoulders, plunging décolletage—the woman generated as much heat as a snowbank dumped on the side of the Kennedy Expressway by a plow of the Department of Streets and Sanitation. Her pale blue eyes were as cold as frozen lakes under icy skies. Her white skin radiated as much warmth as would a field of newly fallen snow.

"Ah . . . and the stern and strict clerics from the prelature of Corpus Christi?"

I was referring to priests from the Corpus Christi Movement, a "secular institute" that was to some considerable extent independent of the local bishop, even when said local bishop was as eminent as Sean Cardinal Cronin. The Corpus folks were considered to be somewhere to the right of Niall of the Nine Hostages.

She dismissed them with a brief movement of her ring-laden hand. "They are more interested in exact numbers of sins than the anguish of guilt and failure."

"So."

"I am going to die very soon, Your Grace," Chantal Cardin replied, ignoring my piety, ice in her carefully modulated voice, "a terrible and painful death. I deserve to die. I want to be certain that I'm at peace with God, despite my wretched life."

For the second time that evening I shivered and for the second time groped for words.

"It is a mistake, Ms. Cardin, to overestimate our sinfulness. Indeed, we are creatures and sinners. But at this time of the year we also remember that we are beloved children."

She turned toward me, frosty blue eyes pondering me, lovely breasts all too close. "Priests ought to be stern with their penitents."

"As Jesus was with the woman taken in adultery."

A flush rose from her chest to the roots of her

hair. A faint upward tug of her lips suggested the possibility of a smile.

"A point to you, Your Grace."

It is worth noting that the title "Your Grace" is not used in our sturdy republic, save in the Archdiocese of Cincinnati and only rarely there. "Your Excellency" has also gone out of fashion. "Bishop" usually does very well, thank you. Or in my case "Father Blackie." However, the Cardins were aristocracy and they lived by their own sense of appropriate manners.

As to my role as an auxiliary bishop, I assume the reader is not unfamiliar with the film *Pulp Fiction* and remembers the Harvey Keitel role. He was the "Sweeper," the skilled and dutiful operator who cleaned up messes for what we are pleased in Chicago to call "the boys out on the West Side" (with a quick nod in the general direction of Taylor Street).

An auxiliary bishop is a "Sweeper" for the local Ordinary, in this case the Eminent Lord Sean Cronin.

The woman in question was Chantal Reynolds Cardin (or, to be more precise, Jane Frances de Chantal Reynolds Cardin, to give the eighteenth-century saint after whom she was named full recognition), the wife of Peter Paul Cardin in whose honor the dinner guests had gathered. The Cardins had been patrons of the Jesuits since the memory of Chicagoans runneth not to the contrary. In recent years, however, the Jesuits had ventured to the left both locally and nationally and the Corpus Christi Movement had moved in on the family. The Cardins had not exactly become "supernumeraries" of the Movement, but they had made generous contributions to them and sought their spiritual advice and counsel. However, the family had also sustained its historic loyalty to the Jesuits. My Lord Cronin had suggested that the Grand Ballroom this evening would be the locale of a fierce tug-of-war for the souls and the checkbooks of the clan Cardin.

I was betting on the Jebs. The Movement had enjoyed enormous success with the wealthy and the super wealthy, but I doubted they were as good at the game as were the members of the Society of Jesus, who, when it comes to charm, are hard to beat. Moreover, they had played the game for a long time and knew how to pull back from being (or seeming to be) presumptuous. If one must raise money, and what religious group can escape that obligation, one should do it with class. Generally the Jesuits do.

Peter Paul Cardin V, Chantal's husband, was the guest of honor that night. He was to receive the "Sword of Loyola," a prize granted either for major achievement or substantial contributions to the University or, preferably, both. The Sword itself was a glittering ornament that would have been as useful in combat as one of the old Fourth Degree Knights of Columbus swords. But the symbolism and the double meaning that linked the Sword both to the University and to St. Ignatius of Loyola, who was a soldier before he founded the Society, had a certain poetic flair to it.

Corpus could never have figured out anything like that.

The Sword's phallic symbolism was generally ignored, save by Freudian psychiatrists like my virtuous sibling, Mary Kathleen Ryan Murphy, M.D., who was also present that evening, along with her long-suffering spouse, Joseph Murphy. I would seek her evaluation of Chantal (no one would dream of calling her "Jane," would they) at the end of the evening.

Before the wife of Peter Paul Cardin could continue her discussion of possible confessors, the rituals of the evening had begun. The master of ceremonies, the Dean of the medical school, introduced those of us at the head table, referring to me as "Bishop John Ryan," a name that I rarely use. He then thanked everyone who had participated in the planning of the dinner, the Cardin family for their graciousness in allowing Loyola to honor them, and virtually everyone in the Chicago province of the Society of Jesus.

Ridley Becker, the young and vigorous Provincial, who was sitting next to me, rolled his eyes. In a well-run Church, Ridley would be named a bishop the day after his term as Provincial ended. The intelligence and zeal of the hierarchy would rise substantially as the result of such a promotion. However, our Church, colorful as it may be, is something less than well run these days.

"Sorry, Blackie," he whispered to me.

"It's a living," I replied.

The Dean introduced the President of Loyola, whose job it was to introduce Peter Paul Cardin V and present him with the coveted Sword. The weapon in question could arguably be of some use in repelling heathen invaders—like Dominicans or Franciscans for example.

The President praised the generosity, dedication, and devotion of Peter Paul Cardin at great but not unmerited length. I noted that, next to his wife, to whom he had not spoken through the entire dinner, the back of his neck had turned red. So. He found the praise embarrassing. That should be counted to his merit.

The theme of the President's remarks was that the Cardin family had never forgotten its roots among the poor and the oppressed and that their generosity to the various Jesuit works among the poor and the oppressed was a tribute to the durability of that memory.

"They haven't been poor for a century and a quarter," Ridley whispered to me.

"They are generous nevertheless."

"That they are."

We Irish don't do aristocracy very well, perhaps because most of our aristocratic genes were eliminated from the gene pool by Oliver Cromwell and those who came before him and those who came after him. I am not precise enough. Rather I should say we don't do aristocracy very often. I am not speaking of the super rich like the Kennedys of Massachusetts who were in fact nothing more than wealthy shanty Irish. (The late Ms. John F. Kennedy was an aristocrat but she was not Irish.) Nor do I mean the affluent Irish like the Irish professional class that has enjoyed comfortable living for a couple of generations (as my own family has) and who would not choose to be aristocrats even if they knew how. I mean rather those few Irish-American families who have been prosperous for more than a century and have become so cultivated, so well mannered, so at ease with their wealth and power, that they don't even look Irish anymore. Such families were the Cardins of Chicago and the Reynolds of Philadelphia of whom Chantal Cardin was a descendant.

Members of such families live in a world all their own, cut off from the rest of us and indeed from the human condition. They buy their clothes in Paris or Milano, ride in chauffeur-driven cars, fly in their own Gulfstream G-3 to anywhere in the world, receive their secondary education in private boarding schools, date and marry their own kind. They tend to be courteous but distant with others, soft-spoken, generous to their favorite charities (college residence halls, medical center pavilions, homes for the retarded), intelligent, extremely private, ruthless in their business dealings, and devout Catholics of the most traditional variety—the kind of people for whom Cardinal Newman was the last great Catholic thinker. Their religious needs, save on solemn occasions as baptisms and marriages and funerals when the Cardinal was required, were ministered to by religious order priests, mostly Jesuits at one time and more recently, since the Jesuits have been radicalized, by numeraries of the Corpus Movement or odd-looking folk like those who appear on Mother Angelica's TV channel.

"It's a matter," Sean Cronin had said to me earlier in the evening, "of how far back our memories go. The first Peter Paul Cardin made his money selling rotten meat to the commandant of Camp Douglas, the place out on Cottage Grove Avenue where thousands of Confederate prisoners died during the Civil War. The second one was as skilled a manipulator as the Chicago Board of Trade ever knew."

"They have become more legitimate in this century?"

"Not necessarily. They've just acquired better manners. Mostly because of the women that marry into the family."

"What will Irish Catholic men ever do if they run out of Irish Catholic women to tell them how to act right."

"Small chance of that ever happening."

I was present at the awarding of the Sword not because I am suited to such affluent gatherings—much less an appropriate dinner companion for someone who was arguably the most beautiful woman in Chicago—but because My Lord Cronin insisted that I represent him. Chantal Cardin doubtless had planned to discuss her general confession

with Cardinal Sean Cronin, by the grace of God
and the remarkable patience and restraint of the
Apostolic See, Archbishop of Chicago. When the
Cardins interacted with the Archdiocese, they in-
variably went to the top. A poor auxiliary bishop in
their eyes ranked with a Jesuit novice. She must be
gravely concerned about the state of her immortal
soul to settle for the short, pudgy, nearsighted little
Bishop—something of a figure of fun in the city—
instead of the tall, handsome Cardinal.

"They're honoring the Cardins tonight," His
Lordship had said to me, as he sipped from a
Waterford tumbler containing my very best Bushmill's Green Label. "It is good of you to volunteer
to take my place."

"Ah?"

I had not volunteered to do anything. I never
volunteer.

"You know I can't stand any of them. They're
creeps."

"They are indeed reputed to be quite serious."

"All of that. Moreover, there's an aura of doom
about them. Something really wrong with them.
Something bad is going to happen there. I feel it in
my bones."

Sean Cronin rarely feels anything in his bones.
When he does, he wants no part of whatever gives
him that feeling. So he turns it over to me.

"Indeed?"

"They're too quiet, too good by half, Blackwood.
There's too much mystery about the old man's death

in that plane crash off the Bahamas, Count Cardin, as he liked to call himself. They all act as if they're covering up some terrible secret."

He had put down his tumbler, leaving some of the water of life still in it. Serious sin.

"But that was years ago."

"I didn't like it then and I still don't like it. You weren't around then, so I couldn't tell you to see to it."

He had stood up.

"There's something scary going on with them now, however," he had continued. "I saw the Countess the other day at a Catholic Charities event. She looked like she'd rode in on her broomstick. I don't like it one bit."

When the Cardinal felt something in his bones, he was rarely able to be specific about what it was he felt.

"Fascinating."

"I figured you'd think so. . . . See to them, Blackwood . . . and don't stare too obviously at Chantal's breasts tonight, marvelous as they are and half bare as they are sure to be."

"I'll endeavor to follow your restraint in such matters."

He had stormed from my room, wild gallowglass laughter trailing behind him.

The President of Loyola had finished his introduction. Peter Paul Cardin rose from his chair, without so much as a glance at his lovely wife, and walked briskly to the podium. He was a tall, broad-shouldered man in his middle forties. His iron-gray hair was combed back from a square, chiseled face, a retired linebacker in excellent physical condition, and, except for his diffident brown eyes, every inch the hard-charging merchant adventurer. Behind the podium, however, his confidence seemed to falter. He fiddled for his glasses, seemed to experience a hard time putting them on, unfolded the text of his remarks—a single page of paper—cleared his throat, and began to speak in a bland and uncertain voice.

"I want to thank Father for his kind remarks about our family. I accept this honor in the name of the family. Everything I am I owe to my family. Everything I may have done has been done because of my family. I hope our contributions are a help to other families, in this time of great crisis for so many American families. That our family has been so strong and happy is not the result of anything we have earned but is rather the result of God's grace. I pray that God's grace will help other American families. I hope that we can continue to do all in our power to sustain other families. I know that Loyola is a university with special concerns about family life. That's why I accept this honor with great gratitude and humility. Thank you very much."

He nodded slightly in response to the applause and, his fingers trembling as he removed his glasses, turned and walked back, briskly again, to his place between his wife and his mother.

He had not mentioned her. He did not look at her.

She did not look at him and had applauded perfunctorily at the end of the speech, her facial expression glacial as ever. His mother—a handsome woman with artificially silver hair—had, however, beamed happily and applauded loudly. He kissed her as he sat down but ignored his wife.

What the hell!

If my wife were so lovely . . . but then that's not a thought that a priest, much less a bishop, should ponder too long. A little bit of pondering, maybe, but no more.

Moreover, his speech had been an anticlimax. He certainly could have found a ghostwriter to put stirring words in his mouth. For some reason he must have deliberately chosen not to do so.

"Will you hear my general confession, Your Grace?" Chantal Cardin asked me as soon as the applause had died down. "Not here of course, but some other time and place?"

Why me, I wondered. But I said what every priest must say in such circumstances. "When?"

"Tomorrow afternoon?"

"Fine."

She obviously did not expect to die that night.

"I could come to the Cathedral Rectory . . ." she said hesitantly. "At four o'clock?"

"Fine," I said again.

"I hope it is not an imposition."

"I will be candid, Ms. Cardin. I don't especially believe in general confessions. I believe that our God is hopelessly in love with us and does not desire such minute examinations of our past sins as much as She requires our reflection on Her great love for us. You do not impose on me at all. But we must be clear that the two of us have rather different approaches to our faith."

"I understand," she said softly.

"Then, not to put too fine an edge on things, why me?"

Implicitly I was asking why, if she deemed her life such that only a bishop could cope with her sins, she did not seek out a more important bishop. Like Sean Cronin for example.

Head bowed, eyes averted, she answered promptly. "Because you are such a kind priest."

That seemed to settle that.

Thereupon she withdrew into herself and said nothing to me for the rest of the evening, a carefully carved and delectable statue of ice.

Chantal Reynolds Cardin wanted to make her final confession to a lowly auxiliary bishop who was South Side Irish, member of a tribe that would not be admitted into the Cardin residence in Forest Lake or their Gold Coast cooperative apartment, to say nothing of their condo in Santa Barbara or their flats in London or Paris or Rome.

Because he was a "kind priest."

Odd.

It did not escape my attention, fascinated as I was by Chantal Cardin, that the aforementioned tribal druid had acquired a generally unmerited reputation for solving on occasion certain small puzzles that had baffled both church and state in our city.

Something, as Holmes never said to Watson, was up.

Peter Cardin's wife was at that moment the picture of radiant not to say regal health, a woman who might very well have spent the afternoon at a spa, an exclusive and expensive spa at that. A little under medium height, she was a few years over forty (the mother of four children, including a surly and sultry teenage daughter who was present at this Jesuit festival—a taller and lusher version of her mother) but looked ten years younger. Her black hair was cut short in a halo around her slim, oval, and expressionless face. Her light blue eyes were as warm as the glow of an acetylene torch. Her thin lips, crimsoned with utmost care, gave no hint of what she was feeling but warned potential predators to stay away. Delicate makeup had banished whatever lines might be on her face, though these would have had their own appeal. Her only jewelry, besides a massive wedding ring studded with rubies, were a string of pearls around her neck and tiny sapphire earrings. Her trim, compact body, doubtless genetically endowed, had been carefully tended and exercised through the years and, as revealed in her daring dress, defied one to find fault.

She had invested careful work, planning, and self-discipline into her physical image. In my judgment of this matter (after all I was sitting next to her even if she did ignore my existence for the rest of the evening) none of this effort would have been required for her to merit her listing by *Chicago* magazine as one of the ten most beautiful matrons in the city. She was a natural beauty.

"Most women would not wear that thing even in their bedrooms," I heard a matron say who would not have made the list. "Even if they had a figure like hers."

"She sure does carry it off though," her companion replied. "As unaffected as a nun in the sanctuary in full habit."

Nice metaphor I thought.

When we were leaving the speakers' table after the interminable rituals and Chantal Cardin was kissing my ring (a practice I abhor), I said, "My mother, God be good to her—and She better or She'll hear about it—would be very upset with me, Ms. Cardin, if I did not compliment you on your lovely dress."

Again she flushed from her breasts to her hair roots. "Thank you very much, Your Grace."

"Some folks think she dresses that way to intimidate men, not attract them," Ridley Becker said to me as the dinner was breaking up. "Some of our guys say that beneath all the ice you will find more ice."

"Indeed!"

"I'm not so sure that they're right. She's got brains and an iron will. She works for us every day over at our Hispanic high school in Pilsen. She's the toughest one in the family. Probably the smartest.

Not that anyone knows what goes on among them."

"Ah . . . I note that the clan is together over there on the far side of the room, ready to receive anyone rude enough to approach them. Would you, ah, identify them for me?"

"Sure. On the far left, the redhead is Lisa, Peter and Chantal's second oldest child. Spoiled brat. Goes to the Pines, the Corpus high school. Feuding with her mother currently, as do all teenage daughters."

"Indeed."

"The next one is Patrick Reynolds, Chantal's brother. Came along with her from Philadelphia as part of the package I guess. Vice President of Cardin Holdings, brilliant and ruthless entrepreneur. Almost as obsessive about making money as Peter Cardin, though he has a hobby and Peter doesn't. Breeds and raises horses. Along with his wife, he is active in the Opera and the Symphony and the Historical Society and the Arts Institute, activities which bore and embarrass Peter Cardin. Pat Reynolds is an outside man as well as an inside man. He has brought the Holdings into airlines and hotels and is a master of the delicate art of derivatives on which the Holdings have made millions . . . you know what they are?"

"Financial instruments that are essentially hedges on interest rates. Often arcane combinations of speculations which apparently take no notice of chaos theory. A man named Souros lost a billion dollars on them, if I am to believe what I read. Procter and Gamble lost over a hundred million dollars. In the hands of unskilled chief financial officers they patently are dangerous."

"You got it. The blonde next to him is his wife Margaret and the redhead next to her is John Mark Cardin's wife Cordelia. Lovely woman but no one pays any attention to them when Chantal is around."

"Understandably."

"Then we come to John Mark Cardin, also known as Jack, allegedly the lightweight of the two sons. Has the odd notion that enough money is enough and the time has now come for the family to enjoy life. Rarely seen at the Holdings offices—which as you doubtless know are in a small suite of rooms in the 310 North Michigan Building. It is not even listed in the building directory."

"Closely held firm."

"You better believe it. The next woman is the matriarch, Regina Countess Cardin. Always call her that even if her late husband's title was only from the papal court. Tall and handsome and not looking her sixty-five years. Very devout, very proper, very moral, and not very bright. Disdains almost everyone who is not a member of her family. Doesn't even like her daughters-in-law."

"Especially Jane Frances Chantal whose fashion tastes she considers scandalous."

"Got it . . . Then there is the new Swordsman of Loyola, Peter Paul Cardin. The Fifth, I think. The most brilliant and merciless entrepreneur yet in a family which specializes in such men. He is supposed to have tripled the Holdings over what he inherited from his father, the largest increase in the history of the family. Not bad for a family which drove teams of horses during the Civil War."

"Indeed."

"He's bright," the good Jesuit continued. "But rigid, humorless, and dull. Obsessive about money. Not a miser; generous to all kinds of Catholic causes, but drives a hard bargain. Thinks about nothing else but the Holdings and their net worth. Possessive of his money, his family, his reputation, his privacy."

"And presumably his wife."

"Presumably . . . not interested in politics but has enormous clout. Can do just about anything he wants. No one dares to mess with him."

"Indeed," I murmured, thinking to myself that there might be some South Side Irish who would not be afraid of him. Or anyone else. Save Herself. Moreover his hands trembled when he read his paper. Perhaps not so ruthless after all.

"At the far end, you will recognize your lovely dinner partner. Lovely and cold."

"And perhaps a bit sinister . . . Standing a bit apart from the others. Does she always do that?"

"I haven't noticed."

"Indeed."

"They look like the House of Windsor posing for a family portrait, don't they?"

"Windsor-Mountbatten," I corrected him.

A tall blonde in his late teens with a radiant smile joined the line, shook hands with Peter Cardin, lifted Chantal Cardin off her feet, spun her in the air, placed her back on the floor, and kissed her cheek.

"And that?"

"That's Petey Cardin."

"Petey?"

"Peter Paul the Sixth. We saw him first, Blackie. No fair poaching."

Ridley thought he saw a future priest. Interesting . . . Ridley didn't miss much.

"Ah? But is he not the legitimate heir to the heritage?"

"Nah, he breaks the mold. . . . He was put in the family car at the age of fourteen and sent off to The Woods, you know, the Corpus High School for young men, at the insistence of the Countess."

"A deplorable fate."

"He told the driver to take him to Loyola Academy. Walked into our headmaster's office and asked if it was too late to register. Headmaster didn't know who he was, but liked the looks of him. It took the clan two weeks to find out what he had done. The Corpus people screamed bloody murder. The Countess had a snit. Petey wouldn't budge."

"Clearly he won."

"Class President, honor society. Point guard. Goes to John Carroll in Cleveland now. Late because of the snow, I guess."

I watched the most recent Peter Paul Cardin work the family line, with a smile and a joke for everyone and a hug for his sister whose smile, her first of the evening, suggested that she delighted in her big brother. I knew him well. The Irish still produce such people. He might have been a precinct captain or a saloon owner or a cop on the street or a funeral director or a parish priest or a criminal lawyer or even arguably a number of these combined. The Irish will produce this kind of man, possibly in as large a number as ever—the quick, witty, enormously attractive Mick who with a wink of an eye and a turn of the phrase could make every man in a room like him and every woman adore him.

Such charm did not necessarily imply virtue. The one who possessed it might be a bent cop or a crooked politician or a lazy priest or a corrupt lawyer. It did imply, however, the ability to attract people and perhaps change their lives, one way or another.

Oh, yes, this latest of the Peter Cardins was a young man who bore watching. He might drag the Cardin clan down to their final destruction. Or, arguably, he might save them.

Fascinating.

"Where you going, Blackie?" the good Ridley Becker asked me.

"Over to thank them as my hosts for the pleasant evening."

I left the good Jesuit frowning, as people often do when they try to figure out what I'm up to—in the mistaken assumption that I do not engage in some behavior for the pure hell of it.

When I do such things, my eldest sibling, Mary

Kathleen Ryan Murphy accuses me, somewhat vulgarly, of being a shit-kicker. I worked my way down their reception line, tolerating the ring kissing and the "your gracing" and the thanking me for coming. Only the Countess pointedly lamented that the Cardinal had been unable to make it.

"Hey, Bishop Blackie." The Petey shook my hand vigorously. "Great to see you. That was a bitchin' retreat you gave us at Loyola last year. Best I've ever made. Everyone thought so."

"Bitchin'," for those unacquainted with the way the natives talk, is high praise—for reasons that escape me.

"It is good of you to say so," I said modestly.

My siblings insist that I am good with teens because I have not truly left my own adolescence behind. I think it more likely that the reason is I was never an adolescent and thus have less folly to repress.

"Mom and Dad," the young man of unquestionable good taste continued, "this is the totally cool Bishop who gave our retreat last year. You remember me talking about him?"

I noted that he somehow managed to pull his mother and father together, one with each arm, so that they were close to one another, comfortably so at that.

"Glad to hear it, Bishop." His father shook hands with me again. "We need to teach our young people the old religious values."

"Perennial values," I said, "like compassion and loyalty and good cheer."

"Of course."

"Petey also said you were a very kind priest," Chantal added. "We need kind priests, more than stern or lenient priests."

So. That explained it. Arguably a very clever woman.

"What think you?" I asked my good sibling Dr. Murphy who, husband in tow, was waiting for me in the lobby. She was wearing a minimal red cocktail dress trimmed in lavish gold, an elegant and lovely sacrament of Christmas warmth for all who loved her.

"Epidemic depression, collective melancholy," she replied. "More colloquially, Punk, a bunch of unhappy creeps. They all could do with a good orgy. Except the kid. He's great."

"Punk" is an affectionate diminutive that my siblings and their children affect in my regard. As in "Uncle Punk!"

"My wife," said Joseph Murphy, M.D., with a twinkle in his eyes, "has a historic weakness for charming Micks with a twinkle in their eyes."

"Just because I married one . . . but if you're supposed to do something about that bunch"—she nodded her head toward the Cardins who were taking their leave in a solemn high procession—"tell your good friend Sean Cronin to forget it. It's a couple of generations too late."

"The woman?"

She didn't have to ask which one.

"Enough raw erotic energy to blow up the whole Drake Hotel. Buried under tundra, alas."

"Indeed."

It was not a judgment from which I could dissent. Sean Cronin had not sent me to the Sword of Loyola Ball merely because he did not feel like attending. Likely, for reasons of his own, he wanted me to do the impossible and salvage the Cardin clan.

As I walked back to the Cathedral Rectory from the Drake (which is part of my parish), the Chicago winter was delivering the second part of its famous one-two punch—first a half foot of snow and then a plunge into the low single-digit temperatures, aided and abetted by the standard northeast wind off the lake. I skidded down the Magnificent Mile, in the full splendor of the Chicago pre-Christmas glory: thousands of white lights on the trees stretching toward the river in the distance, red and green luminescence on top of the buildings, the walls of the canyon in which errant snowflakes swirled and danced. The Water Tower, small in comparison with the sides of the canyon, gleamed in its floodlights like an illuminated medieval outpost fortress. The various lights observed through my misty Coke-bottle glasses suggested that angels might be lurking everywhere—the only ones besides the Cathedral pastor to be outside on such a night.

The aforementioned cleric pondered the folly of the human condition—so much warmth of love available, even on cold nights, and so many people fleeing from it.

See to it, Blackwood.

CHAPTER 2

SEAN CARDINAL CRONIN was waiting for me in my study, in his fatigue dress of black slacks and a collarless white shirt—with French cuffs on which were emblazoned a symbol of three crowns, perhaps at this time of the year standing for the three wise men, Caspar, Baltassar, and McElroy (as I would routinely insist was the name of the last of the wise men). The Cardinal had removed the manuscript of my most recent work, *Tenebrae Liturgy in James Joyce's Finnegans Wake* from an easy chair and was thumbing through it as he sipped from a bottle of Sprite.

Rarely did he wait up for me.

I hung up my coat, a light raincoat that had provided little protection against the December cold.

"This poor bastard was a genius, wasn't he?" he asked, gesturing with the manuscript.

He looked for a place to put the precious document and ended up laying it on the floor.

"So it is argued."

25

He removed his granny glasses.

"Well?"

I continued to shiver. Next time I went outdoors I would have to ask someone to make sure that I was wearing the right coat.

"Collective melancholia. Epidemic depression."

"Like a family under a curse?"

"Arguably."

He lifted a sheaf of xeroxed pages from another vacant spot on the floor—there were few such.

"Consider this," he said, usurping one of my lines.

It was a copy of an article from a 1967 issue of *Chicago History*. The headline asked: A CURSED FAMILY AND A CURSED HOUSE?

"I'm going to bed, Blackwood," the Cardinal said, rising from his chair. "Read that. Seems that a member of the family dies violently every generation because of a curse that a dying Confederate officer cast upon the first Peter Paul."

"Indeed!"

"His wife died in their house on Prairie Avenue, back in the days when it was the Gold Coast. Cops thought he did it. Couldn't prove it. Locked room mystery."

"Fascinating!"

"I thought you'd think so," he said, his normally hooded eyes emerged with a delighted glow. "One minor point. The house was torn down sixty years ago."

"Even more fascinating!"

"A locked room mystery in a house which no longer exists and a crime a century old. Right down your alley!"

He grinned triumphantly.

"Whence came this article?"

He shrugged. "In the mail. Anonymously."

"Intriguing."

He paused at the door, his elegant right hand on the doorjamb, ruby ring of office glowing. "What about Chantal? Does she act like a woman under a curse?"

"Arguably."

"I was afraid so. Is she an innocent victim? One is always tempted to think that a woman with her kind of beauty is an innocent victim. But the hormones can be deceptive."

Can they ever!

"I think her innocence is not improbable."

"I thought as much. Anyway, I want no family curses in the Archdiocese of Chicago. I hope that is understood?"

"Naturally."

"See to it, Blackwood!"

Out he went, accompanied by his usual, manic warrior laugh.

So that's why he sent me in his place, I thought to myself. The feeling in his bones came from the article in *Chicago History*.

Fascinating.

Fixing myself a small sip of Bushmill's Single Malt to take the winter chill out of my bones, I began to read the article. One of my cardinal (you should excuse the expression) rules of the spiritual life is that night is for sleeping. I broke the rule that night. Something indeed was up and I didn't like the smell of it—the smell of greed and death. Oh, yes, something was up all right, something profoundly evil. As I read I continued to shiver but not just from the cold of Chicago's December.

As I began my second exploration of the article, I realized that a number of matters were already obvious. I turned various scenarios over in my mind. In fact, none of them was correct though one or two of them were close to being correct. My mistake, which would cause much suffering, was that I didn't realize how sinister the Cardin situation really was.

CHAPTER 3

A Cursed Family and a
Cursed House?

DID A DYING COLONEL CAUSE
DEATH IN A PRAIRIE AVENUE
MANSION?

A LOCKED ROOM MURDER IN
CARDIN HOUSE
by Eileen Flynn

The recent establishment of the Prairie Avenue Historic Preservation district came four decades too late for the most notorious of the mansions. Cardin House at 1808 South Prairie was torn down in 1925. It had been vacant for more than twenty years and had become an eyesore and, it was said, a threat to public safety. After the Cardins had abandoned it, no owner occupied it for more than a year because

29

of the legend of the Cardin family curse. Now its site is a vacant lot next to the memorial of the Fort Dearborn Massacre. The memory of the home and the curse seems to have been forgotten, though the Cardins are still very much part of Chicago life and the curse seems to be with them still.

Yet, at one time, Cardin House was deemed the most spectacular home in the four blocks from Sixteenth to Twenty-Second Street, which was the site of Chicago's first Gold Coast. The Cardin House was considered a more ornamental castle than the Kimball House across the street and a more durable mass of stone than even the Glessner at Eighteenth and Prairie. It was the one house on Prairie Avenue that tourists knew they must see even if they had no time to walk or ride down this most elegant of Chicago streets. It was the home that was designed, as its first owner said, to endure till the day of the Last Judgment.

While most of the homes of Prairie Avenue have long since fallen victim to the wrecking ball, you can still stand on an early summer evening at Eighteenth and Prairie—the social center of Chicago for a decade and a half— and look south and imagine its glories at their height in the early 1890s. Even today the illusion is helped by the trees and the lawns and the fences that still remain, hinting that one has crossed the border between the present and the past.

You can imagine that you are a European traveler come to see the wonders of the Chicago World's Columbian Exposition. On your right is the massive, stone Glessner House that reminds you of the Central Railroad Station and the Sixteenth Street Armory just to the north, the latter built to protect Prairie Avenue from the threat of workers' riots.

You know that Chicago's new rich live on this street, those whose climb to wealth began during the Civil War, a climb that the terrible fire two decades later only slightly affected. They are all self-made men—Armour, Swift, Kimball, Pullman, Keith, Marshall Field, Potter Palmer. They have made their money in vulgar work—meat-packing, land, dry goods, railroad sleeping cars—and have not yet managed to acquire the easy style of the rich and the noble in your own country. They are ostentatious and pompous. They parade their noisy mistresses proudly in the city's finest restaurants and ride with them down this very street. They hire more servants than they absolutely need: Pullman has seventeen, some of whose work is to polish endlessly the gold and wood surfaces of his great ballroom.

You expect little of this famous street even if you are told that such famous architects as Daniel Burnham and Henry H. Richardson have designed the homes. Yet as you look down the street, you gasp at its magnificence in the soft light of the setting sun. You have visited the most famous cities in the world and beheld some of the finest homes in the world. But never have you seen a sight quite like this. You are overwhelmed by the grandeur, the splendor, the outrageous variety of these majestic homes. As the lamplighter trudges down the street, turning on the gas lamps, you conclude that while the men who own these homes are vulgar, the architects who advised them were often geniuses. You shake your head in astonishment. Chicago might after all become a great city someday. Those who had no taste were at least shrewd enough to hire those who had.

In the twilight, elegant and burnished carriages and broughams and landaus slip down the street, driven by elaborately clad coachmen, often accompanied by footmen in matching livery, and pulled by superb horses. The women in these vehicles are clad in voluminous pastel summer dresses. They chatter brightly, despite the constraints of the tightest of corsets. The men, often bearded, are dressed in white trousers, blue blazers, and boater hats. Again the impression is one of grace and refinement. These people seem too polished, too discreet, to be mere parvenus. They have acquired the veneer of gentility quickly in-

deed. Again you shake your head in astonishment. You admit to yourself that you have
nowhere in the world seen a street like this.
There is a touch of golden magic about it.
Nothing in Paris or London or St. Petersburg
can possibly match it.

And the city has existed only for a couple of
decades.

You walk slowly south and come to the
Cardin House that is reputed to be the most
magnificent of all the homes. Just as the
Kimball House across the street is designed to
replicate a château from Normandy, this astonishing house reminds you of a late medieval
castle, though perhaps one designed to please
Ludwig II, the "Mad King" of Bavaria.

Pete Cardin, you have been told, is "different" than the others. His wealth is no more
dubious than that of any of his neighbors. No
one on this street earned their money by being
virtuous. But Pete Cardin is the only Irish
Catholic on the street, an immigrant who has
clawed his way to the top. His success is
offensive because of the firm belief on Prairie
Avenue that no Irish Catholic can possibly
become wealthy, especially one who like Pete
Cardin honors all the requirements of the
stereotype. Despite his wealth, he remains
a brawling, contentious—albeit charming—
drunk, though now one with a lot of money

and the most astonishing house you have ever seen.

Designed, you remember, by Solon Spencer Beman, who also had been an architect for the Kimball and Pullman, the thick, gray-stone house with its gables and turrets and balconies and battlements and its mansard roofs has been deliberately created to overawe all the other houses on the street. It has its own generator and is alleged to be the first house on the street illumined by electric lights. Rumor has it, your Chicago friends have told you, that Pete Cardin offered electric current to his neighbors but the offer was rejected because no one wanted to have any contact with this vulgar Irishman.

Moreover, he had constructed his own laundry, complete with steam boilers and steam drying racks, powered by an engine in a barn at the rear of the house. No scrub boards for this immigrant whose mother had washed family clothes by beating them against a rock on the side of a rushing Irish stream.

The man must love gadgets, you reflect, as you try to get a fix on the house. Finally you decide for all its superlative design and solid construction, it is a bit too much, a little larger than it should be, larger even than life.

Typical of an Irishman who has a few extra coins in his pocket.

No one is quite certain how much money Pete Cardin has. He is not as wealthy as

Palmer or Pullman or Field—the latter having spent seventy-five thousand dollars for a "Mikado" party for his two children. But he clearly has plenty of money from his packing and real estate and stock market investments and a flair for spending it that exceeds the most grandiose on the street. As you watch the house, you are fascinated by its fortresslike qualities. This Irishman is not about to let anyone take his wealth from him. Indeed, one hardly would need the armory on Sixteenth Street as long as the Cardin House stands.

A vulgar Irish drunk he may be, but he also has pretensions to cultural sophistication. Your friends say that he once paid Theodore Thomas and the entire Chicago Symphony Orchestra to play in his house. His wife, they said, managed to keep him sober the whole evening.

You shrug your shoulders and turn to continue down the street. As you do, an open carriage sweeps into the coach entrance to the Cardin House. In the fading light you catch a glimpse of three blond heads, a woman and two adolescent children.

And what a woman. Your brief view of her as the door of the carriage gate opens leads you to believe that she is the most beautiful woman you have ever seen—tall, willowy, graceful with an angel-like face, blond hair, and a figure that needs no corset to attain perfection. She seems to be too young to be the mother of the children, but they look so much like her they must be hers.

Then the carriage goes through the gate and you see her no more, but you will never forget her hair or her lovely, sad face. Never.

You decide that Pete Cardin is a very lucky man.

As you continue down the street you ponder the glories of Prairie Avenue—beauty, wealth, power, and incomparable women. You do not doubt that this glorious street will last a century at least and that Chicago is perhaps already a great city. The lights go on in the homes along the street, still a mixture of gas and electricity. What, you ask, must life be like for the people who live in these homes, men and women basking in the glow of great wealth for which nothing in their life has prepared them.

Now the scene changes. The time machine rolls back a little more than two decades and moves thirteen blocks south along the lakeshore. You are now a guard in the Union Army at Camp Douglas that has become a prisoner compound for Southern captives. You have been wounded in action at Shiloh and hate the guard duty at the camp. You have no love for the rebs as a group, but you feel sorry for their suffering. Cold, hungry, sick, defeated men, many of them lack the will to live. The camp commandant is not an evil or cruel man, but he knows nothing about sanitation or the prevention of disease. There have never been so many prisoners in a war before. No one wants the men to die, but if they won't give their parole—promise never to fight again in the war—you can't send them home. Thousands have already died, and unless the war ends, thousands more will die. Feeding the prisoners and collecting and disposing of their human wastes is too complex a problem for those responsible for the camp. Moreover, there are rumors of plots by Copperheads and Butternuts to break into the camp, free the prisoners, and burn the city to the ground. God knows that Chicago would go up quickly. Hence it is more important to guard the men than to feed them and keep them healthy.

Sutlers who supply the food to the camp and sell extra provisions to the prisoners with a little money sent by their families are growing rich off the men's misery. They contract with the commandant to provide a certain amount of food at a fixed cost. Their profit depends on how cheaply they can buy the food. Often they bring in spoiled vegetables and rotten meat that aggravate the dysentery that sweeps through the camp in repeated deadly waves.

The worst of the sutlers is a young Irishman named Pete Cardin, a giant, bearded barrel of a man whom even the guards hate. They call him "Red Pete." His meat is always so rotten you can smell the corruption as soon as his carts appear. You always search his wagons carefully and report to an officer if you find spoiled food. But he has bribed some of the officers and more often than not his wagons of death pass into the camp with official approval.

Today is the first day of the belated Chicago spring, a cold day in late April. But the snow has melted, the sun is shining brightly in a clear sky, and the lake is glowing placidly. You close your eyes because you do not want to see a great and good man die. Colonel Thomas Jefferson Pettigrew, the commander of a crack Tennessee outfit called "Pettigrew's Raiders," has pleaded that the guards take him out of the dirty, makeshift hospital and permit him to die under the spring sky. The commanding officer has approved his request, however reluctantly, because the Union guards admire Colonel Pettigrew almost as much as do the Confederate prisoners.

You think once again about how stupid this war is.

The Colonel is a young man, just turned thirty, yet his wasted body and shriveled face make him look three decades older. His once thick mane of black hair is now scraggly and white. His voice, as he thanks the men who have carried him to the parade ground, is like a death rattle. Yet he remains always the polite and courteous gentleman. Some of his own men, those few who can still walk, stand at attention on his left side. You and the other Union guards who have been assigned to supervise his death similarly stand at attention on his right. There are tears in the eyes on both sides.

At Shiloh you had shot a young rebel colonel in a fancy gray uniform between the eyes without a second thought. Now, on the parade ground of Camp Douglas, death seems different.

As the men watch the death agony of Colonel Pettigrew, Red Pete Cardin comes by, driving one of his wagons, the smell of which is stronger than that of the raw sewage flowing into the lake.

"So you're finally going to hell where you belong," he sneers. "One last fucking reb bastard!"

Colonel Pettigrew sits up on his pallet and jabs a bony finger at Cardin.

"I curse you," he croaks, "you vicious murdering bloodsucker! May death haunt you and your family for every generation! May it squeeze the blood out of your bodies and the love out of your life! May this curse lay upon your seed until as many of them have died as my men have died from your poisoned victuals. And may you all burn in hell forever!"

Red Pete roars with laughter.

"I'm not afraid of your f****g Protestant

curses!" he bellows. "They have no power over me!"

The Colonel tries to respond, gasps a deep, agonized breath, falls back on his pallet, sighs once, and dies.

Cardin pushes aside the Confederate prisoners and spits on the dead man's body. Two of the prisoners grab for him. He shakes them off and grins at the Union guards. You lift your musket to kill him. One of your friends restrains you. Cardin grins.

"May his curse come true," you shout.

Cardin just laughs.

The laugh seems to have protected him and his family till 1895. Since then Colonel Pettigrew's final words have haunted the Cardins.

Peter Paul Cardin was born on a farm near Clonakilty in West Cork about 1838—he himself was unclear about the exact day and year. Ten years later his family—two parents and six children—sailed from Kinsale to the United States to escape from the potato famine. He was the only member of the family to survive the cholera that killed most of the passengers on the ill-fated ship. Somehow— his stories often changed—he managed to travel from New York to Chicago where an uncle lived.

No more than twelve years old, he went to work at a packing house on the South Branch of the Chicago River. One way or another—

and again the stories changed often—he was running his own packing operation by 1860. In the next five years he made himself a wealthy man as a purveyor of meat to the Union Army. His enemies said that he carefully gauged how much rotten meat he could peddle to which clients. When he was caught after taking too big a risk, he bribed his way out of trouble.

It is not clear that he ever learned to read and write, though he was reputed to have a natural ear for music and to sing in a rich tenor voice, drunk or sober.

He lived in a common-law relationship with a sometime prostitute from Cork named Peggy McGurn. She died in the late 1860s, of cholera according to Cardin, though his enemies managed to get into one of the Chicago newspapers a rumor that he had disposed of her—or paid someone else to do so—because she was an inappropriate companion for a man who was now wealthy. As far as the records show, there were no children born to this union, though there were rumors of a son whom Cardin had disowned.

In 1870, he married Rose Lennon, the seventeen-year-old daughter of a Richard Lennon, an impoverished lawyer who had wasted his family's wealth at the gambling casinos that were emerging south of Chicago's business district. According to one of the legends that clings to Cardin's reputation, Lennon, in effect, sold his exquisite and refined daughter to Cardin in exchange for the money to pay off his debts. Later, when Lennon's back was up against the wall a second time, Cardin refused to come to his aid. Lennon quietly disappeared, perhaps killed and dumped into the Chicago River by the gamblers who held his notes.

Cardin and his new bride moved into an elegant new home in the West Division at Washington and Morgan. He became an active member of St. Patrick's parish at Adams and Des Plaines, acting as an usher at the ten o'clock Mass on Sunday morning. In 1871, the first of two children, Peter Junior, was born. Two years later a daughter, Rosina, was born.

Peter Cardin continued to make money, selling and buying meat-packing and ominibus companies and purchasing land just before it became valuable. He was accepted as a respectable and honorable gentleman by the West Side Irish Catholic community at St. Patrick's. The parish church still stands at the side of the Kennedy Expressway, just north of the circle interchange; its parishioners, however, have long since moved out and its schools are closed.

Memories of his past ruthlessness, his heavy drinking, and his Irish Catholic background made him an outcast in the Chicago business community—whose morals were not all that admirable.

Curiously enough, the marriage seems to have been successful, even happy, for twenty years. The refined and inexperienced teenager was apparently more than a match for the massive, heavy-drinking brute from West Cork. Despite what seems to have happened in 1895, he adored her. What she felt for him is less clear. Perhaps she made the best of what might have seemed a bad bargain.

The painting of her at the time of World's Columbian Exhibition and the photographic portrait of her a year before her death give no hint of anything but exuberant health and happiness. She seems more beautiful and more self-possessed than the timid child in the wedding picture. The tilt of her head and the gleam in her eyes suggest a woman who was very much in charge of her own life and that of her family.

In the accounts of life on Prairie Avenue in those days, often delicately candid about the romantic affairs of its denizens, most of whom were not at all discreet about their love affairs, there is never a word about adultery by Peter Cardin—though he is often mentioned in passing in other contexts. Nor in a time when the wives of such men were expected to enjoy poor health and to be described as "delicate" or "nervous" is there any hint that Rose Cardin was not a woman of vigorous constitution.

By 1880, Peter Cardin was one of the wealthiest men in Chicago. He had amassed several new fortunes in the construction boom after the Great Fire, which had missed his West Division home by less than a block. He must have decided that he would make a major step toward respectability by building the most impressive home in the new Prairie Avenue district. Not trusting the Pullmans and the Marshall Fields, the Philip Armours and the Potter Palmers to welcome him, he bought the land through an intermediary.

At the same time he also joined the First Regiment of the Illinois Militia (later the 131st Infantry of the Illinois National Guard) that was stationed at the Sixteenth Street Armory and was granted the rank of lieutenant colonel, a phenomenon that led the diary writers of the day to jokingly wonder how much the rank cost him. The anti-Irish *Tribune* printed a cartoon that showed the new Colonel firing carcasses of dead and rotting cattle at a crowd of rioting anarchists.

Cardin had not been able to shake his past.

There is no record of what the neighbors thought when they learned that, like it or not, they had Red Pete Cardin as a neighbor. Not being quite sure what they should do about this prospect, they decided to compromise: they would accept Rose Cardin, more or less, and at the same time pretend that Peter Cardin did not exist. There would be no invitations to the two Cardins for dinner parties, but the wives would invite Rose to "teas" for women and to serve on various boards, especially those associated with the Columbian Exposition. The records show that she was a woman with sensible and decisive suggestions—and not a little political skill.

The Cardins responded in kind. They had dinner parties for their Irish friends from St. Patrick's parish but issued no invitations to their neighbors. Only when they persuaded, doubtless with a huge contribution, Theodore Thomas and the Chicago Symphony to play in their house did they invite the neighbors. Only the Pullmans did not come. Potter Palmer had already moved to the lakeshore and begun the new Gold Coast.

The Marshall Fields and the W. W. Kimballs responded with invitations of their own. Satisfied that some sort of peace had been made, both sides returned to their previous ways.

At the concert Pete Cardin did not do what some of his neighbors expected him to do. He did not insist that the orchestra play Irish melodies so that he could sing to them. Quite the contrary, his behavior seemed to have been utterly respectable.

There is still no evidence that he could read or write. Most of the papers that remain from the house (those that are not sealed in the family archives) are in what is obviously a woman's hand. His signatures are crabbed and

awkward, a man spelling out letters that someone has taught him to produce—someone who
is probably standing over him to make sure
that he does it right.

It is reasonable, then, to assume that the
relationship between Peter and Rose Cardin
was stable and perhaps even happy for twenty-
five years. In 1895 when he was fifty-seven
(approximately) and she was forty-two, the quality of the relationship seems to have abruptly
changed.

On New Year's, the *Tribune*'s headline announced: CARDIN WIFE MURDERED. POLICE HOLD
HUSBAND.

The article reported that the "lovely" Mrs.
Peter Cardin had been found dead in her
bedroom late the previous evening, her head
smashed by a "blunt instrument." Her husband, "Colonel" Peter Cardin, had been taken
into custody by the police and charges were
expected soon. Both Cardin children, Peter
Junior and Rosina, had told police that their
father and mother had engaged in bitter arguments recently and that they had heard the
Colonel make threats against their mother.
They thought their father had lost his mind and
had killed their mother in an outburst of rage
based on some event in the distant past.
Servants confirmed the terrible arguments.

The *Tribune* lamented the death of such a
generous and gracious woman and expressed

its sympathy to the bereft children. It also hoped that the killer would be brought to speedy justice and end up at the end of a hangman's noose.

But the next day the picture changed completely: CARDIN FREE ON ALIBI; SEARCH FOR WEAPON CONTINUES.

The *Trib* grudgingly conceded that the Colonel had spent most of the evening of his wife's death and much of the following morning at a notorious "den" on South Clark Street in the sight of scores of "denizens" of that unseemly place and that indeed the police had found him there completely intoxicated when they were searching for him the morning after the killing. Captain John O'Shea of the Chicago police said that it was impossible for the Colonel to have been the killer.

The "den" was, in fact, Pat McCarthy's saloon, a hangout for Irish immigrants to which the Colonel repaired on many occasions to drink himself into oblivion. He had told many of those present that he had had another terrible argument with his wife and would have to make peace with her the next day.

The *Tribune* ironically commented that he was never given that opportunity.

Moreover, the murder had taken place in the Cardin bedroom to which there were only two keys. One of them was in the Colonel's pocket the next morning. The other was on the table next to the bed. The last one to see poor Mrs. Cardin alive was her daughter Rosina who had spoken to her from the door of the room after the time when witnesses had reported that the Colonel had entered Pat McCarthy's "den." Indeed, Mrs. Cardin had told Rosina that her husband had left from his dressing room for another one of his drinking sprees. She had added that she had locked the door from his dressing room and left the key in it, so he could not come back in at a later hour. When Rosina had left the bedroom, she heard her mother lock the door that led to the rest of the house.

A crude drawing illustrated the layout of the tower in which the master bedroom of Rose and Peter Cardin was located at the head of a spiral staircase to the lower floors. The bedroom was large with dressing rooms on either side and bathrooms adjoining each dressing room, a most unusual convenience for husbands and wives in those days. A much more typical arrangement was the stairway from Peter Cardin's bedroom to the street level enabling him to leave the tower and indeed the house itself without his wife being aware of his departure. No such egress was furnished to the wife.

The next day the *Tribune* reported the story of Colonel Pettigrew's curse, the first time that event had appeared in the press, and darkly hinted that the curse had taken from Peter Cardin his loyal and faithful wife.

The murder weapon was never found.

Peter Cardin died on July 4, 1896, of a heart attack at the family's summer camp at Geneva Lake. After the police released him, he never returned to live in the house on Prairie Avenue. Apparently he was never reconciled with his children, though they both were mourners at the funeral at St. John's Church in Chicago. They continued to live in the house on Prairie Avenue till the time of their marriages.

In 1887 Peter Cardin Junior married Elizabeth Anne Riordan, the daughter of wealthy parents in San Francisco. The newly married couple moved to the new Gold Coast on Lake Shore Drive and Rosina lived with them till her marriage in 1900 to Terrence O'Mahoney of Chicago. Peter Cardin III was born the same year. His mother and father and aunt died in the influenza epidemic of 1918. Terry O'Mahoney acted as trustee of the Cardin Holdings till Peter III came into his majority in 1923. The young man had graduated from Notre Dame and like his grandfather had enlisted in the National Guard. He too rose to the rank of colonel and was killed in action at Bastogne in December of 1944. Peter IV, the current head of the family, was born in 1925. After the Second World War he married Regina Hoban, an heiress from Minneapolis. Peter V was born in 1951.

The Cardins continued to make money dur-

ing the more than half century after Red Pete's
death though their Holdings are private and the
sources and the size of their income is known
only to the Internal Revenue Service. They
also refuse to discuss Peter I or the circumstances around his death—and have brought
pressure on the Historical Society to prevent
the publication of this article.

It is evident, however, that Colonel Pettigrew's curse has worked in every generation
since 1895. Someone has always died young.
In several generations many of the family have
died young.

The accompanying sketch, based on original
architectural plans, illustrates the puzzle of
Rose Cardin's murder. There were two staircases leading to their luxurious tower rooms,
one from the lower floor of the house to a
small anteroom to the master bedroom, the
other from the ground level to Peter Cardin's
dressing room. Both were locked from the
inside, with Rose Cardin's key in the lock to
prevent her drunken husband from returning.
He had a key with which he could have entered
from the lower floors of the house if he had
staggered into the house and did not rouse
anyone as he climbed up to the fourth floor.
However, there were scores of witnesses who
were prepared to swear that he had never left
Pat McCarthy's after he had entered that "den"
the night of the murder—long before Rosina
had spoken to her mother for the last time.

Might there have been secret passages and rooms in the vast Gothic castle? The plans show no such places, but they might have been purposely left out.

There seems little reason to doubt that Peter Cardin killed the wife whom he may have adored for many years of their marriage. But how he managed to do so is and will probably remain forever a mystery.

Prairie Avenue did not long survive its most colorful owner. The younger Cardins moved to the new Gold Coast about the same time others were leaving. Encroaching railroad yards, factories, and Negro immigrants were threatening its tranquillity. Moreover the red-light district was expanding to the south from the railroad stations and the hotels at the south end of what was now the Loop. The notorious "Lords of the Levee," Alderman "Bathhouse John" Couglin and his sidekick Alderman "Hinky-Dink" Kenna with their favorite madams, the equally notorious Everleigh sisters, helped strike the final blow to Prairie Avenue, a street on which none of them probably ever walked.

One suspects, however, that the "Bath" and the "Hink" would have understood Peter Cardin and perhaps vice versa.[1]

---

[1] Eileen Flynn is a graduate student in the history department of the University of Chicago.

CHAPTER 4

THE NEXT MORNING, scenarios spinning in my head, I faced the fierce north wind howling down Michigan Avenue and trudged to Oak Street and the Reilly Gallery where I proposed to take counsel with Superintendent Michael Vincent Casey, a.k.a., in our family, Mike the Cop (though in fact there is no other Mike Casey from whom the former head of the Chicago police is made distinctive by his title).

The snow-laden clouds had swept through the city and were now rushing across Michigan toward Detroit and New York that would be soon blessed with their very own white Christmas. The second of the standard one-two punch of Chicago winters was still upon us: a north wind roaring down over the ice dunes at the edge of the lake and striving to dismember my shivering parish—and its poor pastor in the process. Just to rub it in, the sky was the same crystal blue above Oak Street Beach as in the height of summer.

I could think of scores of ways that one could account for the death of Rose Lennon Cardin,

whether by her husband or by someone else. It
seemed to me that there was no great mystery about
how the murderer had done his horrific deed. The
Chicago cops of those days must not have wanted to
solve the mystery. Nor was the literate writer of the
article in *Chicago History* willing to spoil her story.

Maybe, however, I was missing something.

And why had someone mailed the article to Sean
Cronin? Other than to involve his lowly auxiliary
bishop?

The beautiful woman's face from the article
haunted me. It was Petey's face. Was he to be a
grace to the family just as she had been (in my
judgment) for so many years? Was he to pay with
his life for being graceful?

Romantic that I am (like all the other Ryans), I
was prepared to believe that although the first Peter
Cardin had in effect bought his seventeen-year-old
bride, they had come to love one another. The
privacy and the luxury of their tower suite suggested frequent and joyous sexual activity, behavior
of which the species was aware before 1960, though
men and women who came of age since then think
they invented sexual pleasure.

Nor could I imagine such a suite being designed
without Rose's agreement. She did not seem to be
the sort who would have permitted a single detail of
the house to escape her notice. Arguably she had
designed the suite herself.

The line between passionate love and murderous

rage is often thin. So perhaps he had killed her. But I wasn't ready to decide that yet.

And what did all of this have to do with the poor woman, surely no surrogate for Rose Lennon, whose "general" confession I was to hear that afternoon?

I had no reason to believe that there was any connection at all. Yet, while I didn't believe in curses, there might be a connection. No harm would be done to anyone if I tried to sort out the mystery that was now a hundred years old. Had the house been torn down seventy years ago? Is that an insurmountable obstacle to Blackie Ryan? Or a challenge?

Arguably both.

Why would anyone challenge the aforementioned Sweeper to Milord Cronin to a duel of wits?

There were ideas teasing the edges of my mind that seemed promising—and dangerous—though I could not quite get at them.

I turned down Oak Street and found shelter from the wind if not from the zero temperature. I was forced to tug at the door of the Reilly Gallery to gain admittance, as it was half frozen.

"Not many customers today," I observed to the proprietor of the now elegant, though once haunted, gallery.

"Blackie," Annie Reilly protested, "how dare you come out on a frigid day like this without a hat? Don't you know you'll catch your death of cold?"

Knowing how useless it is to respond to this

question, so beloved to all mothers, particularly of Celtic background, with medical truth, I nonetheless replied, "Colds result from infections by opportunistic viruses and not my uncovered pates."

"A lot you know about it," she answered smugly— as all Irish mothers routinely do when challenged by something as insubstantial as fact. "And you don't have your scarf tied properly. It won't keep you warm hanging over your shoulders that way. And when was the last time you had it cleaned? Why aren't you wearing gloves?"

The reader will perceive that these are rhetorical questions that do not require and indeed do not admit of answers.

Annie thereupon hugged me. I confess that I was partially healed from the December cold.

"An extra ration of your chocolate chip cookies might warm me up," I suggested. "One needs more energy on days like this."

Usually on my visits to the Reilly Gallery I am allotted two medium-size chocolate chip cookies to accompany my pot of raspberry kiwi herbal tea (which this year had replaced the more traditional apple cinnamon tea). The limits to my permitted consumption of cookies were based on the utterly mistaken assumption that I would put on weight if I ate too much chocolate.

"I'll see," she promised with little conviction. "Now that you're over fifty, you can never tell what will happen."

On the most recent September seventeenth, I had

entered the golden years, a fact that family and friends and clerical colleagues proclaimed on every possible occasion.

"Arguably."

Annie was still clinging to me, doubtless in the mistaken conviction that I had saved her life and sanity once in this very gallery. One takes womanly adoration, however, wherever one can find it.

"Himself is in his studio. Wait till you see what he's working on. It's the best yet. Really, Blackie, it is."

When Mike Casey had retired from the police force, he had done four things—in the order of importance:

1)He had won to his marriage bed his childhood true love, the aforementioned Annie Reilly.

2) He had taken to producing impressionist paintings of Chicago, each one of which now often commanded fees several times larger than his salary as Superintendent of Police.

3) He had organized his own private security force, appropriately if uncreatively known as Reliable Security, made up of the best of off-duty and retired cops (of both genders).

4) He had been enrolled, without his consent, into a loosely organized group of allies and advisers, whom I called with intent of a literary allusion the North Wabash Avenue Irregulars. (732 North Wabash being the address of the Cathedral of the Holy Name.)

The work in question, I discovered in Mike's

studio, may well have merited his wife's fulsome praise. I sighed in approval.

"Like it, Blackie?" he asked with a broad grin, knowing full that I would.

Mike looked like a silver-haired Basil Rathbone playing Sherlock Holmes.

"It does show some merit," I admitted. "The Loop from the new Roosevelt Road Bridge."

It was a winter scene, of mural proportions, on a gray day like yesterday with snow lurking in the clouds and a touch of sunlight illuminating the Loop and its south foothills in delicate pastel colors.

"It's harder for me to be impressionistic these days," he said. "The city seems to be imitating my paintings."

"Arguably."

Both Mike the Cop and his wife glowed with satisfaction, leading me to believe that since they had hardly ventured into the cold, they had recently indulged in lovemaking, a virtuous habit to which they are addicted.

"Sit down," Mike invited me, gesturing with the brush he was cleaning. "I got your E-mail this morning about the Cardins and dug up whatever I could. Handy thing E-mail."

"Indeed."

All the North Wabash Avenue Irregulars are now on-line.

"An interesting bunch," he said. "Not quite our kind of Mick."

There is some discussion about the exact nature

of Mike the Cop's relationship with me. Those who
would wrongly compare me with G. K. Chester-
ton's Father Brown claim that he is my M. Flam-
beau. Annie denies this vigorously, contending that
I am rather Mike's Dr. Watson. While there may be
some truth in both comparisons, the reality far
escapes them. Mike the Cop is simply Mike the
Cop. Let literary characters look to their own
laurels.

His good wife appeared with the tea and a plate
of oatmeal raisin cookies for me. Another advantage of E-mail in that the tea would be ready upon
my arrival.

"Oatmeal raisin are better for you than chocolate
chip," she assured me.

Perhaps so, but I was not about to debate the
matter.

The three of us sat at a table beneath the
Roosevelt Road Bridge.

"They're very private people," Mike began, shuf-
fling through a stack of notes and faxes. "The goal
of their lives for almost a century has been preserv-
ing the family 'holdings' as they call their wealth.
That means keeping the 'holdings' at the same level
of real value, net of inflation, and adding modestly
to them by cautious and conservative investments.
They do not seek to control or manage companies
and are anything but your modern corporate raider
type. They have a small staff of accountants and
lawyers down at 310 North Michigan. According to

one of my sources, they are quick to cut their losses and even quicker to cut their gains."

"More interested in money than in power?"

"And not all that given to pleasure either. There is hardly a whiff of scandal attached to their names for a couple of generations."

"Sounds like a dull life," Annie observed.

"They don't seem to have much fun," her husband agreed.

"How much money do they have?" I asked.

"That's a big secret. They know and the Feds know, but no one else. They're not big-time players like Kerk Kerkorian of Warren Buffet, though they probably could have been often in the past and still could be today. Celebrity is not high on their agenda. . . . Anyway, Blackie, to answer your question, my sources say no less than a billion and probably no more than two billion, though the upper figure is less certain."

"Indeed!"

"Given the size of the wealth at their disposal, they lead relatively modest lives. No big parties, no contacts with the elite in Hollywood or New York. When they go to their apartments in London or Paris, they are as private as they are here."

"And the Feds leave them alone?"

"Of course not. They're too tempting a target for the Service to overlook. So agents are on them every year. For the last couple of years, the Feds have people in their office every day going over books and punching numbers into calculators. So far they have come up with nothing. There was talk that Peter IV was going to be indicted just before his plane crashed back in '85. Something about wrongfully claimed capital gains. The U.S. Attorney had some dubious theory about money made on a string of malls in Canada. There were rumors that the Justice Department was not enthused about the can of worms involved. They didn't want to scare the Republican big guys who were claiming the same kind of exemptions and deductions. Moreover, the people in D.C. thought the local man's theory was pretty weak."

"Anything suspicious about the plane crash?"

"It was the family Gulfstream. He was going somewhere on Christmas Day, allegedly to check on irregularities in a resort in the Bahamas of which they owned an interest."

"Alone?"

"With a lawyer and an accountant. All of them were killed. The plane crashed in the ocean on a remote approach to the airport at Nassau."

"Bodies found?"

"I knew you'd ask. The answer is no."

"Casino?"

"Sure."

"Connected?"

"I suppose so."

"Indeed."

"They rarely own a controlling interest in anything. They're more interested in the profits of a venture than in what it actually does. As long as they weren't responsible for managing a casino, they didn't care how it made its money or who was paid off. There must have been something going on which could have tainted their reputation. No one knows what."

"The Outfit go after them?"

"As far as I can figure out, not overtly. Our friends on the West Side and their allies around the country are pretty cautious people these days. Presumably the Cardins steer clear of them too."

I paused to ponder the information that Mike had so quickly compiled.

"They nonetheless invested in a casino. Surely they realized what lurked behind such places?"

Mike sighed. "The funny thing, Blackie, is that the various Peter P. Cardins—after the first one—seemed to have little taste for their work. They presided over the holdings because it was their duty. But ever since the founder from West Cork, they seemed to have needed someone at their right hand to goad them into the occasional risk that was necessary to stay ahead of the game. They have usually been dull, plodding men, obsessed with their family and their family's wealth. Well, Peter Junior was one of the great Board of Trade barons at the turn of the century, but he learned the trade from a drinking buddy of his father's named John O'Donovan. Story is that he had planned to be a priest until his father died. Turned the holdings into a family vocation in honor of his father. It's the myth they've lived by ever since. When he died from the Spanish Flu, Terry O'Mahoney, his brother-in-law, presided over the holdings in the name of the family, a kind of Cardinal Richelieu of the money game. Terry is supposed to have said when he died that not even someone as dumb as Peter III could ruin the holdings."

"Fascinating!"

"Yeah . . . Peter IV, who took over when he came home from a cushy desk job in England after the war, had the red hair of his great-grandfather and something of the buccaneer spirit. Maybe not the brains, however. He put a lot of money into suburban developments."

I noted with some dismay that the last of the oatmeal raisin cookies had vanished. I lifted up the plate to see if they had been hidden somewhere. Annie produced another plate somewhere out of the blue and poured me another cup of the delectable raspberry kiwi tea.

"Was not that a very wise strategy in the late 1940s and early 1950s?"

"He seemed to pick the losers—developments that were either too expensive or too far away from transportation. Then he signed on a young accountant named Steve Quaid, a taxi driver's son who went to school on the G.I. Bill. Quaid apparently played the Terry O'Mahoney role, but with a bit more willingness to run a risk. Hence the string of hotels with casinos."

"A chain of casinos!"

"Yeah. Story was that maybe Quaid was not above

taking something on his own now and then. . . . Anyway, Pat Reynolds, the current brother-in-law, is the grand vizier in this generation. An absolutely brilliant operator, I'm told. People tell me that Peter VI, though he's still in college, has made it clear he is not going to keep the tradition alive."

"Ah?"

"So until now"—he pulled out a page of his own notes—"the holdings have been sustained by a shadow behind the throne and wives carefully chosen from Irish aristocracy down on their luck, matriarchs who keep alive the family myth."

"So. The various Peter Pauls are hollow men, prisoners, as it were, of shrewd businessmen and domineering women?"

"That's what it looks like," Mike said, stacking up his notes. "Handsome, empty men . . . well, the present guy may be better than the rest. They say he is more active than his father, doesn't spend all the day in his office pouring over accounting sheets. Nice man too. We did some security for him once, and I couldn't help but like the guy. I heard he'd like to buy the Chicago Bears from the McCaskey family lest they move the team out of town."

A redeeming grace!

"Remarkable."

"You know the present matriarch?"

"The Countess, as I believe she is called?"

"He lives in mortal fear of her. Might live a very different life if she wasn't on him all the time."

"A real bitch," Annie agreed, using language that rarely passes the lips of a woman who was a sodality prefect in high school. "Arrogant and dumb. But in control, absolutely in control. Under the power of those Corpus Christi priests. Big fight when her grandson decided to go to Loyola instead of their school."

"If I am correctly informed, the young man won."

"I hear that his father stood up to her, egged on by his own wife."

"The next matriarch?"

"Chantal Cardin?" Annie hesitated. "I don't know, Blackie. She's unreadable, not that anyone sees much of her. Really beautiful. Something of an iceberg, however."

"When we were doing the security—there were threats she would be kidnapped—she seemed to be a nice woman," Mike continued. "Tense but with more class than anyone in the family. You've met her?"

"Oh, yes."

"I like her, Blackie," Annie said in the tone of voice that one of her kind uses when issuing a definitive opinion of approximately equal merit as an infallible declaration by the Pope. "And I feel very sorry for her. Are you going to take care of her?"

"That remains to be seen," I said guardedly.

"She needs help."

"Arguably . . . now about the brother and brother-in-law?"

"Regina presided over the decision to keep the Reynolds family out of the slums." Mike picked up another sheet of paper. "It looked like they were getting a two-player purchase for their money. Chantal to bring class and intelligence to the family and Pat to be the greatest grand vizier yet. He and Peter are apparently quite a team. They have made a lot of money, more than any other team since the old man himself. Hard to sort them out, to figure out what each of them contributes. The talk is that they're going to move into the communications field in a big way. Get involved in the big media mergers going on. They have certain stock investments scattered around, though not enough to be big players yet."

"Interesting."

"Pat is a charmer too. Has Regina under his thumb. His wife, Margaret, is equally charming. . . ."

"Flirt," Annie insisted. "At least Chantal isn't that despite the clothes she wears . . . you see her in evening dress, Blackie?"

"Oh, yes."

"What did you think?" She leaned forward, eager for a clerical opinion on the subject of Chantal Cardin.

"I quote my sibling, Mary Kathleen: enough erotic energy to melt all the ice on Lake Michigan."

"Interesting." Annie sat back to ponder the verdict of her good friend. "Do you think she dresses to please men or to offend women."

"To please herself," I said firmly.

"Is that good?"

"Oh, yes."

"The Reynoldses," Mike continued, "are a little less private than either of the Cardin brothers and their wives. Have contacts and a few friends in the world beyond the family. Show up in Vegas and Monte Carlo on the odd occasion. Feds have been watching him closely, but they don't have anything on him yet. The current U.S. Attorney thinks Reynolds is the one who will stumble and then the Feds can pull down the whole Cardin empire."

"Destroy someone or something or preferably both: the way a hardworking U.S. Attorney can get himself elected to public office . . . are they also watching, ah, John Mark Cardin and his Cordelia?"

Another pot of tea appeared, this one smelling of orange mango. And yet a third plate of cookies.

"You will spoil your lunch," Annie said severely.

"Not hardly."

"Sure, the Feds are watching them. When they watch a family enterprise they keep an eye on everyone. If I know how they work, they figure that since John is kind of the playboy of the family, he might be the weakest one, the first to crack when they lean on him, the kind of guy who might betray the whole enterprise to avoid jail. He couldn't care less about the holdings and the two of them love the good life. But they're enough afraid of Regina to avoid scandal which might cost them the good life."

"Works for the holdings?"

"They all do. He spends some time at the office each day, I suppose, and then is off to the golf course or the tennis club. Collects his check whenever it's paid. The family could never accept the scandal of cutting him loose."

"Hmm . . ." I said, wondering what good all this useful and concise information would do when I faced the mysterious and delectable Chantal this afternoon.

"And Chantal?" I asked.

Mike the Cop threw up his hands. "Impenetrable! I agree with Mary Kate's description. No one has a fix on her. The Feds are reluctant to mess with her."

"Uhmm."

"You have to help her, Blackie," Annie insisted with the full fury of a woman who sympathizes with another woman. "I'm sure she needs help."

"Perhaps."

Perhaps she had already asked for it.

"You're not afraid of all that erotic energy, are you?"

Not hardly.

I fixed her with my most steely stare that, I fear, has all the consistency of a burnt marshmallow.

"Woman, how could you of all people ask that!"

She and her husband both laughed happily and I was favored with another hug.

Nonetheless, they took my point.

As I returned to the Cathedral, my scarf properly tied to protect me from any viruses that were mad enough to be riding on the north wind, I pondered the various mysteries in the sad history of the Cardin family.

They were a monumentally dysfunctional family. Probably had been since the death of Rose Cardin, if not since the death of Red Pete Cardin's parents on the trip to America. They were bound together by the obligation to protect a family heritage based on wealth—wealth that seems never to have brought anyone happiness. A clever outsider had always presided over the actual protection of the wealth and an outside matriarch had always bound the family together. The actual Peter Paul Cardins were puppets dangling by the two outsiders in protection of a fortune to which they were slaves.

One needed no curse from a dying Confederate colonel to account for the family's dysfunctionality. They had managed to do it all themselves.

Yet might a solution to the mystery of the locked room on Prairie Avenue free them from their bondage? Or perhaps give a hint of the precise nature of their demons? That was too romantic an assumption even for Blackie Ryan.

Almost.

The family, however, would have to reconstitute itself if it were to survive any longer. I wondered if Chantal Cardin was perhaps the crucial player in such a challenge. Or might her firstborn son, the legendary Petey, be the grace everyone needed.

And why would a man with a wife like Chantal permit himself to be obsessed with the pursuit of more money than he could possibly spend?

CHAPTER 5

PROMPTLY AT FOUR that afternoon, Megan came into my office on the first floor of the Cathedral Rectory and announced with a toss of her long brown hair, "There's a *woman* to see you, Bishop Blackie, in the first counseling room."

"Indeed."

Megan is one of the four porter persons, the teenage women who answer the door and the phone after school hours and thus add a good deal of charm to the interface between rectory and people. All four of them are named Megan, which simplifies matters. While they differ in most other respects (including race and ethnicity), they are also similar to one another in the confident conviction that they could run the parish better than I do, and the Church better than the Bishop of Rome does.

Perhaps they are right.

This Megan, like the others, attends St. Ignatius College Prep, and indeed wore a sweater announcing this fact against the cold of the day. She was the Mexican-American Megan—as opposed to the African-American, Korean-American, and Irish-American Megan.

"You should have an armed guard in there with her. The coat and suit and jewels are worth at least six thousand."

"So." I turned off my new Pentium computer.

"Gorgeous too," Megan continued. "Real pretty boobs. Scared I think. But she's kind of neat. I like her. Totally righteous!"

That was a definitive enough verdict. No mention of ice. Interesting. If a Megan—any Megan—liked a visitor to the Cathedral Rectory it must be counted strongly in that person's favor.

So now there were two votes in Jane Frances de Chantal Reynolds Cardin's favor—Annie Reilly's and Megan's. Three if one counted that of my virtuous sibling.

As I walked down the hall to the counseling room (no more harsh rectory offices to deal with problems), I heard the Cathedral Choir singing "Stille Nacht" in the original.

"It is good of you to take time to receive me, Your Grace."

She was wearing a gray, tailored suit, a gray knit blouse, and a red and green scarf at her neck, only a modicum of makeup and no jewelry besides her wedding ring. The suit, I judged, was close to the thousand-dollar range. Even in such modest garb, she was as distracting as she had been the previous night—and as distant.

She stood and reached for my ring, which I was not wearing.

"I don't think I should be bothering you, Your Grace."

"Ah?"

"The Corpus Christi priests say we should go only to them for confessions, especially general confessions."

"Do they?"

"Yes, Your Grace." She bowed her head and, novicelike, averted her eyes.

"Well, you're not constrained to remain."

"No, Your Grace," she said hesitantly.

I was supposed to say something to reassure her.

"Would it surprise you greatly if I were to say that I don't think that the priests of the Corpus Christi Movement have a monopoly on virtue or wisdom or the power to preside over a person's reconciliation to the Church?"

"No, Your Grace, it would not."

"Well?"

"I'll stay if you let me, Your Grace."

"Sit down, Ms. Cardin," I said briskly. "And, by the way, that is not the correct form of address in this country."

"Oh?" She drew back in embarrassment. "I always thought it was."

I was not looking forward to the encounter. I would be wrestling with her for a life, maybe a couple of lives. I didn't hold the high cards. So I would have to establish a certain context for the relationship.

"What should I call you, then?" She returned to the couch across the coffee table from my easy chair—in which I sank with a weary sigh.

"Call me Blackie."

A line for which my affection is notorious. She knew the right answer.

"Not Ishmael? . . . I can't call you that."

"Bishop Blackie then . . ."

"I'm Jane," she said evenly. "Better, Janie."

"Janie?"

"That's my real name. I mean Chantal is elegant and I don't dislike it. But I'm really Janie. My older son is the only one who calls me that. I can't stop him."

A trace of an indulgent smile flitted across her lips.

"To annoy your mother-in-law, doubtless."

"Of course."

Same trace of a smile.

"Now who is going to murder you?"

"My husband."

"Why?"

"He claims I have been unfaithful."

"Have you?"

"No. But he pays so little attention to me, I might easily have been."

"A rival?"

"The holdings. My husband, Bishop Blackie, is a possessive man. When he thinks he might lose something that he possesses he becomes irrational, even if he has paid little attention to it for years."

"Indeed."

"Our marriage was a merger of two distinguished families, one very rich, the other . . . well, impoverished. Looking back on it I was only nineteen and my parents sold me to the Cardins."

"Ah?"

As the Lennons had made a similar transaction more than a century before. I didn't like the similarity.

"I fear I was not as responsive as I might have been in the early years, though I did care for him. He is very attractive and very kind unless the family and its holdings are in jeopardy. Then when I understood responsiveness and wanted to enjoy it and him, he had lost interest. Most of the time. Occasionally he has made efforts to renew intimacy. Sometimes we both were pleased with the result. As I said, I was fond of him . . . I astonish myself by saying that oftentimes I still am. I have done worse things to him than he has done to me."

Her response in our terse exchange was as concise and as cool as though she were discussing a problem with her rose garden. Nonetheless, I marveled that like so many women she was willing to trust a celibate priest with the details of her intimate life.

"How so?"

"After the birth of Ellen, my youngest daughter, four years ago, the doctors said my womb was badly damaged. It should be removed because, while it was no threat to my health unless I was pregnant, it would almost certainly rupture if there were any future pregnancies and I could easily bleed to death."

"I know of similar situations."

"Father Lawrence forbade me to have the operation. He said I should be brave and trust God. My husband wanted to continue the, uh, affair we were having at that time with the use of contraceptives. Father Lawrence ordered me to refuse him. My husband accepted that decision."

"Bastard," I said softly.

She looked surprised. "Is that proper language for a bishop?"

"In the circumstances, most proper."

"Do you mean my husband or Father Lawrence?"

"Father Lawrence."

"I know that most Catholics practice birth control and that many Catholic doctors approve of the removal of the womb in circumstances like mine. But I don't want to take chances with my eternal salvation. I want to make sure that I keep all the rules."

"You know that even forty years ago, many Catholic teachers said that in circumstances like yours it would have been all right to accept your husband's wishes about contraception in order to save the marriage."

"Yes"—she nodded solemnly—"but Father Lawrence said they were false teachers. And he tells me that Cardinal Ratzinger said recently that the operation would be wrong."

"Who knows whether an organ is diseased, Janie, a doctor or a cardinal?"

I could not in good conscience consign Father Lawrence and all his kind to hell. But I would not have objected if the Almighty in Her wisdom would see fit to banish them to purgatory for a good long time so they would see what evil their arrogant assumption of a monopoly on Catholicism had done to many good, if naive, people.

"I don't know, Bishop Blackie." Tears appeared in her eyes. "I wanted to be certain. Now I'm not sure about anything anymore. Except that I have done terrible things to my husband and my children. If I had it to do over I would not have listened to Father Lawrence. I would have listened to Father Wren."

The latter was a younger Jesuit (there are really no *young* Jesuits) who would have given exactly the opposite advice.

"I'm to cast the deciding vote?"

"I know what you would say, Father, I mean, Bishop Blackie. I wouldn't have come unless I knew that. I know now that I did wrong. It doesn't matter anymore. Because I will soon be dead and poor Pete will be able to find another wife."

"Why do you realize that your response was wrong."

"I'm beginning to understand that my faith is about compassion and forgiveness, not about rules.

Petey has persuaded me of that, though of course he doesn't know what my problems have been."

"Yet you still think that maybe Father Lawrence might be right?"

"Perhaps. But it doesn't matter. I will die very soon."

"Ah, yes. Your husband will kill you. Tell me, does he have any grounds for suspecting infidelity?"

"Like many women in Forest Lane, I have a personal trainer who comes to our home every morning. He is a blond Adonis. My mother-in-law disapproves of trainers—even of women exercising. She played the Iago role, Bishop Blackie, and created suspicions in my husband's mind. My daughter began to spy on me. . . ."

"Your *daughter*?"

"We are at that stage of the mother/daughter relationship where she hates me. It will pass, but by then it will be too late. . . . Foolishly I let my trainer kiss me. I guess I was in desperate need of affection, even from a man who is gay. Lisa was watching. With a camera."

The house of the Borgias!

"Passionate kisses?"

"Hardly. They were mortal sins, just the same."

The hell they were, but I didn't argue.

"How often?"

"Twice. Lisa was there both times. Fast film."

"And?"

"I was immediately excluded from the family.

We all live on the same street. Even my own brother had his wife pretend that I don't exist. I am not permitted to speak with my younger son and daughter who now live with Patrick and his family. There is to be no divorce. Not in our family."

"You told them that the young man was gay?"

"No. It would not matter."

Her facial expression did not change, nor her voice become warm as she described her fate. Not icy so much as drained of affect.

"This all under the seal of confession, Bishop Blackie?"

"As you wish."

"I do not want to make matters worse for my family. I am prepared to die."

Was there no will to resist, to survive, to fight back against the cruelty that was trying to destroy her?

"What makes you think you will suffer Desdemona's fate?"

She removed a file of papers, held together with a paper clip, from her shoulder purse that she had placed on the coffee table next to my book on the Catholicism of James Joyce and passed the file over to me.

"These notes, unfolded and without envelopes, appear beneath my bedroom door every morning. I don't have to tell you that my husband and I no longer share the same bedroom."

The notes had been printed by a laser printer on the parchmentlike personal stationary of "Peter Paul

Cardin"—with the upside-down cross of St. Peter as a logo.

"I will not be home tonight," the first one said. It was signed "Peter" with an elaborate flourish.

What kind of a weirdo sends notes to his wife printed on parchment stationary by laser printer?

I considered the print—600 DPI (dots per inch), probably a HP Laser 4M or something like it.

"I must fly to London," the next informed her.

"I am concerned about Henry's grades."

"You will not attend the Christmas party at John Mark's tonight."

Less and less did I like this Peter Paul Cardin. A certified nutcake.

The next letter confirmed that conclusion

"You are an adulterous woman. For that crime you will die. Moreover it will be a slow and painful death so that you will expiate the pain you have caused me. It will do you no good to try to escape or seek help. As you know I have the power to do what I want with all that is mine, including you."

Off the wall and over the top.

The next one followed the same theme.

"Remember these frigid days that at the depth of hell there is not fire but ice. That is where you belong and that is where you go. Soon."

The rest of the stack of notes were of the same sort. Household instructions and threats of death, the latter often rich in obscene detail about what would happen to her sexual organs in the pit of hell.

I put the file back on the coffee table.

"You have gone to the police?"

"It would make no difference, Bishop Blackie. My husband does what he wants to do."

"Has he ever been physically abusive to you?"

"No."

"Verbally."

"No . . . I've been part of the scenery except on those rare occasions in which he feels some desire. There is no need to abuse me. But that is not his weakness, Bishop. Possession is his vice, avarice, greed, whatever. A major corporation tried to take away one of the holdings two years ago. Illegally, he felt. He not only held them off, he destroyed the careers of the executives who concocted the scheme. Or he had my brother do that. I am a threat to his privacy, his reputation, his family. I must be eliminated."

"The times you were intimate?"

"Oddly, Bishop Blackie, he is a good lover, capable of great tenderness and respect. I'm like the Lyric Opera to him."

"Indeed?"

"He was very active in the Lyric. Loved opera music. Then he stopped attending. The music distracted him the day after and he could not work. He had to work. For his children and for the family. He will never have enough money."

I picked up the sheaf of notes and glanced through them again. There was something wrong with them but I could not figure out what it was. It would come to me eventually, I told myself.

"I did not come for help, Bishop Blackie. No one can help me. I will be dead by New Year's. In a way that will be a relief. I have time to prepare to meet God. Will you hear my confession now?"

"Any man who writes notes like this should be served immediately with divorce papers."

"A strange thing for a priest to say."

"We no longer tell women to put up with a madman for the sake of the marriage and the children. Well tell them to get rid of the man. He should be history in your life, Janie. Archive him."

"He is my husband. I still love him, as mad as that may sound."

"He's crazy."

She shrugged, the first gesture she had permitted herself since I had come into the counseling room.

"I cannot go to a divorce lawyer, Bishop. I'm a Catholic. Please hear my confession."

"Very well."

Amazingly I managed to find a purple stole of the sort she probably needed to be certain that my priestly exercise was valid. I reflected that Chantal Cardin had lived all her life in a hermetic world, sealed off from the rest of humankind, a world of medieval pieties and medieval punishments. What seemed insane to us might seem perfectly normal to her.

She fell to her knees, and head bowed in contrite humility, she began to recite the sins, real and imagined (mostly the latter), of her life. Though convinced she was a terrible sinner, she was in fact a virtuous matron who had done her best in the isolated context in which she was forced to live. God loves all of us. I'm sure She especially loved Chantal and therefore expected me to clear away the obstacles to Chantal's responding to that love.

Typical of the usual impossible demands She makes on Her priests.

Perhaps the Jesuits were right, under the ice was more ice. But underneath the second layer of ice there was fear and generosity and confusion. The ice was protection.

The "general" confession was a difficult process because, foolishly perhaps, I tried to modify her deep but mistaken religious convictions.

"I don't think I've made a valid confession since I was sixteen," she said.

"Oh?"

"I engaged in passionate kisses with a boy at a Christmas party. I was afraid to confess it when I went back to school. I've confessed it often since then, but I don't think I've ever confessed all of the sins that I committed after that invalid confession and which were not forgiven at subsequent bad confessions."

"God is an accountant?"

"Certainly not."

"Then why should you be an accountant in your dealings with God?"

"Because priests tell me that unless I go into all the details of my sinful life, I will go to hell."

"Father Wren tell you that?"

"No . . . only Father Lawrence and the other Corpus priests who have given retreats for our family."

"Do you think you will ever be able to make what Father Lawrence would call a good confession?"

"No," she said, bowing her head in dejection. "But I must try if I do not want to go to hell."

"If I get the deciding vote, I go with Father Wren. You knew I would or you wouldn't be here. My verdict is that you've never made a bad confession."

"The passion with the boy?"

"Trivial."

She thought about that. "I guess it was."

"I'll tell you what, Janie, when you talk this over with God, tell Her that She should blame me for bad advice."

She actually laughed at that.

"Oh, I won't do that. I'm sure God is on your side."

The woman was torn between despair and hope, between the worst of the old Church and the best of the new Church, the latter preached to her, no doubt, by her remarkable son. But her hope was tenuous. Immediately she went back to the old Church.

"I spend much of my time," she said, "enhancing my physical appearance."

"If you want to confess your sins, Jane Cardin, that's all right with me, though I am dubious about the wisdom of general confessions, but we can dispense with a list of your virtuous behavior."

Anger flashed briefly in her eyes. "What do you mean?"

"Proper care of one's body is virtue not vice."

"I spend too much time on my body."

"No you don't."

"You're not giving me a chance! My immortal soul is in jeopardy!"

"No, it's not. You told me last night I should be stern with you."

"About my sins! Not about my not being sinful!"

"If you stop to think about it for a moment, you'll realize that such a statement is unworthy of your obvious intelligence."

"You're assaulting my religious convictions!"

How could she say that when earlier in our conversation she had admitted that those convictions had led her to the destruction of her marriage.

I bounded up from my easy chair and pointed my finger at her—a patented Blackie gesture that usually has some effect.

"God has made you very beautiful, woman, as you well know. Not to protect and present that gift as best you can would be an insult. When you follow your instincts to conserve that beauty, you do God's will!"

"May I please go on with my confession, Bishop?"

I had not moved her an inch from her self-rejection and despair.

Finally she finished her catalogue.

"Please give me absolution for these and all the sins of my life, especially those I have forgotten."

"No. Sit down on the couch, Janie, we're only beginning."

For once she was startled.

"No?"

She obeyed me and returned to the couch.

"No firm purpose of amendment."

"I finally resolve to amend my life," she repeated the formula.

"No you don't, not as long as you are not prepared to take due precaution against a premature ending of your life."

She was silent for a few moments.

"If I do not promise to go to the police or a divorce lawyer, you will not give me absolution and I will go to hell?"

"God has far too much good taste, Janie, to send you to hell. She made you what you are so She could enjoy having you around in heaven. Forget about the possibility of hell. She adores you even more than you adore Her. That's what Jesus came to tell us. But you cannot be reconciled with the Church unless you take steps to defend yourself."

Thus I slipped in the back door, so to speak, the new and traditional doctrine about the Sacrament of Reconciliation. I also wondered if she had chosen me for her confessor instead of one of the Mother Angelica creeps because she thought maybe I would find a way out for her.

"It will destroy the family."

"And maybe save your kids."

"There is that too."

"The family needs to be destroyed."

"That is possible."

We waited.

"You want me to fight back?"

"I say you have an obligation to fight back."

I don't normally do the spirituality of obligation, but it was an interim rhetoric that this woman could understand.

"Very well," she said briskly. "Two days after Christmas I will bring these to a divorce lawyer. I promise. On my honor, such as it is. Now may I have absolution?"

"No. You will call a lawyer first thing tomorrow morning. You will see the lawyer tomorrow afternoon. You will give the lawyer these notes. You will then tell your husband what you have done. Before the day is over tomorrow. You will tell him to his face, not in a note. You will emphasize that if anything happens to you, your lawyer will go to the police with the notes. That will protect your life."

"I don't want to."

"Then you do not regret the sin of endangering your life."

She took a deep breath, outlining for a moment her exquisite breasts.

"My life is worthless. It has always been worthless."

"Janie, the essence of our faith is a dream, a vision, a possibility. It may be that love has over-

whelmed the world. It may be that we can all live
with one another in peace and affection. It may be
that the whole of humankind can become one
family. This is the story Jesus told us. This is faith
that keeps us Catholic; this is the vision we see in
the eyes of our children before they fall asleep
at night. It is not a faith of rules, though perhaps
rules are necessary. It is rather a dream about what
is possible if God really loves us the way Jesus says
He loves us. In light of that dream, the worst of all
sins is to say that one is worthless."

She thought about that.

"If I could only believe that . . ."

"If you don't believe that, woman, you have no
right to claim to be Catholic."

She closed her eyes and leaned back against the
couch.

"Moreover, the only hope for the husband that
you inexplicably but perhaps not unwisely still love
is to believe that you are far too precious to die a
senseless death that you can avoid."

Eyes still closed, she nodded slowly.

"Fight him to save him?"

"Perhaps. No guarantee, but perhaps."

She opened her eyes.

"That's really the only way, isn't it?"

"What do you think?"

"All right, Father Blackie," she said briskly. "I
will do what you say. I will really amend my life. I
will try to believe in my head that you're right when
you say that I am precious. I will fight them all."

"And bring down that horror of a family."

"Smash it." She banged her fist on the couch. "Will that do as a firm purpose of amendment?"

"For the moment . . . call me tomorrow afternoon and tell me that you have done what you promised."

That was perhaps an outrageous demand. She did not think so.

"All right, I will . . . and, oh, Bishop Blackie, I've also thought about committing suicide. I don't know how often, but"—she giggled—"I suppose that you'll say I don't have to tell you the exact number of times"

"You did not, however, commit suicide?"

"I guess not."

"Why else does temptation come, save that man may meet it, master it, and so be pedestaled in glory?"

"Browning," she said automatically as she knelt, unnecessarily it seemed to me, for absolution. "And for these and all the sins of my past life, I'm heartily sorry."

So I said the words that she still considered to be magic and that I considered to be a call for the Church to rally round her and protect her.

As she left, she murmured, "Thank you very much, Bishop Blackie. You are a wonderful priest."

"You helped that woman a lot," the Megan interrupted my reflections. "She was crying when she left the rectory. She looked like she needed a good cry."

"Arguably."

Even then it was clear to me that the scenario was all wrong. I had wrestled for the soul of Jane Frances de Chantal Reynolds Cardin on the premise that her soul and her life were the issue. What else is one to do but to accept the facts as a penitent presents them? Had she wanted me to urge her to fight for her life? Had the good Ridley Becker recommended me as a kind of St. Jude of spiritual advisers, someone who deals with the impossible—as Ridley was quite capable of doing?

Or were there deeper and more sinister energies at work of which I had now become a pawn? Had the scene in the counseling room been an act? But if it were, why? And could she be such a superb actor?

I had in my possession even then all the clues to a resolution of the puzzle I needed. But, distracted as I was by the overwhelming demands of Christmas at a Catholic parish, I missed the clues with catastrophic results.

In my study late that evening as I worked on my Christmas homily, part of which, one might not inappropriately suspect, Chantal Cardin had already heard, a vague notion that had been bothering me suddenly crystallized out of the fog. I reached for the phone and punched a number of a phone in the John Hancock Center.

"Casey."

"Strange, I was about to call you."

"You just did call me, Blackie," he seemed

mildly irritated. I could never be certain with a call
to that number that I had not stirred someone out of
a bed of passion. Well, neither the bed nor its other
occupant would go away.

"I neglected to ascertain why the Gulfstream
crashed on the approach to the airport at Nassau."

"The pilot reported that both engines stopped
without warning. It was night, though the skies
were clear. They got search planes and boats out in
a hurry, but it was too late. They assume he ran out
of fuel."

"Indeed . . . an inexperienced pilot?"

"No. You think that might be important for
whatever you're poking into."

"Oh, yes."

But I had no idea why.

CHAPTER 6

THE NEXT MORNING, after I had presided over the Eucharist, eaten a modest breakfast (nine blueberry pancakes drenched in maple syrup), and deputed responsibility for the Cathedral of the Holy Name to my senior associate, I wended my way south on Michigan Avenue in my 1955 turquoise-green Ford Thunderbird convertible (top on, of course). Actually the car isn't mine but is a family heirloom that has been loaned to me temporarily so long as I promise to keep it in one of the Cathedral garages. In truth, I ought not to be trusted with the car because while I did usually manage to remember to put it in the garage, it was not completely responsible of me to take it out on a day when the third punch of Chicago's one-two winter punch was working: slush. If I were wise I would remember to have the car cleaned before anyone in the family saw it.

If they should take the car away from me the only other option was to loan me the gull-wing

Benz—or buy me a new car, which is a very difficult thing for any of the Ryans to do.

I turned off Michigan Avenue at Fourteenth Street and ventured over to Indiana Avenue, passing on one side Soldier Field, home of the hapless Bears, the Illinois Central tracks, and the new Central Station town house development, whither our Mayor had withdrawn from the Royal Borough of Bridgeport. It was a nice touch that the Mayor's address was on Prairie Avenue, though the modest town houses (which had replaced the Illinois Central Station) were not in the tradition of Prairie Avenue. I noted mentally that I must once more remind Milord Cronin of the necessity of restoring to this old neighborhood turned new its recently suppressed parish church of St. John's by the Roundhouse, the very parish church from which Peter Cardin Sr. had been buried.

The corner of Eighteenth and Prairie did not look picturesque in the accumulating slush, though, having been there before in the summer, I could not dissent from the romantic view of the locale advanced in the article in *Chicago History*.

As I parked on Eighteenth Street along the massive north wall of the Glessner House, I wondered why I had permitted my instincts to lead me here during the busy pre-Christmas season at the Cathedral. The puzzle of the untimely death of Rose Lennon Cardin was an intriguing one. But the guilty parties as well as the innocent ones were long since gone to other and better places. Whatever curse had battered the family for the last century had been of their own making, even if its remote origins were to be found in the long since demolished tower suite of Red Pete's castle.

Yet someone had sent the *Chicago History* article to Sean Cronin, someone perhaps clever enough to want me to delve into the mystery, someone who for twisted reasons of his or her own wanted me to find parallels between then and now.

In the Glessner coach house, headquarters of the foundation that presided over the Prairie Avenue Historic District, I was greeted warmly and offered a tour of the house. Someone asked if I were trying to solve a mystery, a question I often hear these days wherever I go. I replied that I was rather trying to explore an old puzzle about the Cardin House. All the eyes in the room widened and there were a few soft gasps. Apparently they had read the article from the 1960s.

"Do you believe in the curse, Bishop Blackie?"

"The only curses that are dangerous," I responded, "are those that we make for ourselves."

They agreed and my reputation as a wise person remained intact. I did not add that sometimes there are energies out of the past that can slip into the present and make common cause with our own self-induced slaveries. I know that to be true, but I don't like to have to explain how it works, in substantial part because I don't know.

They gave me the detailed plans of the house— library, office, ballroom, dining room, kitchen, butler's pantry, servants' quarters, private steam laundry, electric generator, bedrooms, classroom for the two children, music room. They also handed over a small book of photographs that had been taken inside the house. Quite a place, I thought to myself, but perhaps not all that comfortable to live in. Still, it was a long way from West Cork to South Prairie Avenue.

I retreated to a desk in a spare corner and began to study the plans and the pictures. If the outside of the house was Victorian Gothic, the inside was more baroque marble and oak columns, heavy ceilings, vast urns, wide staircases, heavy draperies. The servants' quarters seemed quite roomy, better than the ones in *Upstairs Downstairs.* Apparently Red Pete was considerate of his servants. Or maybe it was herself who was considerate.

I turned the page of the book and discovered a full-page print of a formal photograph of Rose Lennon Cardin, a much better print than the one in *Chicago History.* She was a striking young woman, brimming with energy and vitality. Her piercing eyes, blue presumably, seemed to leap out of the page and catch mine. She should not have been brutally struck down in the prime of her life. If she had lived, the family history would surely have been different. This woman would not permit the protection of wealth to become a family obsession. An import, a purchase even, from a more aristocratic family, she was nonetheless no haughty Regina Hoban, Countess Cardin, nor much less a terrified Jane Frances de Chantal Reynolds Cardin.

No indeed. Life for her, I suspected, was to be lived in the present exciting moment, neither in the future nor in the past. Petey had inherited not only her face but also, I fantasize, her character.

Red Pete had surely met his match.

I told you I was a romantic.

I murmured a brief prayer for the two of them and turned the page. It displayed a picture of Red Pete, in full white tie elegance, in his library, a touch of a smile above his beard and beneath his eyes that seemed surprisingly soft and mild. Perhaps he was laughing to himself at the thought of his portrait surrounded by books, none of which he could read—if the *Chicago History* research was right that Red Pete was illiterate.

I was drawn back to the previous page and to Rose Cardin's eyes. Whoever had turned off those two blazing lights had done a terrible thing, an evil that persisted even to the present. I permitted myself to imagine that she was pleading for me not so much to avenge her as to strike down the evil.

Had she wanted her son Peter Junior to be a priest? What Irish mother of that generation would not have supported the idea? Had he given up the thought when he was faced with the obligation to protect the world that his mother and father had built? Would young Petey correct that decision?

I turned the page quickly. My romanticism was turning into fantastical sentimentality, an indulgence that would help no one, especially the staff back at the Cathedral who might legitimately need my presence during the pre-Christmas rush.

Not that they would ever admit it.

After the library there was a full-page picture of the master bedroom—baroque the way baroque could never be with not only separate dressing rooms but separate baths and, according to the plans, good-sized bathrooms at that. The bed, king-size long before the term, was much wider than most beds of that era would have been. Drapes pulled back to reveal its full splendor, more masculine than feminine perhaps, it appeared to offer a candid invitation to rest, comfort, and peace.

To pleasure also?

Perhaps, but elegant and tasteful pleasure. No bordello this room.

I checked the plans. The spiral staircase from the third-floor hall was broad and graceful, its banisters ornately carved. One did not sneak up to the tower of Peter Cardin's house. Rather one ascended to it.

There was, I noted, a servant's stairway to the tower too. For Rose's maid, for surely she had one, and for Pete's valet for which I very much doubt he had any use. The servants' access to the tower was out of sight of the massive and richly paneled oak door that served as an entrance to the bedroom. Some could lurk at the top of the servants' stairs and watch who was coming in or out of the bedroom. The same stairs could also perhaps have served as an egress for someone leaving the bedroom who did not want to use either the main stairway or Pete's exit from his dressing room.

What did herself think of that, I wondered. Or did she take it for granted that such a convenience was simply part of every house on Prairie Avenue. Perhaps she was secure enough in her hold on her man that she thought it most unlikely that he would seek release in one of the brothels of the encroaching Levee.

Was I deceiving myself about Rose Lennon Cardin—aided by the fantasies of the author of the article I had read the night before last. Perhaps she was a shrew, a scold, a domestic tyrant, whom all the servants avoided whenever they could and from whom her husband often fled in terror.

I now could elaborate many scenarios to explain her death. The locked room mystery need not be a mystery. But I had no way to choose among the possible scripts unless I knew more about who might have had a motive to kill her.

Might it be Rosina who hated her mother because she would not protect Rosina from the father's sexual abuse? Might it have been her son Peter Junior defending his sister from his mother's cruelty? Might it have been a servant whom Rose had beaten or hassled? Might it have been a lover whom she had teased and then rejected?

It *might* have been any of those, but there was nothing to confirm any of these suspicions. The most obvious suspect was her husband. But he was drunk in a saloon at the time of the murder.

Or was he?

I closed the book and rolled up the drawings. I

was at a dead end. In the absence of more data, the mystery of the death of Rose Cardin would remain a mystery.

"Bishop Blackie," a docent said to me, "are you interested in the history of Cardin House?"

"Indeed."

"We've recently received an archive of letters from a servant girl who worked there between 1892 and 1897 to her younger sister in Ireland. We haven't had the time to screen them or catalogue them yet, but if you would like to glance at them . . ."

"I might have a few moments to take a brief look," I said in the biggest understatement of a lifetime of effort to control enthusiasm.

"The younger sister eventually migrated to America too. She brought the letters along. The girl's ancestors discovered the letters in an attic only last year. We have the originals in the safe. I'll bring you a xeroxed copy."

The letters were from one Clare Raftery, an immigrant form Bekan in the County Mayo, to her sister Mary Ellen. The former may have been all of sixteen when she began to write. "Little Sister," as she often called her sibling, was one year younger. Clare was a young woman with strong opinions and a strong will, but was nonetheless unfailingly tender in her affection for her "little sister."

The messages, written in bold and clear block letters gave a remarkable portrait of life inside the Cardin House during those years. I went through them very quickly, pulling out the more pertinent ones to copy.

August 15, 1892

Dear Little Sister,

Well, here I am in America and meself over the terrible seasickness that never once left me in the whole trip. But I have the job that our cousin Delia promised me and it's a grand job too. I thank God and Blessed Mother for taking such good care of me and I hope you and the others pray that my good luck continues.

I'm a maid of all work in the most glorious house in all the world on a street they call Prairie Avenue which is more grand a street than you can possibly imagine. The people who live on it are all toffs, the richest people in Chicago. From the looks of some of them I get out the window, I wouldn't want to work for them. They look mean and cruel.

But our Master's name is Cardin and he came here as an orphan from County Cork. I haven't seen him yet, but Delia says he's a grand man, generous and fair and not wanting anyone to work too long or too hard. The Mistress is even nicer, she says, sweet and gentle, though you would not want to get her mad at you. She spoke to me the other day, and you wouldn't believe how beautiful she is. She said that I should feel free to come to her if I ever feel homesick.

Can you imagine that!

They have a son who is a few years older than I am and he's away at college at a school called Notre Dame in a place called Indiana because there are so many dangerous red Indians there. I wonder that the Master would send him to such a place.

Then there's a daughter that's about your age and she seems nice too. She always smiles and says thank you like she really means it.

Well, I'd better turn off the lights now and get some sleep. Delia and I share a room and it's a grand time we're having together.
Pray for me.
Your loving sister,
Clare

September 3, 1892

Dear Little Sister,

Well, as I've often told you, a girl has to be careful of men or they'll be the destruction of you altogether. There's a coachman here called Tony O'Boyle and he's the Master's favorite coachman because he's a Cork man and himself from Skibeereen. He's a big husky man with a loud mouth and no manners save when he wants to have them. He's got a lot of growing up to do, let me tell you, and himself already nineteen.

Doesn't he pretend that he's sweet on me and don't I tell him that he's a terrible amadon altogether.

*Well, the other day, he's trying to talk to me
and meself cleaning one of the ground floor
windows from the outside. And doesn't the Master himself come up to us.*

*The Master's a fine-looking man with red hair
and red beard and always a pleasant smile and a
kind word, though they say he's a terror in the
business world.*

*"Is this gosson troubling you, Clare," he says,
and himself knowing everyone's name. "If he is,
won't I send him back to the bogs of West Cork
where he belongs?"*

*"Sure, wouldn't West Cork be too good for the
likes of him?" says I as bold as brass.*

*They both laugh and me face gets terrible hot.
"Now you're from Mayo, aren't you, Clare?" the
Master says.*

*"God help us," I say, now being terrible
embarrassed.*

*"Well, I guess you can take care of yourself
then," he says with a laugh. "But don't be too
hard on the poor lad. He means well."*

*And they both laugh, but it's Tony O'Boyle's
turn to blush and good enough for him says I.*

*But you can see what a grand place it is. In a
way it's like I never left home with all the Irish
voices around the house.*

*You should be careful with them fast-talking
boys, Mary Ellen. Someone like Tony O'Boyle
has only one thing on his mind. And you know
what that is.*

Pray for me and tell everyone that I love them and miss them.
Your sister,
Clare

November 20, 1892

Dear Little Sister,

We're working awful hard this week because there's a big American feast on Thursday called Thanksgiving. I don't mind working hard, though that little snip Jenny Kinane gets away with doing almost nothing. Quinlan the butler is sweet on her and she leads him on, though she's really chasing that big oaf Tony O'Boyle who still looks at me with those big dumb eyes of his, even though I won't give him the time of day.

There's a man who comes around here sometimes, a Joe Carey, who looks at me real dirty. I don't like him and he has no business trying to flirt with me. He's not a servant, but works for the Master in his business. I don't think he does good things to people, though the Master and the Mistress are both very kind to him.

Did I ever tell you that our house has electric lights? You wouldn't believe how bright they are, especially these days when it gets dark so early. A lot of the houses on this street don't have electric lights though the swells in them are real rich. The Master makes the electricity in a barn in back of the house and has offered it to the neighbors, but they won't take anything from someone who is Irish.

We also have a steam laundry in the basement and we are the only house on the street which has one. It's terribly hot down there but we only have to work there one half day every two-weeks so I don't mind.

The house is heated by some kind of hot water that comes around in pipes, so we don't even need fireplaces to keep warm, though we light the fires every morning just the same. "In case the boiler breaks down," Quinlan says.

So we'll be all snug when the snow comes. Delia says the weather is terrible in winter.

I love you, Little Sister, and I'm saving my money to bring you over here too.

Pray for me.

Your loving sister,

Clare

December 26, 1892

Dear Little Sister,

Well, we had a glorious Christmas here in Chicago. The Master and the Mistress gave each of us parlor maids ten dollars. I felt like a rich woman. The Mass over at St. John's Church was lovely and the Master had the coachmen drive us over there because it was so cold.

Wasn't it my bad luck to get in the coach which that amadon Tony O'Boyle was driving (and don't you ever DARE say again I'm sweet on him because I'm NOT!). I haven't said a word to him for six weeks, but I had to wish him the best of Christmas time. Didn't he smile at me like no one else had said it to him all day.

This morning I felt sad, despite all the good times, because I wasn't with you and Ma and Da and the rest of them. So I was crying when I was dusting the library, which I'm supposed to do every day, except when the young Master is around because he's in there reading and we're not supposed to be in a room with any of them unless they call for us.

Well, doesn't the Mistress come in and hear me sniffling and doesn't she take me in her arms and let me cry my eyes out. She doesn't ask why I'm crying because she knows.

Then when I'm through crying and I go back to work she tells me that I can dust it even when the young Master is in because, she says, he gets so absorbed in his reading, he doesn't even notice pretty girls.

Well, I tell her I'm not pretty and she laughs and she asks me what I think about the young Master, which I thought was a strange kind of question.

So I says to her, as bold as you please, "The way he prays in Church, Mistress, I think he has the mark of the priest on him."

She smiles and says, "Well, that's all in God's Providence, isn't it?"

So you see how nice everyone is here, except Quinlan some of the time and that Joe Carey all the time.

I love you, Little Sister, and I look forward to the day you can come and live here with meself and Delia.

God bless everyone at home.
Your loving sister,
Clare

March 20, 1893

Dear Little Sister,
It's still winter and a terrible cold winter when you have to go outside, even with the warm clothes the Master and the Mistress give us to wear.

The young Mistress and I have become good friends. Quinlan doesn't like it and that little hussy Jenny Kinane makes fun of me. The young mistress goes to St. Xavier Academy where the mercy nuns teach, but there's no one her age to talk to on this whole beautiful street with all its empty people. So she talks to me and the Mistress doesn't mind.

"God knows, there's no more wholesome or healthy young women on the whole Prairie Avenue, Clare Marie Raftery," she says to me.

So I feel strange about it, but Delia says it's all

right. *The poor child needs someone her own age to be a friend in this terrible house.*

I don't know what's so terrible about it.

Anyway, the young mistress Rosina tells me that I should treat that big amadon Tony O'Boyle nicer than I do. Her Da says he's a bright lad and a harder worker and will amount to something in a few years.

"Well," says I, "what difference does that make to me?"

"But he loves you, Clare," the child tells me. "He loves you like you're the one true love of his life. Everyone can see that!"

"He does not!" I say real firm.

And she laughs and says that if I don't believe it I should ask him and of course I'd never do that.

That Joe Carey person is back, looking terrible, all worn out and dissipated and so thin you'd think there was nothing left to him. He doesn't stare at me that way anymore, thank the Lord God.

The Master and the Mistress are very good to him, though I don't know why. The Master seems just a little bit afraid of him, but the Mistress, God bless her, isn't afraid of anyone.

He still does things for the Master, but I don't know what they are. Delia says the Master pays him well for this work and his advice and then he goes away and spends all the money on drink and women and then comes back for the Master's help.

'Tis a strange house, though I don't think it is terrible like Delia says sometimes.

Anyway, beware, Little Sister, of gombeen men like Tony O'Boyle, even if someone tells you that he's a hard worker and is going to amount to something.

I love everyone at home. I can hardly wait till you come to America.
Your loving sister,
Clare

August 15, 1893
Mary Day in Harvest Time

Dear Little Sister,
'Tis been a year since I wrote you my first letter and I'm in a terrible state altogether because of that terrible Tony O'Boyle. I finally did what Rosina has been teasing me to do. I asked the big, dumb amadon if he loved me.

Then he said terrible things altogether, so terrible that I ended up weeping. I'm not any of the wonderful things he says I am. I'm certainly not the finest woman in all the world, as you well know. I surely am not the best thing that ever happened in his life. I am not more beautiful . . . well, I'd better not even write that.

But what am I to do with him?

We're having a grand party this week for the young Master's birthday. All the pretty Irish

Catholic girls in Chicago will be here, and their mothers and fathers too.

The Master says to the Mistress, "Sure, let him be a priest. I don't mind that. Some of them are good men. Still, he should at least know what he's missing."

And she says, "Not all that much!"

And he laughs and she laughs with him.

And he says, "Well, maybe he won't be as lucky as I was."

I think I know what they mean, but I'm not sure.

And I'm terrible confused by my big dumb ape from West Cork.

Love to all.

Pray for me.

Your loving sister,

Clare

October 3, 1893

Dear Little Sister,

Happy Birthday to you, you're now sixteen, the same age I was when I came here. I miss you and Ma and Da and the little kids so much. When you're finished with the National School next year, we'll set a date for you to come to America. I won't settle for anything less.

No, Tony has not kissed me yet. He wouldn't dare. And don't be asking such foolish questions.

You asked me about the Mistress. She's been very kind to me and I love her very much. She is so incredibly beautiful. She must be about forty or so, but she looks like she's twenty-five. She has the most gorgeous long blond hair, and blue eyes that see right through you. She's never mean, but if she catches two of us giggling when we should be working (like she catches myself and Delia more than once) she just shakes her head and says something like, "Girls, you really know better than that."

And we both want to collapse for shame. And we apologize and run off to cry our eyes out. She's a tough woman. I wouldn't want her really angry at me. When she bawls the Master out—and it doesn't happen often and only when he's had too much to drink—he looks like he wants to cry too.

She's like an empress or something.

If only she didn't look so sad when she doesn't realize that anyone is watching her.

And I won't answer any questions about Tony O'Boyle, do you hear!

Pray for me.
Your loving sister,
Clare

December 20, 1893

Dear Little Sister,
I don't know what's happening in this house. Joe Carey is back and the Master is sullen and the Mistress looks sad and everyone is nervous,

even poor Rosina. The Master is drinking too much again, even Quinlan hints at it.

We're all waiting for the young Master to come home from Notre Dame for Christmas. He cheers everyone up. Even when he spends most of the day in the library reading, he makes everyone laugh when he comes home. I tell you, Little Sister, the mark of the priest is on him and a good priest he will be.

Oh, I almost forgot, Tony O'Boyle finally got around to kissing me last night. It wasn't much of a kiss and you would have thought the oaf was going to die of fright. In the end I did most of the kissing.

He is a little sweet. For a big oaf.

I hope you all had a good Christmas.

I miss you and the others.

Pray for me.

Your loving sister,
Clare

January 6, 1894
Little Christmas

Dear Little Sister,

No, I am not going to marry Tony O'Boyle. At least not right away and probably not ever. I'm only seventeen and he's only twenty. I have to save money to bring you over and he has to save money to buy his own team, though the Master has promised he'll pay half of it.

I don't even know if I love him. He is a very

nice boy. Very gentle and respectful despite his big Cork mouth.

But all of that's a long way off.

It's a happy house again. The young Master was wonderful during the Christmas holidays. The Master stopped drinking and the Mistress had two glasses of wine a couple of times and laughed a lot. Even before she drank the wine. And that awful Joe Carey is gone. Delia says he has something on the Master and Tony says he's good at spotting land that the Master ought to buy. He also says that the Master has made so much money that he doesn't hunger for it anymore, though he can't turn down a good opportunity.

I think Tony is right. He usually is.

Now don't go telling anyone that I'm in love with him.

Rosina is happy again too, over the worst of the flu she had before Christmas. She sings a lot down in the music room and the Mistress plays the piano.

I miss you, Mary Ellen, I miss you something terrible.

Pray for me.
Your loving sister,
Clare

May 13, 1894

Dear Little Sister,

Ah, don't I miss all of you something terrible. During the day when I'm working hard and don't have time to think, I don't notice the lump in my heart. But at night when I'm falling asleep, I think of dear Bekan parish and all of you. I see the sun coming up over the lake and hear the birds and the cows and Ma singing in the kitchen and I wish I were home. Almost every day I wish I were home. America is a wonderful place and I'll make my fortune here but I will pine for County Mayo.

God help us!

You ask what I do all day when I'm not spying on the Cardins.

WELL, I don't spy on them. Not exactly anyway. It's just that they're such powerful interesting people, if you take my meaning. I wonder if when I have a lot of money I'll be as unhappy as they seem to be a lot of the time. Faith, I hope not.

Well, as to what I do, it depends on what Quinlan the butler and Mrs. Lyne the housekeeper tell me to do. I'm still a maid of all work, you see. Some days, especially the day before or the day after a big dinner, I'm in the kitchen all day cleaning china and silver (and being careful not to break anything) and preparing vegetables and wiping up mess. Other days, I'm making beds and turning mattresses and airing rooms and dusting and mopping and scrubbing and polishing and changing linens and towels and cleaning bathrooms and heaven help me if I do anything wrong should Quinlan or Mrs. Lyne find out.

Neither of them like me much. They say that I'm currying favor with the Master and the Mistress. And I'm not. I just try to smile and be pleasant as Ma taught us.

We are supposed to always be ready when one of the family signals for us on the buzzer. They must not be kept waiting. But when they don't summon us, they are not supposed to see us. We have to be invisible except when they need us to do something for them.

Whether they can do it themselves or not.

"Clare, would you bring me a cup of tea?" the young Mistress asks very polite like.

"Yes, miss," I say and dash off to get it.

Then when I come back she looks at me with those pale sweet eyes of hers and says, "I don't think it's fair either, Clare."

"Yes, miss," I say real polite.

She sighs and says, "Thank you, Clare."

"Yes, miss."

I realize that we're both caught in something neither of us likes very much. And I admire her even more. And feel sorry for her because there is sadness in her pale eyes.

In the morning I wear a gingham dress with a small cap and a large apron and in the afternoon and evening a black uniform with white collars and cuffs and a white apron and a big white sash. Some days I have to work in the laundry which gets me out of a lot of purgatory but is a lot better than the other laundries on the street with the scrub boards.

When the Master and the Mistress have guests I take the ladies' cloaks and put them in a closet and then give them back to them when they leave—and if I confuse one with another Quinlan gives me a tongue-lashing.

If there's a shortage of serving maids, sometimes I'm even permitted to wait on table for guests and I think the Mistress holds her breath for fear I'll spill something on one of her posh guests or break some expensive piece of china.

Naturally I don't do that.

Sometimes men make little comments about me that are rude, but not rude enough to anger the Mistress. I bite my tongue, but it's hard not to tell them what I think of them or spill soup on all their fancy white tie suits.

When everyone has gone from a dinner I often have to polish the silver and then go around and make sure all the lights are out. First thing in the morning I have to turn on the lights and you know what I'm like first thing in the morning.

Some days every bone in my body aches. I'm glad I'm young and strong and God takes care of me. Still, there are times when I want to quit and would if I could.

Only of course I can't.

Life was hard in Ireland too. But I had time to think and I didn't have Quinlan and Mrs. Lyne

watching me every minute and themselves look-
ing for an excuse to discharge me.

I have all I want to eat here and the house is
always warm and I'm earning money, though
only half of what the men make and that isn't fair.

Some nights I'm so tired that I fall asleep as
soon as I go to bed, and Delia wanting to gossip.

But I'm young and strong and I don't intend to
spend all my life as a maid of all work.

Anyway I love you and all the family and I will
always miss you.

Pray for me.
Your loving sister,
Clare

July 4, 1894

Dear Little Sister,
I'm writing from a place called Geneva Lake
which is in another place called Wisconsin. It's a
long day's carriage ride from Chicago. The
Master has bought a summer "camp" here for
the family when the weather gets hot. As far as I
can see it's just as hot here as it is on Prairie
Avenue and we servants have to work just as
hard. Life is simpler here but the Master and the
Mistress bring fewer servants.

I'm not complaining because it is a beautiful
lake. There is a big lawn in front of the white
house and a pier extending into the lake and a
steam launch to ride around the lake in. Several

*days of the week at the end of the day the servants
are given a chance to swim in the lake. The
Master and the Mistress even bought swimming
costumes for us. Not everyone swims of course.
Some are afraid of the water and others are
afraid of what they will look like in the costumes.
Well, I have no fear of either. The water is a lot
warmer than in County Mayo.*

*This morning because it's a big American feast
in honor of them getting rid of the bloody English
the young Master and the young Mistress took us
for a ride around the lake on the steam launch. I
was afraid I'd get sick again, but the ride was as
smooth as you please. There are lovely homes all
along the lake, places where the posh can get
away from the city but still have their servants do
the work. At least we're treated better than the
rest of them.*

*I asked the young Master what American stood
for and he talked a lot about liberty and equality.
"If there's so much equality," says I to him, "why
do some people live in such beautiful homes and
others in those terrible slums in Chicago and why
are the niggers treated like slaves even though
they've been free these thirty years?"*

*That was pretty bold, but I like the young
Master and he tolerates my loud Irish mouth.*

*First he laughs and says to me, "Clare, you've
already become an American."*

*Then he gets very serious and says it isn't right
and that America is changing but it isn't chang-*

ing fast enough. "When my father came here there was a chance for everyone. There isn't anymore. If I were one of them I'd be an anarchist."

I'm not sure exactly what an anarchist is, I guess it's kind of an American Fenian.

Sure, doesn't he have the look of a priest in his eye when he says something like that. Or of a Fenian.

"It's meself that's not knowing my place," *I says, coming all over shy.*

Doesn't he laugh again and say my place is at the top of the mountain?

Wasn't that a strange thing to say?

I suppose you're wondering about that big oaf Tony O'Boyle. Well, he's up here too, of course, and himself staring at me in my swimming costume and telling me at night that none of the men can take their eyes off me because I have such a wonderful figure.

I tell him to stop talking dirty. But I'm afraid I blush happily when he says it.

We go walking along the lakeshore at night sometimes, just the two of us. So I suppose it could be said that we're walking out, but we're a long way from what that would mean back home. He does kiss me something fierce in the dark. I don't mind a bit, though I pretend that he has no right to do it. Sometimes when he seems afraid to start the kissing, don't I start it? Good enough for him says I?

Am I in love with him?

Well, not yet.

We do a lot of singing up here. Before we left Chicago, the Mistress heard me singing when I was scrubbing the steps to the floor where the bedrooms are (all except hers which is up in the tower). It was the lullaby in the Irish that Ma sings all the time.

"You have a beautiful voice, Clare dear," she says.

"Thank you, ma'am," says I.

"It's never been trained of course?"

"No, ma'am. If I ever marry and have a daughter I'll see that she takes voice."

"I'm sure you will marry," she says with a laugh, "and that you will have a daughter and she will sing just like you."

The Mistress looks terrible sad these days. No one knows why.

"Yes, ma'am."

"Would you ever sing a trio with Rosina and me?"

"Oh, ma'am," says I, "that would be beyond my station and besides I couldn't read music."

She laughs again. "All right, you raven-haired little schemer. You've said your piece. Now you will be in the music room at half four this afternoon, won't you? And you'll love every second of it!"

I laugh too and grin like I always do when someone has caught me out.

Well we don't sing anything very elaborate and they teach me the music and I pick it up quickly like I always do and we have a grand time. The young Master plays the piano and the Master himself comes down to the music room and asks where all the angels have come from and then sits down and listens.

At one of these singing things I discover a terrible thing about the Master. He can't read! I hand him a leaflet which has the words on so he can sing with us. He sings all right, but he's looking at the wrong page!

Delia says everyone knows that. He hides it well, but he always brings along someone like Joe Carey to read a contract for him before he signs it. So that's what Joe Carey does—he reads for the Master! He must know everything about him.

Isn't that terrible, Little Sister, the poor man has all that money and he can't read!

Of course Ma and Da can't read much either but they're not wealthy.

Weren't we the lucky ones to have the National School?

Well, darling Little Sister, I can make you a promise. In September of 1896, I'll have the money to bring you over. Just two more years and meself so longing to see what a beautiful young woman you've become. I thought it would take longer, but the Master and the Mistress are generous and I don't waste any money.

Won't it be wonderful to be together again! And then we can bring the others as want to come over to this land of freedom and equality. I don't want a house of my own on Geneva Lake. But if I ever have a daughter and she has a nice voice I hope I can pay for singing lessons for her.

I'm sorry the letter is so long. It's so quiet and peaceful up here tonight, especially because Tony had to drive the Master back to Chicago this afternoon.

He's only gone a few hours and already I miss him.

God bless all at home.

Pray for me.
Your loving sister,
Clare

October 14, 1894

Dear Mary Ellen,
The Mistress has been ill for the last two weeks. She's better now. But she's still pale and takes a nap every afternoon. The Master and the young folks were very worried.

Delia says that most of the women on Prairie Avenue are in poor health because their husbands have no time for them, being too busy with their work and their mistresses. But our Mistress is not that way.

Do I rave on about them, Mary Ellen? They

are such interesting people. But there seems to be much sadness in their lives.

One night a few weeks ago I couldn't sleep and so don't I sneak out of bed and walk along the servants' corridor. I think about sneaking outdoors for a breath of air but instead I walk up the servants' stairs to the tower. I've never been up there before because I'm not the Mistress's maid, not even her parlor maid.

Well, the hallway up there is something terrible grand, and the door to their bedroom looks like it is as thick as the walls of a cathedral.

I tell meself that I'm a disgrace and ought to be ashamed of meself and in my bare feet at that.

Then I hear the most terrible screams, like a man who is being tortured to death. It's the Master and he sounds like the Devil himself has taken his soul.

God forgive me for it, but I put my ear to the door and listen. The Mistress is saying real soft like that it's another of those terrible dreams and everything is all right. Then the Master sobs like he's a baby.

I run back to my room and jump under the covers and try to forget it all, only I can't. I don't ask Delia or anyone else because I don't want to admit that I've been a sneak. If the Mistress found out, she'd fire me for sure and without a reference, as much as she likes me.

I did hear Quinlan tell that horrid Joe Carey

that the Master was having them dreams again and they both laugh.

I hate that Joe Carey, hate him, hate him, hate him. He stares at me like he's taking off my clothes and it makes me feel sick.

Tony looks at me that way and I don't mind at all. But that's different. I say to him, "Well, do you like what you see, Mr. O'Boyle?"

"What do you mean?" says he, coming over all flushed.

"Do you like me when your imagination takes off all me clothes?"

"I'm not doing that," he says, embarrassed something terrible.

To tell the truth, Mary Ellen, I don't mind all that much.

"Yes you are," I say real haughty like. "You men only want one thing."

And he says, real serious like, "I want you, Clare Marie Raftery, and I mean to have you someday."

I'm feeling like my legs are turning to melted butter.

"That will be as may be," says I as pert as I can. "But keep your imagination to yourself until then."

He just grins and turns red again.

"I'll imagine what I like," says he, "and you can't stop me."

I flounce out of the room, burning up all over. And feeling very happy. Hadn't he proposed marriage and hadn't I accepted? Mind you, he's going to have to be a lot more formal than that.

I wouldn't stop him from looking that way at me if I could.

The young Master has finished college and is working with the Master, though his heart doesn't seem to be in it. I think they have agreed that he'll work for two years and then he can go off to the seminary at Baltimore.

He's working now at a place they call the Board of Trade which sounds to me like a gambling den, but when the young Master comes home and sinks into an easy chair in the library he looks exhausted and happy, just like lads back home after they've won a hurling match.

"It's crazy, Clare," he says to me when I try to sneak out of the room without him seeing me. "But it's a lot of fun, like a football game down at Notre Dame."

"Hmnpf," says I as I leave, "sounds to me like a gambling den."

"The biggest in all the world. No salvation to be found there, Clare, but a lot of excitement."

No one asks me, but I think that place will make it all the harder for him to go off to the seminary.

Well, enough for now. My love to all the family. Young Paddy must be growing into a strapping lad by now, God bless him.

Pray for me.
Your loving sister,
Clare

November 19, 1894

Dear Mary Ellen,

I have had a terrible suspicion lately. I think the Mistress wouldn't mind if the young Master fell in love with me. I know she'd be happy if he went off to Baltimore to become a priest. But she'd be happier if he stayed here and married someone and lived in a house down the street like Mr. Marshall Field's son does.

I don't understand why she'd pick a little chit of a servant girl from Mayo with the brogue in her voice and the smell of the bog on her skin and a loud mouth and terrible inquisitive nose in her face.

Still she talks to me about him like she was trying to find out whether I might be willing to be her daughter-in-law. All very gentle and in-direct, but she knows what she's saying and so do I.

I'm flustered something terrible when I finally figure out what she's saying.

To tell the truth, Mary Ellen, I'm also terrible flattered. Meself a great lady on Prairie Avenue! Sure, I'm enough of an actress to learn how to play the game. Clare Marie Raftery one of the swells.

The young Master finds me amusing, I think, but there's nothing between us. I've watched him with women at the parties they have here (and meself peeking through the door of course) and he's very nice, but he keeps his emotions under control.

Could I attract him?

Ah, that's the question now, isn't it?

Probably I could if I set my mind to it. Certainly the Mistress thinks I can or she wouldn't be hinting the way she is.

So I think about it all and lose a couple of nights sleep, tossing and turning and trying to figure it all out.

Why me? I keep asking.

Then finally I know what my feelings are.

I'd sooner have Tony in my bed than any of the toffs on Prairie Avenue, even a nice toff like Peter Cardian Junior.

So the first thing the next morning, don't I sneak out into the stable where Tony is polishing the brougham and sneak up behind him and kiss him on the cheek and whisper, "I love you, Anthony O'Boyle, and I always will."

I run away as quick as I can, giggling all the way.

So that's how I deal with the temptation to be a posh. I'll have to tell the Mistress some way or the other.

I don't regret it one moment.

Like Da always says, once you make a big decision, you stick with it and you never look back.

Pray for me that I'm able to work it out with the Mistress, I don't want to hurt the poor woman's feelings.
Your loving sister,
Clare

CHAPTER 7

I PAUSED IN my study of Clare Raftery's letters. A substantial amount of destiny was locked into place in that stable on Prairie Avenue that November day in 1894. Presumably Tony O'Boyle knew then and after what a fortunate man he was. If he ever forgot it, she would have reminded him in no uncertain terms. The history of the Cardin Clan would have been very different if the bold honesty of that young woman had been introduced into their lives. I would not be worried about the quagmire into which five generations of misguided and unenjoyed avarice had led them.

Clare's decision was the proper one for her, a good one for Tony, and the loss of a last chance for the Cardins, a chance that perhaps was now being granted again.

The "young Master" seemed a curiously bloodless young man—intense, studious, high-minded, and so easily mesmerized by the Board of Trade. Petey was perhaps cut from a different bolt of Irish linen. I hoped so. I had a hunch that before this struggle was over he'd be a useful and necessary ally.

I wondered that Rose Lennon Cardin would be willing and even eager to break the rules of her caste—and she surely was a woman who was raised with servants all around—to try to recruit this fierce young Mayo woman for a daughter-in-law. The admirable characteristics evident in the letter must have been even more evident in the person. Rose saw Clare as a grace. Clare saw the Cardins as a trap. Both presumably were right.

Christmas Eve 1894

Dear Mary Ellen,

This is the third Christmas away from those I love and my poor heart is breaking. Mistress caught me weeping as I scrubbed the bath on the second floor. She hugged me and told me that it was all right to cry and that I'd see all my family again.

That made me feel better. She isn't mad at me for telling her that I loved Tony O'Boyle.

The way I did it was tell her one day when we were talking (and meself hiding from Mrs. Lyne) what a terrible young man Tony was. I went through all his defects, though to tell you the truth he doesn't seem to have any. She laughed and laughed and told me that it was obvious I was in love with him. I denied it hotly but she said he was a lucky man and I was a lucky woman (not "boy" and "girl" you notice).

So that was that, but there was so much sadness in her heart I wanted to cry for her. She knows that her son really doesn't have the mark of a priest on him after all and that he needs someone to love who will save him from . . . well, I don't know what, but from <u>something</u>.

She has a daughter so that's all right, but she needs to have a daughter-in-law too.

This is a very unhappy house for Christmas Time. The servants are all happy and laughing and singing carols and writing home like I am now. But upstairs there is sadness. It fills the place like the smell of peat fire. The Mistress and the young Mistress have both had the flu again. The Master has too much of the drink taken every day, though he's even more polite to us when he's fluttered. The young Master strides up and down like he's an animal locked up in a cage.

And, do you know, Mary Ellen, I don't think any of them knows why they're sad.

Joe Carey is back to spend Christmas with us, evil man that he is. And he has some woman out in the coach house who he says is his mother. I haven't seen her, but don't all those that have say she's a horror. But they're not the cause of the misery in this house. It was here before they came.

I'm giving himself a red woolen scarf for Christmas so he'll be warm when he takes the landau out. He's giving me some lovely ribbons, though I'm not supposed to know that.

And two Christmases from now, you and I will be together, my dear Mary Ellen.

And just maybe I'll be a married woman by then. No promises about that, however. Your man has yet to speak of such things—at least clearly enough so I can say "Yes."

My very best love to all.

Keep praying for me.

Your loving sister,

Clare

January 12, 1895

Dear Mary Ellen,

Well, I've been promoted. Now I am the young Mistress' personal maid. She's never had one before but now that's she going on seventeen, the Mistress decided that I ought to be the maid for her daughter.

Not that I mind. It will be a lot easier than scrubbing floors. The young Mistress is kind and sweet like her mother and sad like her mother too, but she doesn't seem to have as much willpower as the Mistress.

Few women do.

Quinlan and Mrs. Lyne are furious because

they hate me so much. Jenny Kinane won't speak to me, which is a blessing. Even our Cousin Delia has her nose out of joint, but she'll get over it.

I didn't ask for the job and am as surprised as anyone that I got it. The young Mistress told me that Quinlan and Mrs. Lyne actually argued with the Mistress that I was unsuited for the task. She shut them up pretty quick. You don't argue with the Mistress.

So I guess she's not mad at me because I didn't want to be her daughter-in-law.

The Master stopped me in the corridor when I was trying to scurry by him and congratulated me. The smell of the creature is on him as it often is.

"It appears that my coachman has excellent taste in women," he said. "He agrees with my wife, so that leaves no doubt about it."

"Ah, isn't he a terrible amadon altogether?" I stammered.

"Isn't he now?" he laughs again.

I didn't think he even knew who I was.

"I know we can't be friends, Clare," the young Mistress says to me, "but we can be friendly to one another, can't we?"

Well, I'm taken aback by that too. All I can say is, "Friendly it is."

Of course we're friends. In a couple of days we're "Clare" and "Rosina" to one another and we're gossiping about our men, me about the big oaf and she about Terry O'Mahoney, on whom she has her eye, a big, genial man who works with the young Master. If he doesn't have his eye on my pretty young Mistress, he's a fool. But as I've told you often, Mary Ellen, men tend to be fools.

I must let none of this go to my head. I'm still a greenhorn serving girl from the bogs of Mayo.

I still try to figure out why such pleasant, generous people with so much to live for are so sad. Even the young Mistress with so much of her life ahead of her.

Her eyes shine when she talks of Mr. O'Mahoney and they grow dull and she says, "But life doesn't work out the way we want it to, does it, Clare?"

"I haven't lived long enough to know," I says.

If a beautiful girl like that says something so sad, she must have heard it from her mother. Still I don't see what the Mistress has to complain about.

Maybe it's those screams from the Master when he's dreaming.

You know me well enough to know that I still sneak up to the tower floor to listen for those screams. He shouts about a "curse," so he's afraid of something all right.

The Mistress tells him that he's a superstitious fool, but real tender like.

Then sometimes I hear other noises and she's the one who screams, but not in pain, if you take my meaning.

Sure, it's a nice scream, I say to meself and go back to my room to dream that I'll scream like that someday. Soon I hope.

The Master does get fluttered, more often now I think than when I first came here. But he's a quiet, sad man when he's fluttered, tears in his eyes. He doesn't hurt anyone.

If a man of mine got fluttered often because he was afraid of something, I suppose I'd be sad too.

What do I know of life and suffering?

I'll be counting the days till you come, dearest Little Sister. Tell Da and Ma I'll pray every day for a good crop this year and especially on St. Brigid's day.

Pray for me.

Your loving sister,
Clare

February 14, 1895

Dear Mary Ellen,

Didn't I get a fancy lace valentine from your man today and a pound of candy? Some women would have been angry because he should have been saving his money instead of wasting it on foolish and trivial gifts. I'll never do that. Whenever my man gives me something I'll hug him and kiss him and thank him.

Then I'll give him my gift—warm gloves to match his scarf. We do a lot of kissing and

*hugging these days, mostly out in the stable where
no one will see us. It's more fun each time we do
it, but as the young priest used to tell us back in
Bekan, kissing leads to other things. I don't mind
that, but only in my wedding bed. Which he
knows even though I have not said it or even
mentioned it to him. Well, not in so many words.*

*"When I finally have you for me own, Clare
Marie Raftery," he says to me, "I'll play with you
all day every day. I won't give you a minute's
peace, I won't."*

*Well, I like the sound of that, but I don't tell
him.*

*"That will be as may be," says I, "but there's a
few little formalities which will have to come first."*

He just laughs.

*Poor Rosina asks me about men. What can I
tell her?*

*Well, I have to say something. So I say, "To tell
the truth, I think they are more afraid of us than
we are of them and need us more than we need
them."*

*That interests her. "You mean Terry, uh, Mr.
O'Mahoney is afraid of me."*

*" 'Twould be a foolish man who was not afraid
of someone as pretty as you are," says I.*

She just giggles.

*I think I'm beginning to understand why they're
so sad.*

*I ask Rosina bluntly one day, while I'm helping
her with her corset before a big dinner party, why
I'm her maid and not Jenny or Delia.*

"Does it have to be that tight?" she gasps.

"Only if we want to get that dress on you. If you ask me, you'd look fine without the thing . . . You were saying?"

"My mother wanted you. She knew I liked you, but that had nothing to do with it. Even if I didn't like you, you still would have been my personal maid."

"But why did she want me?"

She shrugs her pretty shoulders. "She says you know what life means."

"Do I now?" I says, astonished as you may well believe.

"Uh-huh. She says that your parents raised you to work hard and not to complain and to be nice to everyone and not to think money is the only thing in life."

"Oh."

"My mother and father are afraid of money. My father was once terribly poor. My mother's parents were well-to-do but lost everything during the War. My father earned money the hard way and he's afraid of losing it. They both are. They want to have it and everything that money can buy for them, but they fear the effects on me and Peter and on themselves too. And sometimes I think my father feels guilty about the way he earned his money before they were married. Sometimes he says money is a curse. And my mother says, well, you can always get rid of it. He groans and says she knows he can't."

"Oh."

"Does it make any sense to you, Clare?"

"I don't think so," I tell her.

In my head, however, I think all the parts are fitting together. The Master must have killed people to make all the money they have.

How horrible.

I hope poor Rosina never figures that out.

It's a crazy world, isn't it, Mary Ellen?

Pray for me as I do for you and the family all the time.

I miss you something terrible. Only a year and a half more.

Your loving sister,
Clare

Young Clare had figured most of it out. Yet she had no idea of the cloud of tragedy that hung over the house of Cardin and would hang over it for another century, at least. Just as well; for all her insight and courage there was nothing she could do to stop it.

May 8, 1895

Dear Mary Ellen,

My heart is like to breaking. I'll be separated from my love for at least two months and maybe all summer. The young Mistress and the Mistress are going to the camp at Geneva Lake this week.

The rest of the family will join them on the Fourth of July when the camp "officially" opens.

It's been a terrible cold winter, the worst in years they say. Delia and I shivered in our snug little rooms and the "hot water" heat pipes were not much help. So we had to build fires in all the grates in the house, even if we were someone's personal maid. I thought I'd die of the shivers. Still I should thank God and the Blessed Mother that I didn't get the flu.

Quinlan tells me that only a "skeleton" staff will go up on the train with them. Tony will go because the Mistress trusts him more than any of the other drivers. The Mistress's personal maid will "do" for the two of them. I should not count, he said, on another summer of leisure up there because others more deserving than I would join the skeleton staff in July. I was back to being a maid of all work again.

Quinlan told me this with a smirk on his lips. Mrs. Lyne stood behind him with a wicked look in her eyes. They knew what they were doing to me.

The Mistress has been sick for the last month, with the flu, they say. The young Mistress is worn out from all the parties celebrating her graduation from St. Xavier. There was a terrible mess when they had a "coming out" ball for her at the Palmer House. The Master had made careful inquiries of the men on the street and they promised him that they and their wives and their children would come to the ball.

No one came. Apparently the wives got together after they sent their acceptances and ruled against it, the terrible women, says I. It didn't bother the young Mistress much because she danced most of the night with her Terry. But the Mistress, who got up out of her sick bed to come, wept most of the evening. The Master, of course, got himself fluttered, the fool.

So they're off to the camp to recover. The young Master says he'll be going to Baltimore in the autumn. But there's talk about a young woman with black hair and calculating blue eyes from San Francisco who is visiting relatives here and who has set her cap for him.

She's a grand beauty but I don't like her much. Neither does my poor Rosina. I don't think the Mistress would like her either if she weren't so sick with the flu.

I know this Betty Riordan as she's called will get the young Master. Maybe she'll be good for him. Maybe like I heard the Master whispering to him, "She'll give you more direction in your life. And she looks like she'll be good in bed, if you lay down the law with her in that regard. Doesn't she?"

The young Master didn't say a word in response. He looks at this Miss Riordan much the way he might look at a flower in a garden or a spider on the wall.

Not the way me love looks at me.

There I go rambling on about these poor people when I should feel sorry for meself about losing my man for several long months.

He says to me before he leaves, "I'll be faithful to our love, Clare."

And I say back, "That will be as may be, Anthony O'Boyle. But if you're not, I might just murder you."

Well, I wouldn't go that far, dearest Mary Ellen. Not quite.

Anyway, write to me a lot because I will be so lonely.

I'm happy to learn that the crops are doing well this year. Praise God and the Blessed Mother for hearing our prayers.

Pray to both of them for me.
Your loving and lonely sister,
Clare

Poor young people, I thought to myself. All three of them would be dead in 1918, wiped out by the Plague of the Spanish Lady as it was called. Only Terry O'Mahoney, perhaps with a broken heart, perhaps not, would remain to carry on their generation.

Did the flu also carry off Clare and her Tony? Somehow I rather thought not.

May 18, 1895
Geneva Lake

My dearest Mary Ellen,
As you can see, I did join the Mistress and my poor Rosina and me love here at Geneva Lake.

The country air and the lovely spring revived the Mistress's spirits and they say her health. She looks dreadful pale to me, though not as sick as she did in March and April. Darling Rosina is exchanging love letters with her Terry and is perfectly happy.

WELL, the Mistress wakes up one morning, feeling better than she had in months, and looks around and asks where Clare Raftery is.

She's told by her own maid who likes me what Quinlan and Mrs. Lyne have done. She cranks up the funny-looking thing that they call a telephone (which was installed both here and on Prairie Avenue so the Master and Mistress can talk every day).

Before the day is over the young Master finds me scrubbing the floor of the kitchen. "Clare, my mother talked to Quinlan and Mrs. Lyne and you're to go up to the camp tomorrow."

"I'm supposed to walk, is it?" *I say, knowing what makes him laugh.*

"No, you're to ride up on the train to Williams Bay with me and Miss Riordan. We'll be picked up in the phaeton by someone whom I think you know."

"The young Mistress is it?"

"She'll probably come along too," *he says with another laugh.*

I'm not at all eager for a long train ride with Miss Betty Riordan, but it's better than walking.

She's not all that delighted when she sees me at the Northwestern station. Her quick glance says that she doesn't like me and would like to push me in front of the train. On the other hand she sees that the young Master likes me, so she's polite to me, even sometimes addresses a comment to me, usually about how wonderful San Francisco is.

I couldn't possibly be a rival she tells herself. Well, I'm not a rival and that's good for her because, calculating wench that she is, I'm an even more calculating wench. And besides, though God forgive me for thinking it, I am better-looking than she is.

Rosina and me love do meet me at the train. She kisses me, but he doesn't dare. At night he made up for that.

We had a song session almost as soon as we arrived at the camp. The two Mistresses and I doing the singing and the young Master playing the piano. Miss San Francisco doesn't look pleased.

"I'm so happy you're with us now, Clare," Rosina whispers to me. "That terrible Joe Carey is up here with that old woman of his. I don't like the way he looks at me."

"He looks at every woman that way," I says. "Why does the Mistress permit him to be here?"

"I don't know. He's always polite to her and she seems to trust him. He's a big help to Daddy."

"What am I supposed to do about him?" I ask Rosina.

"Well, if he gets fresh, you can drive him away."

"More likely we'd get that O'Boyle man to do it. He's not very smart, but he is a strong brute."

She laughs at me and says, "I knew you'd say something like that. My father says he has a great future because he is honest and diligent and very smart. I agree with my father."

" 'Tis your privilege," I say with my nose up in the air. And we both laugh.

It's much easier for me here than on Prairie Avenue because Rosina requires very little attention.

So I'm looking forward to a long summer's holiday.

If something more doesn't go wrong in this sad family.

Say a prayer for them when you're praying for me. And remember when this summer is over it will be only one more year and you'll be able to come to America.

Your loving and very happy sister,
Clare

June 29, 1895
Geneva Lake

Dear Mary Ellen,
The Master and the young Master and Mr. O'Mahoney have come up for a "couple of weeks" of golf. More servants too. So we're very busy. The Master is not drinking but he looks

haggard and gray while the Mistress is her old self again. They seemed happy to see one another, which is the way a husband and wife should act, isn't it now?

Though, I'm not supposed to have any duties except taking care of Rosina, I help out on everything else because both the family and servants need it.

"You're the hardest-working woman in the place, Clare Marie Raftery," the Master says. And he's not fluttered.

"Well, someone has to do the work," I says "and the menfolk playing golf and lollygagging all day long."

"Ah, your man is a lucky man," he says.

"I don't have a man yet, Master," I tell him, "and when I do he'll know he's lucky because I will tell him so every day."

He laughs at that, not the mild little laugh you usually hear from him but a big, rich, happy laugh.

God knows he needs a laugh now and again.

They have been very good to me ever since I arrived at their house on Prairie Avenue, so I will not criticize them, even if that terrible Joe Carey continues to loiter here. The Master and the Mistress are always friendly with him, almost affectionate. That seems crazy to me.

My love agrees with me. "There's something wrong somewhere, Claire," he says. "You can almost smell it. And whatever it is, it gets worse."

"Too much money," I says.

"Maybe," he says. "Too much bad money."

Which is what I'm thinking too, but I didn't want to say that until he said it first.

We walk along the shore of the lake every night holding hands and stopping often to kiss. It's so hot in America this summer that I think we'll all perish with the heat.

Tony said it was even worse the summer before I came to America. "It's either too hot or too cold here."

So last night I did something very wicked. Not sinful, mind you, and I'm not going to tell a priest. And don't you dare show this part of the letter to Ma and Da.

I was so hot when we came to the place in the woods where we usually turn around and go back and I was so dry and dusty that I said to himself, "I don't care what you're going to do, Tony O'Boyle, but I'm to have a swim for meself."

"You have no swimming costume, Clare," he says, shocked half to death.

"I don't need one," says I. "It's so dark tonight that there'll be nothing to see."

So don't I take off all me clothes and jump into the water. It felt so wonderful that I thought that heaven might be like this.

Your man comes along after me and himself falling into the lake.

"You're a desperate woman, Clare Marie Raftery," he says.

"A lot you know," says I.

Well we splash around and swim and talk in whispers. We're careful not to get too close to one another, himself being more careful than I.

"You'd never do that on a night with a full moon," he says as we walk home.

"You just wait and see," I tell him.

"I'll do that," he says, not knowing whether I'm serious or not, but hoping I am.

When we come up the path from the lake, we have to pass the house on the way to the servants' quarters. Don't we hear the poor Master cry out again in his sleep.

"Glory be," says my frightened love. "Isn't that the cry of a lost soul? A banshee out on the lake!"

"There are no banshees in the United States of America. I think there's a law against them," I tell him. "That was the Master having one of his bad dreams."

"Poor man," he sighs.

"I hope he's not a lost soul," I says, making the sign of the cross. Tony does the same thing.

He kisses me good night like he usually does and I kind of groan like in his arms.

"God protect us from that kind of dream in our life ahead," he says.

Normally I would have told him to speak for his own life, not for mine. But not that night, not with the Master screaming again. I squeeze his

*arm and say, "Holy Mother of God, protect us,
now and at the hour of our death. Amen."*

*Are you wondering, Little Sister, whether I'll
swim Indian style as they call it here some night
in a full moon? Sure, you know me well enough
to know that I'll do it, so you won't have to ask in
your next letter!*

*Pray for me and for this poor troubled family
that has been so kind to me.*
Your loving sister,
Clare

September 1895

Dear Mary Ellen,

*We're back in Chicago and the weather is
beautiful again. The Mistress talks like her old
self, but I think she still looks sick. The Master is
drinking again. The young Master did not go to
the seminary and even went out to San Francisco
for a week. My Rosina is going to parties several
times a week, but not on Prairie Avenue or with
any of the young people who live here. She says
the Catholics from St. Patrick's parish over on
the West Side are more fun than the Prairie
Avenue snobs. Besides, Terry O'Mahoney lives in
St. Patrick's.*

*The dolt whom I love acts as if we were going
to be married next year after you come. I pay no
attention at all. He has to ask me formally or
there'll be nothing like that happening.*

He also says that he is going to leave service here next year and begin his own livery company. He says it's up to me whether I want to continue to work. I ask why shouldn't I work? Who's going to support me? Saint Joseph?

I ask Rosina whether the rule against married maids applies in this house.

"Of course not," she says with a big grin. "We're Catholics here and marriage is a sacrament. We'd be proud to have a married woman here. Don't worry about that, Clare dear."

I feel my face grow hot. "I've no plans at all, at all. I was just curious."

"I understand, Clare, you have no plans at all, at all."

And she giggles, like she knows I'm lying. But I'm not really lying. Well not exactly.

I might work a little while here until Tony gets his livery company going. But I'd rather slave for my own children than for wealthy people, even nice wealthy people.

The amadon better have a ring for me Christmas, just a tiny inexpensive ring. Otherwise, he'll get his marching orders.

It sounds like I'm not in love?

Oh, Mary Ellen, my darling, I'm hopelessly in love!

And as for swimming Indian style on a moonlit night up at the camp? Haven't I been after telling you that I'd provide no details.

But we did it and it was wonderful and nothing else happened. Are you satisfied now?

Just another year, Little Sister, and I'll have you with me. If we can earn enough money we'll be able to bring along young Paddy and even that little lad Tim. Won't that be grand!

I'm glad that the farm was such a success last year. I wish I were there. But, like it or not, my destiny is to be an American.

The Master and the Mistress argue all the time now. She keeps saying, "Why didn't you tell me?"

And he says in that quiet voice of his, "I thought you knew."

I don't like the sound of that.

My love to everyone.

Keep praying for me.

Jesus and Mary and Patrick be with you all.
Your loving sister,
Clare

December 25, Christmas Day, 1895

Dear Mary Ellen,

Jesus and Mary be with you.

This is the happiest day of my life. So far. Am I not wearing an engagement ring that my love gave me at Mass at St. John's by the Roundhouse? I didn't think I was going to get it and my heart would break. Sure, I ought to have had more confidence in my man than that, ought I not?

I was the last one to know of course. I think he'd showed the little gold Claddagh ring to everyone in the house before he gave it to me.

It was his grandmother's ring, she that died in the famine, poor dear woman, at the age of twenty-five. I don't care how small it is and that there are no diamonds in it. It will be my engagement ring and my wedding ring together for the rest of my life. I'll always think of that good and kind young woman who wore it first and pray to her that God will protect our love.

Maybe it's just me, but somehow everyone in the house seems especially happy this Christmas Day.

Poor dear people.

May Jesus and Mary and Patrick be with you during this joyous season.

Tell everyone I said happy new year and that I love them all.

Your loving sister,

Clare

January 1st, 1896

Dear Mary Ellen,

May the Good Lord have mercy on us all!

A terrible thing has happened here. The Mistress is dead. Murdered in bed on New Year's Eve.

Her maid couldn't get in the door this morning. She pounded on the door and tried to awaken her. Then she told Rosina who became hysterical. Mrs. Lyne and Quinlan dithered. So I went to the stable, got my love and a couple of the lads and they came up to the tower and battered down the door.

I'll never forget the sight. The room was covered with blood, some of the Master's whiskey bottles had been smashed and the room smelt of the creature. The Mistress was lying on her bed, her clothes torn off and her face beaten into a terrible mess. They had interfered with her and even shoved a crucifix inside her. They had also cut her body many times with the broken bottles. If it wasn't her room, I would not have recognized her.

Most all of us vomited.

Quinlan would not summon the police, so I told my Tony to ride over to the station and get them. Everyone kind of shied away from Rosina and Peter. I called Terry O'Mahoney on the phone, first time I ever used the thing, and it took a long time to get through to him. When I did it, he sounded like he was in the next room. I tried to console the young Master and the young Mistress as best I could, holding them both in my arms as they sobbed on my chest. I don't know where the Master is. The police think he did it in one of his drunken rages. But he never had rages. They're out looking for him now. Everyone here thinks his arrest will be in headlines in all the papers tomorrow morning.

It's snowing again, big heavy flakes that dance in the gaslights outside. I say to meself that it's like they're doing a dance of death.

The police questioned us all day. Some of us, Tony and meself, could have told them what had happened, but they weren't interested in what we knew, only in making a case against the Master.

They were very hard on me.

"You were the one that took charge, were you not?"

"I was not."

"Didn't you order that the door be broken down."

"No."

"Others say that you did."

"When Rosina couldn't arouse her mother I went and asked the stable lads to break into the room. I have no authority to give orders in this house."

"You ordered the coachman to go to the police station?"

"I suggested it to him."

"You're only a common maid of all work, aren't you?"

"I am Miss Rosina's personal maid."

"Could you not have let the butler and the housekeeper take charge?"

"They seemed unwilling or unable to do so."

"So you usurped their authority."

"If I had waited for them, the poor Mistress

would still be in the room and you'd still be in your police station."

"You took a lot on yourself, did you not?"

"I don't think so."

"And you weren't surprised when you saw the inside of the death room?"

I glared at them for a moment.

"I was shocked and sickened."

"You thought she was dead, didn't you?"

"The Mistress has been sick. I thought she might be very sick."

"Come now, you knew she was dead."

"I did NOT and them that says I did are liars."

"Why are you protecting Mr. Cardin? Was he your special friend?"

"If you weren't a police officer I'd claw your eyes out for saying that."

"Where is he now?"

"I don't know."

"You're lying!"

"I am NOT."

"What time did Mr. Cardin go out last night."

"I have no idea."

"Wasn't it odd that he didn't take one of the coaches?"

"No. He often walks over to Clark Street."

"You think he's on Clark Street?"

"I don't know. Why don't you look for yourselves?"

And so it went. They finally gave up on me with

a warning that if I was caught in my lies it would go hard with me. I laughed at them.

Some of us could have told them who had killed the Mistress. They didn't want to know about anyone but the Master.

They didn't ask me where I had been when the Master might have gone out. The truth was I was in the coach house talking to my fiancé. Only talking, Little Sister. I kissed him good night when the clock struck twelve and went back to my room, and meself able to walk a straight line despite the few sips of the creature I had taken.

"You won't get off so easily next New Year's Eve," he says to me with a big happy grin on his face that made my poor legs turn to butter.

"What makes you think you'll get off easy?" I says over my shoulder.

I'm sure the murder took place after that.

Well that's the end of this horrible story. For now anyway.

Jesus and Mary and Patrick be with all of you and may God grant eternal peace to this poor dear woman whom I loved.

Your grieving sister,
Clare

P.S. My Tony just came to me and said, "They took the phaeton and the horses."

"It was there when I left," I said.

"I was dead to the world and the other lads

had so much of the creature taken when they came in that the whole stable could have vanished and they wouldn't have noticed."

"They're out of their minds!"

"We have to find them, Clare. We can't let them get away with this."

And we won't, Mary Ellen, you can depend on that.

January 6, 1896

Dear Mary Ellen,

May Jesus and Mary be with those I love.

We buried the Mistress this morning. Out at Mount Olivet Cemetery, miles and miles from here, in the frozen ground. I couldn't go to the cemetery because I had to work on the preparation of the meal after the burial. But I did sneak out in the terrible cold and run over to St. John's Church for some of the Mass. Bishop Foley himself preached and he preached powerful well, praising the Mistress's good works as well he might. Everyone was crying, the Master worst of all.

He was not fluttered like he was all three nights of the wake.

The Bishop said that money had meant nothing to the Mistress. Maybe that was true in a way, but money is the cause of all the problems in this terrible house.

The Master is out of jail. He had a good

alibi—he was dead drunk in a saloon with lots of men as witnesses. The papers and the police say they are not finished with him, but that's only talk. They know he didn't kill his wife.

There was a story in all the papers about some kind of curse put on the Master and his family by a rebel officer during the Civil War. I don't believe any of that nonsense, though maybe the Master did. The only curse in this house is money—too much of it come too easily and maybe in the wrong way.

The wake was terrible—three nights in the ballroom and ourselves working every minute to keep the house clean and neat. The young Mistress hardly knows what she's doing. That Betty Riordan hussy who came in on the train from San Francisco may be part human after all. She broke down and wept and I had to hold both her and the young Mistress in my arms. She thanked me very politely afterward.

"You're an amazing young woman, Clare," she says. "I'm sorry I was rude to you last summer."

"Thank you, miss," I say back to her.

Only late at night after everyone has left the ballroom, except the Master who never sleeps, do I go up to the casket and kneel down to pray. The woman in it doesn't look at all like the Mistress. I pray a long time.

"She loved you too, Clare Raftery," the Master says to me when I get off my knees, his voice

slurred with the drink. "Almost like you were a daughter."

"Yes, Master, I know."

And I loved her almost like she was a mother, but I didn't say that. Maybe I should have.

Anyway, it's all over now. She's at peace. She has the joy we all want.

The rest of the family?

Pray for them, Mary Ellen. They need a lot of prayer.

Jesus and Mary and Patrick be with all those who love me.

Your loving sister,
Clare

March 4, 1896

Dear Mary Ellen,

Jesus and Mary be with all I love.

A wonderful thing has happened for all of us! It's all so sad that I'm still weeping.

The Master doesn't live in the house anymore. The tower floor is locked and no one goes up there. He's staying in a suite at the Palmer House. He comes by here once in a while to tend to business. He looks terrible, like an old man, though he's no older than our Da.

This morning the young Mistress, who is still dazed, says to me, "My Father would like to see you in the library, Clare."

So I go down to the library with my heart in my mouth, wondering whether he has found out.

I wonder even more when I see that my Tony is already there.

"Sit down, please," says the Master, like we are distinguished guests.

So we sit down.

"My wife," he says and his voice catches, "was extremely fond of both of you, as you no doubt knew."

He pauses, trying to prevent the tears from flowing. I think to meself that he won't be with us long either. The mark of death is upon him.

"Ours was perhaps a strange love," he begins again. "But we truly and deeply loved one another."

"Never a doubt, Master," I says because someone has to say something.

"Her death was cruel and brutal. The doctors tell me that she died from the first blow and that . . . all the other things were done to her afterward."

Neither of us say anything.

"It was mercifully quick, however," he stumbles on, "to the death she was facing. She would have lived perhaps another year and eventually died in terrible pain. Her . . . her killers in a strange way did her a good turn."

I'm astonished as you may imagine, Mary Ellen. I think I knew she was dying but I was afraid to say it even to meself.

"I have told this to the children. They will tell others I presume. All our lives are in the hands of God, are they not, Clare?"

"They surely are, Master."

"I have retained the Pinkerton Agency to find the criminals responsible for her death. They assure me that neither of them will ever harm anyone again."

Neither himself nor I say anything.

"I regret," his voice catches, "that she had to suffer for my sins."

"Jesus suffered for all our sins, Master," I says, the words leaping out before I can stop them. "And He and the Blessed Mother love all of us, sinners that we all are."

He looks at me for a long moment as if he is wondering whether to believe me.

"I should tell Bishop Foley that he has an able missionary living in this house," he says finally with a sad smile.

We all laugh, a very quiet and melancholy laugh.

"In any event, I have consulted with the children about what I am going to do now and they enthusiastically agree."

He takes two envelopes from his coat pocket and puts them on the desk.

"I know that you will be married in the fall and that you, Tony, will start your own livery agency and that you, Clare, will bring your sister over with the money you've saved. We thought it

*would be helpful to you both if we gave you a
small wedding present early. Clare, we hope you
will stay with us here as long as you can. Rosina
and Peter will supervise the house as I am not yet
ready to live in it. They would regret losing either
of you. And, Clare, we'd be delighted to have
your sister work for us here."*

*My love and I look at one another. We're not
sure what to do. We don't pick up the envelopes
he has pushed in our direction.*

*"Please take them," he says. "Your accep-
tance of our gift will give us a little light in these
dark days."*

*I look at Tony. He frowns and nods, but with a
hint of a question in his nod.*

*"Thank you very much, Master," says I. "We
accept these generous gifts in the spirit in which
they were given and with much gratitude to you
and the young Master and the young Mistress.
And we'll always stay close to them, one way or
another."*

*"You really don't know they're generous,
Clare," he says, his old big Cork grin coming back
for a moment. "You haven't opened them yet."*

*"Ah, Master," says I with my best smile. "You
have never been anything but generous."*

*We shake hands and leave the room. I glance
back into the library. He is looking out the
window on the gray March day, his head bowed,
his shoulders slumped.*

We don't open the gifts till we get to the coach house. There's five one-hundred-dollar bills in mine and ten in Tony's. We weep in each other's arms. It's a sweet gift but bittersweet, Mary Ellen, if you take my meaning.

Well, the good news is that I can bring not only you over here but young Paddy and Little Tim. Tony can begin his business with a couple of cabs instead of only one.

So I'm very happy.

And very sad.

"Should we keep the money?" Tony asks me.

" 'Twould be rude not to," says I. "We don't have much choice."

"Do you think he knows?" Tony says.

"Maybe," I say. "But he would have given this gift anyway."

"We'll never be certain this side of paradise."

And I reply with a hug and a fierce kiss and he caresses me, very lightly I might add.

So we both write notes to the Master thanking him and say that we'll both stay here till the wedding and meself after the wedding.

May Jesus and Mary and Patrick be with those I love.

I'll see you very soon now, darling Little Sister, sooner than I thought. As soon as we can book passage. I can hardly wait.

Your loving sister,
Clare

I glanced through the rest of the letters. The last one recounted Red Pete's death at Geneva Lake (as the lake is properly called, though few know that anymore) and his quiet wake and funeral. The great men of Prairie Avenue boycott the wake as they have everything else that happened in that tragic house. Clare is sad but not surprised at the Master's death. She promises to meet her sister at the Central Station the day she comes from New York.

Then the correspondence ends because her "little sister" is now in Chicago. I presume that Mary Ellen had brought all the letters with her.

I thumb through the letters again. I must have missed one.

I cannot find it, however. The family must have removed one letter.

I sit at the table and ponder. The mystery of the locked room on Prairie Avenue is now for all practical purposes solved. Only one or two points need to be cleared up. Does that mystery illumine in any way the present apparent crisis in the Cardin family?

Perhaps, though not necessarily directly.

Clare Raftery was right about the essential flaw—money. And that was the flaw that still haunted the family.

I stacked the xeroxed copies in as neat a pile as I am capable of and returned them to the helpful docent.

"Are they interesting, Bishop Blackie?"

"Very. The Foundation should think of publishing them. She is a remarkable young woman and her letters are a vivid account of the life of an immigrant serving girl at that time."

"I'll tell them what you said. You're the first one to have read them."

"Ah," I said, one of my important questions answered before I had asked it. "Is the name of the family who donated the letters a secret?"

"Not at all. It was the Phelans from Beverly. Dr. Phelan, the cardiologist. Clare O'Boyle was Mrs. Phelan's grandmother. Both of them lived into their eighties, Clare and her husband that is."

"Indeed."

Into the 1950s or '60s. Perhaps I had seen them at Mass at our parish church when I was growing up. Good for you, Clare, you and your man survived the Plague of the Spanish Lady.

"Yes. They found the letters in a closet at the family summer home at Lake Geneva."

"Very interesting."

And ironic.

The Phelans lived right down the street from the virtuous Dr. Mary Kathleen Ryan Murphy. I must make a call on them immediately after Christmas.

Back at the Cathedral Rectory I endeavored to exorcise the vivid images of Prairie Avenue in the 1890s that Clare's letters had created. There were Christmas preparations to be supervised—not that my supervision was essential or important or even noticed.

After supper I allowed myself a few minutes to

reflect on Clare Raftery's letters. Too many questions remained to be answered about both past and present.

Megan, tonight I believe the Korean Megan, buzzed me on the phone.

"A call for you, Bishop Blackie, a Ms. Cardin."

"Of course."

"Father Ryan," I said.

"I've done what you told me to do, Bishop," Janie said breathlessly. "It was terribly difficult, but I did it anyway."

"And your lawyer said?"

"That my husband was a fool to put such threats in writing and especially to sign them."

"And your husband?"

"He was astonished. Divorce never happens in his family. A disgrace. Couldn't we work out something short of divorce. He even said he did not want to lose me."

"You told him you had turned his notes over to your attorney?"

"Just as you said I should."

"And his reaction?"

"Was to promise me a generous settlement if I agreed to a separation instead of a divorce."

"And you said?"

"I told him to talk to my attorney. He was quite flustered. Apparently he thought I would never defy him."

"He made no further threats."

"No. He just strode out of the room. He does that when he's angry and can't express the anger."

"And how do you feel?"

"Relieved, Bishop. And alive. And free."

"Excellent. Stay in touch with me."

"I will. . . . And thank you very much."

I too was relieved. The urgency had been taken out of the case. Or so I thought.

I could not have been more wrong.

CHAPTER 8

TWO DAYS LATER the Cardin problem intruded itself again—and in a puzzling way. As I was emerging from the F.A.O. Schwarz store in my parish (on the Magnificent Mile that is also in my parish though most of its denizens are unaware of the fact) burdened with a vast array of toys I had purchased for various young persons of my acquaintance, a very large Mercedes pulled up and stopped in explicit violation of the traffic ordinances of the City of Chicago. Out of it, in morning suit and bowler hat, stepped Peter Paul Cardin.

"I want to talk to you, Bishop Ryan," he said curtly, his breath turning to steam in the near zero air.

"Call my office for an appointment."

"It will take only a moment or two. I am a good Catholic. I do not believe in divorce. I do not accept this annulment nonsense that you men are permitting. My wife is my wife, whatever has happened. There will be no annulment, do you understand?"

He spoke calmly enough, respectfully, even sadly,

but as a man who is accustomed to giving orders and being obeyed.

Burdened as I was by my precious gifts, I had to pause to put them on the sidewalk so that I could respond properly.

"Are you threatening me, sir?" I asked affably.

"We have friends in high places in the Church, even in Rome. There will be no divorce, much less no annulment in the Cardin family. I want that clearly understood. We will simply not tolerate it. Our family honor is at stake."

"I'm afraid sir, your family honor is mostly a false legend."

He did not respond for a moment. Words were trying to form themselves on his lips.

"You have no right to judge my family honor, Bishop," he said meekly enough.

"Ah?"

"Nor do you have any right to recommend my wife see a divorce lawyer."

"I will not discuss my conversation with your wife."

"She is my wife. I have the right to know everything about her."

"Your friends from the Corpus Christi Movement may think that. I don't."

He looked acutely uncomfortable, apparently surprised that an innocuous-looking little priest would stand up to him.

"I will talk to the Cardinal."

"Be my guest."

"As I said before, Bishop, we have powerful friends in Rome. We will go to them if necessary."

"You are a rich and powerful man, Peter Paul Cardin," I said, jabbing my finger at him, just as I had jabbed it at his wife. "In some venues during the course of history that would have enabled you to tell the Catholic Church what to do. But not in the Archdiocese of Chicago and not today. The Pope himself could not make me violate the seal of confession in my relationship with Ms. Cardin. Don't mess with us, don't even think of messing with us."

His mouth opened and then closed. He bent down to pick up my packages.

"Riches and power do not bring happiness, Bishop."

He piled the packages into my arms.

"Hardly an original thought with you."

"No, it isn't. . . . And I still love my wife. I don't want to lose her. Maybe if I have one more chance . . ." His voice trailed off weakly. Then he turned and reentered his limousine just in time to escape the wrath of a young African-American woman cop who was descending on him like the Fifth Horseman of the Apocalypse.

"I got his license number, Bishop Blackie. Should we go after him?"

"Not this time, Sophie."

The exchange with Peter Cardin made no sense at all.

The blood had run thin since the first Peter Paul

had, in a desperate gesture of expiation, made dreams come true for a young immigrant couple who were much in love. So too perhaps the genes had turned thin, if genes do that. This man was incapable of anger. All he could do was repeat empty threats that he had heard from someone else. Then at the very end, in words of pathetic frustration, he would claim that he loved his wife.

Whom he had threatened with a horrible death.

What the hell was going on?

I thought about it as I walked down Chestnut Street, past Quigley Seminary where I had attended high school and the new Loyola Tower (which had violated the solemn Jesuit vow against attractive buildings) and over to the Cathedral.

I have always felt that every successful return to the Cathedral Rectory was something of a miracle. I am, you see, easily distracted by thoughts when I walk.

There was something wrong with the whole Cardin picture. Someone was playing games with me. That is a very serious mistake. For a moment I thought I had a fix on the game if not on the person. But then the image drifted away. Again Christmas distracted me.

That afternoon while I was in my study proofreading the bulletin for Christmas Day (a bootless effort because others would catch the mistakes I had missed and point them out to me in excruciating detail), the house phone buzzed.

"Father Ryan."

"This is Megan, Bishop."

"Indeed!"

"I bet you don't know which one."

"Only the Irish Megan would put me to the test."

She giggled. "You win. This time. Righteous!"

"You wanted me for some purpose, Megan?"

"Oh, yeah, Bishop. This totally gorgeous boy, and I mean over the top gorgeous, wants to see you. And he goes like his name is Pete and you know who he is and what I want to know is, if you know who he is, why haven't you introduced him to me and he's like sweet and nice too."

"And rich, Megan."

"What difference does that make?"

She wasn't joking either.

"Show him to one of the counseling rooms and tell him I'll be right down."

"Fersure."

As I might have expected, an animated conversation was taking place in the counseling room. Megan, who might have been Clare Raftery reincarnate, had deserted her post and was entertaining Pete while I came down the steps.

"Would you believe, Bishop Blackie, that he goes to John Carroll and, like, that's where I might go next year."

Megan's college plans varied from day to day.

"It is alleged that some people even like Cleveland," I said.

"Not many," Pete Cardin said amiably. "I wanted to be close to home. I thought about Marquette, but they don't have a football team and John Carroll does. And you don't have to be very good to play there. If you can catch a pass, you're first string wide receiver."

"I like to watch football, but we don't have it at St. Ignatius," Megan observed.

"We did at Loyola," Pete replied.

"Well," said Megan, exercising some tact, "I'll let you guys talk. Nice to meet you, Pete."

"My privilege, Megan."

"Cute kid." Pete lifted an eyebrow as the door closed behind her.

"Indeed."

I warned him about the four Megans in case he should return to the Cathedral Rectory.

"That one is by far the most pushy of the lot, though they all think that they are administering the parish."

"She's Irish, isn't she, Bishop? What else would you expect?"

"And charming."

"Give my poor kid sister Lisa another year and she'll be just like Megan."

"Ah."

He was wearing gray slacks (not jeans) and a heavy brown sweater (not Aran Isles variety). A jacket (not a letter jacket) had been casually tossed aside. His frank and open face glowed with physical health and a walk in the cold.

"I wanted to talk to you about my parents, if I might. I don't want to violate any secrets or anything like that, but I thought my input might be useful."

He talked a different language than the Megan. I believe it was English, but it has been so long since I heard it from one of his generation that I wasn't altogether sure.

"Perhaps," I said cautiously.

He spread his hands in a gesture of appeasement. "Bishop, they're both cream puffs, cupcakes, pushovers."

"Indeed."

This was certainly a new take on his parents. But somehow it did not seem all that implausible.

"I could have gone to Georgetown, which I would have liked. But Cleveland is close enough to home that I can keep an eye on them, not that my eye has helped all that much lately."

"So?"

"They're two really nice people who'd be very happy both as individuals and as a couple if only they weren't hung up on this family stuff."

"Indeed?"

"It's not just my grandmother either, though she's a lot of the problem. My grandfather, before he died in the plane crash, bought into it too. I think Gram wanted no part of it when she first came here from Seattle. But it was so important to her husband that when he died in the plane crash, she took the family myth over and made it her life."

"Your mother has not done that, however."

"Not yet, Bishop, not yet. But it's like a disease.

It permeates the family, even my little brother and both my little sisters buy it some of the time."

"You don't, however?"

"No way. The Cardin string ends with five. My father has given up already on my joining the holdings. Not a chance. Gram tells me that I am betraying the heritage and I say so what. I don't think much of the heritage."

It occurred to me that there were some letters out at Glessner House that this young man should read.

"I see."

"And that creep, Father Lawrence—excuse my language, Bishop—keeps telling them that they have an obligation to make more money so that they can use it for the good of the Church. He means for the good of his outfit."

Doubtless. I liked the use of the word "outfit," though I did not think that young Pete knew the connotations that referred to "our friends over on the West Side."

"The family has more money than they know how to enjoy even now, so what's the point in piling up more? I'll take my cut of the loot and run."

"Where?"

He shrugged his broad shoulders. "I don't know, Bishop. Not yet. Maybe to medical school. Maybe to the University of Chicago so I can be a college teacher. Maybe to the seminary . . .."

"Indeed!"

"I'm not sure. And every time I run into a woman like your friend Megan, I have my doubts."

"She is still a child," I said.

"In two years she won't be." He rolled his eyes. "And she's an interesting half woman even now. Transparent and knows it and doesn't care."

"Arguably," I agreed.

"I just wish poor Mom had the same kind of self-confidence. That's most of her problem."

"Arguably," I said again.

"Anyway, my decision about the priesthood will not rest finally on the charms of the Megans of the world. I gotta make up my mind that I want to do it. That's what counts isn't it, Bishop? Not the feeling that you have to do it, but the feeling that you want to do it more than anything else and that you'll enjoy it more than anything else. Right?"

"Oh, yes. . . . Presumably the Corpus Christi Movement would not prove attractive to you."

"They wouldn't take me!"

"I think not."

"No, I'd either be a Jesuit like Father Becker or a diocesan priest like the ones in parishes around the city, Old St. Pat's for example."

Ellen Flynn had been wrong about the future of that historic place, totally wrong. They had even reopened the school.

"We could make you an offer," I said politely.

"Yeah?"

"We could guarantee you a life that would never be dull."

"That's an interesting offer. I'll take it—what

would my father say—I'll take it under advisement."

He leaned back on the couch and smiled contentedly.

"We could arrange the details on a later occasion."

"Yeah. . . . Hey, Bishop, someone said that the second Peter Cardin, let me see,"—he counted on his fingers—"that would be my great-grandfather wouldn't it?"

"Great-great."

"Anyway, my uncle said he wanted to be a priest and then his father and mother died and he had to take over the holdings. I wonder if that is true."

"Oh, yes, it is true."

"You know about him, huh? Was he like me?"

"No way. Absolutely no way."

"I'm glad to hear that. I can't see myself ever doing that sort of thing. But the family stuff drives people crazy. . . . How do you know about him?"

So I told him in as much detail as was necessary about the Raftery letters, as I had begun to think about them. I left out the blood and gore.

"Wow! Hey, I'll have to read them."

"I can arrange that. You'll find them very interesting."

"Was this Clare anything like your friend Meg up in the front office?"

"You must judge when you read the letters."

"Your opinion?"

"Some would say the Megan is almost a clone."

"Yeah! Interesting."

"There are no family curses, Peter. And no family blessings either. There are heritages perhaps, good and bad, but there is nothing inevitable about them. Don't ever forget that."

Well, I half believed that. Heritages could be turned into curses and that's what had happened in his family.

"Yes, Bishop . . . and that brings me around to my mom and dad again, which is why I thought I came here."

"Ah."

"Look"—he leaned forward and jabbed his fingers (both of them I note) at me—"what we really need to do is to get them away from the family. All of them, even the little kids for a month or two, maybe longer. So there's just the two of them. No distractions. Then they'll get in sync. That's their problem. All through their marriage they've been out of sync, emotionally and physically and every which way. It's no good."

An arguably insightful diagnosis. Alas, things had gone too far for that. Besides even in the best of situations, they would need sustained therapy.

"But how would that goal be accomplished?"

He leaned back in the couch and threw up his hands. "I don't know, Bishop, I really don't. I tell my mom that and she says it's much too late, which I know it isn't. And I tell my dad and he says I know nothing about the nature of his relationship with my mother."

"And you say?"

"I say that I know more about it than he does."

"And then?"

"The steam goes out of him like it always does and he says maybe I do. But starting over again is usually impossible. And I say it's still worth a try. And he shrugs and finds an excuse to change the subject."

"Remarkable."

Again I had the feeling that someone was playing games with me. But who?

"I'm not trying to tell you what to do, Bishop. I don't think either of them will do any better if they try someone else. I'm prejudiced naturally, but I think they should give it another try. Nothing to lose, is there? But they've got to get away from the family. It's sick, Bishop, really sick."

No doubt about that. Even to the third and fourth and fifth generation. But it was a seamless and impermeable neurosis. We would do well enough to save his mother's life and his sanity.

"I'm glad you came to see me, Peter," I said. "Your 'input' casts matters in a different light. You may well be right. I'll keep it in mind. Given the confidentially involved, I can say no more."

It did cast matters in a different light, though it was a murky and problematic light.

"Great, Bishop." He bounded to his feet. "That's what I was hoping you'd say."

"No promises, Pete."

"I understand that . . . hey, Bishop, can I say one more thing."

"Certainly."

"Do you mind if I take her out?"

"Who?" I said, demonstrating how far I had drifted from my understanding of young people.

"Herself"—he nodded toward the front office—"like I said, or was it you, she may be only half a woman now, but half is better than none, isn't it? Kind of going long on a future as they say at the Board of Trade?"

"If she raises the charge of sexual harassment in the workplace, I will not be responsible."

"I'm not going to harass her," he said quickly, fearing I was serious. "And I won't try anything with her either. I promise. I'd be handed my lunch if I did."

"Bank on it."

We walked toward the door of the counseling room. Before we parted, he asked one more question. "Does she know who I am?"

"Not from me surely. I doubt it. When she hears your name, however, she will ask around as those of her gender do."

"I know. What will she think?"

"Lake Forest wealth will not be counted in your favor."

"Great! That's what I was hoping."

Indeed.

There was no doubt his invitation would be

accepted and equally no doubt that his wealth would be held against him, but not irrevocably.

Back in my study, I ignored the bulletin for a few moments and pondered the case of Peter Cardin VI. Would he become a priest? That was a toss-up. His eagerness to escort Megan on a date said nothing either way. Given the nature of the human condition at that age in life, someone who would not want to do that would not be an appealing priest.

As to his parents . . . here the light became very murky indeed. His mother's life was in danger because of his father's threats. He could not know that. Nor could he know that his mother's lawyer had the stupid written threats that his craven father foolishly put in letters with his signature on them.

Peter Cardin V, I decided, needed not only extensive therapy but a long time locked up in a mental hospital. A trip to a place where the sun shone in December would hardly be enough.

Perhaps when Chantal's physical safety had been assured and Peter V's sanity restored, one might consider it.

Yes, but . . . but what? But what's going on here?

The house line buzzed. I knew that it would be Megan.

"You'd never guess what, Bishop Blackie," she said breathlessly.

"He asked you out."

"How did you know! . . . Do you mind?"

"Am I the monitor of your social life, young woman?"

"I don't want you to think I'm trying to seduce every good-looking boy who comes into the rectory."

"There have been no previous cases, I believe."

"First opportunity," she said tersely. "I wasn't *really* flirting with him. Honest."

Yes, she was *really* flirting with him. That, however, was to be expected from a woman of her age with the usual hormone count. She was astonished by the result, however.

"You accepted his invitation?"

"Well, yes, but I could change my mind . . ."

"Have a good time, Megan."

"Yes, Bishop," she said in a voice brimming with happiness.

"It's up to You," I informed the creator. "You're the one who got me into this case and You're responsible for what comes out of it. At least the Megan is not from out of town, like all the other matriarchs since Rose Lennon."

And the chances of her ever buying into the family myth were at absolute zero.

I hoped.

CHAPTER 9

THE MOST IMPORTANT Eucharist at the Cathedral at Christmas was still the Midnight Mass. It would be packed with people, especially young adults. Many of those in attendance had not seen the inside of a church since Easter. Some of my colleagues in the priesthood think that we should denounce them for their lack of devotion. I felt rather that we should rejoice that they still wanted to participate in the liturgy marking the coming of the Jesus child and win them by the elegance and warmth of the ceremony.

Fortunately, Milord Cronin, who would preside over the Eucharistic celebration, shared my view of things. "Trick them into thinking we're not all assholes, eh, Blackwood?"

"Something of the sort."

However, a new custom was rapidly assuming equal importance—the Eucharist for Children at five o'clock on Christmas Eve. The Santa Claus Mass as it is often called. Virtually every child that could walk on up to maybe sixth grade would be there and many who were still babes in arms.

With their parents of course.

Naturally the small and inoffensive Bishop was expected to tell them a Christmas story, usually with some small child sitting in his lap.

This was a work of no little artistry because the natives under ten are, as the reader doubtless knows, extremely restless on Christmas Eve. The smallest of them are also likely to protest at phenomena that displease them.

At the top of their voices.

So I went through a certain period of preparation for this task.

I was in the middle of that preparation when the house phone buzzed.

"Father Ryan."

"There's a woman here to see you, Bishop," the Megan in resident said. "She claims to be some kind of countess. She's totally postal. Do we have countesses in the Church anymore?"

The slang word meant slow-witted. Teen slang improves in its imaginative qualities every generation.

"Now and again, Megan."

"Yeah, well, she takes one look at me at the door and about dies. Then she treats me like I'm poor white trash."

"That, Megan," I said, "is the last thing anyone could possibly think about you."

The Megan, patently the African-American one,

giggled (all Megan giggles, regardless of ethnic background, are fundamentally the same). "Well, I told her I was the affirmative action porter person. She was definitely not amused."

"You may inform her, porter person, that the Bishop is preparing his sermon for the children's Mass and that he will be down when he is finished. It may require ten or even fifteen minutes."

"Bitchin', Bishop!"

Please note the comma between those two words.

I continued to work on my presentation to *les enfants* and then donned not only my clerical collar and my black suit jacket, but even my St. Brigid pectoral cross. I stopped short in this quest for authority from also wearing my Episcopal ring both to deprive the Countess of the opportunity to slobber over it and because I could not find it.

She was definitely not amused when I entered the counseling room.

"You have kept me waiting twenty minutes, Your Grace," she said, glancing at her jewel-bedecked watch. "I am not accustomed to being kept waiting."

She had made no move to slobber over my nonexistent ring.

"Madam," I said quite formally, "you did not have an appointment. I make it my business never to keep anyone waiting who has an appointment. (Slight exaggeration.) But it was necessary for me to finish preparations for the children's Eucharist at five o'clock."

She dismissed that with a wave of her hand, a

hand that bore the burden of both an emerald and a ruby.

"That does not fulfill the Christmas obligation," she dismissed my excuse.

"I disagree, madam. Whatever your friends from Corpus may have told you, it does fulfill the obligation. There are specific responses from the Code Commission on that issue, which I will be happy to share with you. In the meantime, might I suggest you sit down."

She was, as I have said, a well-preserved woman in her early sixties, carefully made-up and wearing an expensive dark green suit. A long mink coat was tastefully arranged on the easy chair. Patently the Megan had not been trusted with it.

"Why do you have a person like that at the door?" she asked, removing from her purse a long cigarette and a jeweled lighter. "Obviously she will disturb many of your parishioners. What if she is a drug dealer?"

"This is a smoke-free rectory please, madam," I said mildly. "And Megan's father is an orthopedic surgeon on the staff of Northwestern Hospital. I am confident that she does not deal or use addictive drugs, like nicotine for example."

She jammed the nicotine stick and the lighter back into her purse. I concluded that despite her clothes and her jewels and her makeup and her thousand-dollar suit, the Countess was innocent of class. In fact, titled papal nobility or not, she was vulgar shanty Irish.

"I am going to write a letter to Cardinal Ratzinger

about you," she warned me. "He is a good friend of ours."

"Doubtless," I replied.

"I will accuse you of trying to destroy my son's marriage."

"Indeed."

"You will get a letter from him demanding an explanation."

"Madam," I sighed loudly, "hardly a day goes by when we do not receive a letter from our Eminent Brother or one of his aides. They always request an explanation and we always provide one. In this case I will personally reply that I cannot answer the charges against me because that would force me to violate the seal of confession."

"You can't hide behind that dodge," she snapped.

"It is not my intent to hide, madam." I sighed loudly and glanced at my watch. "It is rather my intent to protect the confidentiality of the Sacrament. I would not violate that even for the Pope, not that he would expect me to."

"Our family does not have divorces, Your Grace. We simply do not have them."

"An admirable record."

"We will not tolerate that woman divorcing my son."

"Indeed."

"We will stop her one way or another."

"I note the threat, madam. I observe that it might constitute a violation of the law."

"Not of God's law," she shouted triumphantly.

"What God has put together, let no man put asunder."

I sighed again. The conversation was going nowhere, but I had to listen to her to find out just how sick this dysfunctional family really was.

"I am constrained to point out that from the time of the Apostle on, the Church has recognized valid exceptions to that principle."

"What apostle?" she shouted.

"Paul, of course."

"I disapproved of that woman from the beginning," she continued her tirade. "I said she was a slut. And she has proven herself a slut. Not even in the bedroom would a decent woman dress like she does in public. We should get rid of her now."

"How do you propose to get rid of her?"

"She should be taken out and horse-whipped, that's what should be done."

She knew all the clichés.

"I must observe to you, madam, that you have not invoked any privilege in this conversation. If I am asked by civil authorities, I will be constrained to reply that you made threats against the well-being and arguably the life of your daughter-in-law."

"There will be no divorce, Your Grace. Do you understand that, Your Grace? There will be no media scandal in our family."

"That will be as may be, madam," I said, and realized only after saying it that I was quoting my friend Clare Raftery O'Boyle.

"I will stop at nothing to prevent it, is that clear?"

The woman was patently over the top, totally

postal. It did not follow, however, that she was actually capable of the mayhem that her fury suggested.

"Perfectly."

"We are the most honorable family in the Archdiocese. Nothing has tainted our honor for a century and a half. You should be doing everything possible to protect our honor so that it might be an example to others less fortunate than we."

"Come now, madam, we are both not unaware, I take it, of how the founding patriarch made his money in the Civil War. Moreover, some of us remember the family's unfortunate investment in Mafia-linked resorts . . . ."

I resisted the temptation, cruel but accurate, to connect that investment to her husband's unfortunate death.

"I will see that you are destroyed. I promise that. I have important friends in important places. You are finished."

"Indeed," I said, standing up. "But now, if you'll excuse me, I must preside over the Eucharist for the little children. I see no useful purpose to be served by continuing this discussion."

"I will report you to the Cardinal," she yelled.

"Megan," I said calmly.

"Yes, Bishop?"

"Countess Cardin is about to leave. Would you be so good to show her to the door."

That was pure Sherlock Holmes.

"Certainly, Bishop."

"I don't need a nigger to find my way to the door."

Megan, as pretty as a picture in pink sweater and skirt, froze. I gulped. This was truly over the top behavior. I'd better find something to say. Now.

"Should your good friend Cardinal Ratzinger actually write to me, I shall respond to him and describe your gratuitous racial slur, Countess. I urgently ask you to apologize to Megan. If you fail to do so, I will ban your admission to this rectory permanently."

"I'll ban you," she shouted as she exited the rectory, mink coat still over her arm.

"Thank you, Bishop Blackie," Megan said with a happy smile, tears promptly exorcised. "I'll tell the other Megans she's under interdict."

One must note what is happening to the Church. High school children know what an interdict is.

Patently I had no authority to impose that version of excommunication, which is incidentally no longer one of the canonical penalties. Nonetheless, she would not enter Holy Name Rectory again, not as long as I was the pastor.

"Explain to Megan Anne that she is Pete's grandmother, not his mother."

"Oh, good, she has a date with him, you know."

"So I have heard."

On the way over to the Santa Claus Eucharist, in my full Episcopal purple that I almost never wear, I stopped at Milord Cronin's door.

"Yes, Bishop," he said, looking up from his

breviary. "I don't believe I know you, but you're certainly welcome to this rectory."

"I have imposed a personal excommunication on the Countess Cardin," I informed him. "She is banned from this rectory."

"That's indeed a good work. Gives us one more reason to rejoice this joyous season."

"Do you want to know why?"

"I'm dying to find out. You rarely become that medieval, Blackwood."

I rehearsed the conversation and ended with the slur on Megan (Megan Joy being her full name). The Cardinal's lips tightened and his normally hooded eyes flashed in fury.

"You should have made her *vitanda*, Blackwood."

He was referring to an ancient and honorable and now abandoned practice of attaching a penalty of excommunication to anyone who associated with an excommunicate.

"Alas, that thought never occurred to me. In any event, you should be prepared to hear from her. Most likely on the phone since the door is barred to her."

"I think I'll send a note to our brother Josef Ratzinger about this woman who storms into my rectory, claims friendship with him, and indulges in racial slurs. It'll be nice to put him on the defensive for a change."

"Admirable."

"And, Blackwood, nice work!"

"I try," I said with a loud sigh.

After the Santa Claus Eucharist, the Cardinal and I hastened through the newly fallen snow to the Chancery office where he would record his five-minute message to the people of Chicago and suburbs, a custom I had talked him into. I knew that it would play on all the ten o'clock news programs and then on the news the next day too, since normally nothing much happened on Christmas. Most of the news personnel do not work. Nothing really happens anymore unless the cameras are there to catch it. Sean Cronin was always good copy because he was strikingly handsome in a Renaissance way and said powerful and at times shocking things—always without a manuscript or a note and with his blazing blue eyes looking right into the lens. He would finish right on time too. My job was to warn him when thirty seconds were left, since no director in Chicago would have the nerve to shut up a cardinal.

It was, as one may imagine, quite a scene—a tall, somewhat haggard-looking cardinal sweeping into our tiny studio in his full crimson robes, smiling brightly at the assembled journalists and technicians, wishing them a happy Christmas Eve, and then asking, "Are we ready?"

No desk, no chair, no podium—just the Cardinal standing tall and erect and confident, a posture that seemed utterly natural and that took only three or four weeks of the practice the first time, until he finally said, "Blackwood, you want me to be perfectly natural?"

"Fake that," I replied, "and we've got it."

He never offered to show me a manuscript and I don't know whether there ever was one. That night he raised the question of whether there might not be neighborhoods in Chicago and in the suburbs where the Holy Family was as unwelcome as they were in the inn at Bethlehem because their skin color was too dark. No one who claims to celebrate Christmas, he informed the people of Chicago and vicinity, can exclude anyone whether by reason of race or ethnicity or religion or gender or age or sexual orientation. He concluded with the James Joyce theme (lifted from one of my books, since he had never read Joyce) that Catholicism means here comes everyone.

He finished right on time, shook hands with everyone in the studio, gave them Christmas pictures for their families, and departed, striding down Erie Street in his full crimson robes with a coat tossed carelessly over his shoulders.

"Not bad, huh, Blackwood?"

"Very effective."

"I hope your friend the Countess was listening."

"I had assumed it was meant for her."

"She called while you were telling the kids about the Mother of Jesus and the Grinch or something of that sort. It must have been good because everyone applauded."

"Indeed."

I was not about to ask what the Countess had said.

"I took a very tough line with her. Cut her off at the beginning and went after her on the charge of racism and cruelty. She gave up pretty quickly. Going to report me to Cardinal Ratzinger too."

"Indeed."

"Are you seeing to that situation."

"Oh, yes," I said with more confidence than I felt.

"Good!"

On our way back to the Cathedral, he shook hands with a score or so of people, and hugged Sophie, the black woman cop on the corner.

When he set his mind to it, Sean Cardinal Cronin can be a one-man solemn high procession.

Back at the rectory as I tried to collect my thoughts the Megan-in-charge (now the Korean one, Megan Flower) informed me on the house phone, "Ms. Cardin on the phone, Father Blackie."

Not the Countess again!

"Father Ryan."

"I did it, Bishop," Janie said to me. "My attorney sent me to the best divorce lawyer in Chicago and I gave him Peter's notes. He said I have excellent grounds for a separation and eventual divorce. He's going to turn the notes over to the Chicago police next week."

And thus will end the century-old privacy of the Cardin clan, especially if the cops leak the letters to the media, as they surely would. And Chantal would be safe—if everything she said was true.

"How do you feel about it?"

"Scared. Guilty. Proud."

"You told your husband?"

"Before he left to celebrate Christmas in Naples, Florida, with the rest of them. We all have condos down there. Well, Petey is still around. He has a date to go to Midnight Mass with some girl."

Half woman actually.

"Indeed. . . . What did your husband say when you repeated your previous warning?"

"He said that he was sorry I had taken such a drastic step without first attempting a reconciliation."

"What!"

"His very words, Bishop."

"He did not seem worried about the police reading his notes to you."

"Puzzled, but not worried. I think he's losing his mind, poor man."

"I could understand that," I murmured.

"Speaking of that, I heard you had a run-in with my mother-in-law."

"One might call it that."

"I was forbidden to accompany them. I'm glad. It made it easier to betray them."

"They're betraying you."

"I think I can understand that. It's still hard."

"You're in Chicago?"

"No. Up in the Forest Lane. I'm sort of making a retreat and I need peace and quiet."

She would not be in danger for several days more. Then the news about her husband's threats would appear on the five o'clock news. By then it would be too late to harm her.

I next went back to the Cathedral to hear confessions. While that terrible Christmas Eve custom of hearing all the confessions in the parish has been replaced by the more benign and beneficial communal penance service, there are still old-timers who show up for their last-minute dash into the box. I sat in the confessional for some time before the Midnight Eucharist so that these loyal members of the People of God would not think that their Church had abandoned them.

There were only a few penitents, most of the old-timers even preferring the communal service, in this matter, as in so many others, not agreeing with the Pope.

Thus I had time to think about the absurdities of the Cardin puzzle. There was something wrong in the story, badly wrong, but I couldn't figure out what it was. At that time I had most of the pieces of the puzzle available, enough to smell one very large rat in what I had been hearing. I cite the mad rush of Christmas Eve in a contemporary Catholic parish not so much as extenuation for my stupidity as an explanation for why what Hercule Poirot calls the "little gray cells" were not working as well as they might.

Try as I might in the dark confessional before the solemn midnight celebration of the coming of Grace into the world, I could make no sense of it at all.

I did understand, however, that I had to read the missing letter from the indomitable Clare Raftery.

CHAPTER 10

ON ST. STEPHEN'S Day, on impulse, I called a certain news editor at a Chicago paper that will remain nameless.

"Are you guys going to do anything about the Cardin curse story?"

"On its hundredth anniversary?" He laughed.

"Indeed."

So this New Year's Eve would be the hundredth anniversary of the death of Rose Lennon Cardin. The legendary Blackie Ryan had missed the fact that 1995 minus 1895 equaled one hundred.

A shiver ran through me as the Cardin case became suddenly much darker.

"Well, we got that article from *Chicago History* that someone sent around. But we're not sure that we should hang the Cardins on something that happened in the past."

"Impressive restraint."

"Maybe our New Year's resolution will be not to destroy any more prominent people than we absolutely have to."

"Virtuous."

"We may do something. Public's right to know and all that. But I kind of doubt it."

"Let me know if you change your mind."

"Sure. . . . Anything special going down?"

"Maybe. I'll let you know."

"Thanks, Bishop. I won't forget that."

So the article had not been aimed only either at Sean Cronin or at me. Every media outlet in town almost certainly had it. Someone would use it on New Year's Eve or New Year's Day. On January 2 it would be forgotten.

Whoever had sent the article had not seen Clare Raftery's letters. I was the only one who had read them, besides presumably the Phelans before they had donated the letters to the Architectural Foundation. So whoever had mailed copies of the article had no inkling about the content of the letters or even about their existence.

I knew that fact was important, but I didn't know why. My gray cells were deteriorating at a dangerous rate. Yet I had remembered the names of all my grandnieces and grandnephews at the Ryan family party at the Redmond Kanes in Lincoln Park the day before, a remarkable feat that surprised and delighted by siblings and their children. It seemed the decay of my brainpower after my fiftieth birthday might not be irreversible.

It was time to find Clare's missing letter.

I drove out to my ancestral parish and parked down Longwood Drive from the house of Mary

Kate, my senior sibling. Perhaps after I left the Phelans' old Victorian house, built at the same time as Prairie Avenue but not as big or as famous, I could borrow a cup of eggnog (without the rum) from that virtuous woman.

Rob and Marian Phelan were genial people with a high level of tolerance for the peculiarities of the clergy. So they affected not to be surprised when one such showed up at their house at ten-thirty in the morning on St. Stephen's Day. I was ensconced in front of the fire and offered a cup of eggnog, with or without the rum. Since I was driving I forsook the rum, which I have never liked anyway.

"I visited Glessner House last week."

"Interesting place," said Rob Phelan, giving nothing away.

"And I read your grandmother's diaries," I said in Marian's direction.

She brightened immediately. "Aren't they fascinating. She was a remarkable woman. They were married for more than sixty years. She survived the Spanish Flu, too tough to die, Gram would insist. Both of them lived into the late 1950s. Loved each other to the end. She was a strong woman and very, very sweet. I'll never forget her."

"Indeed not."

Marian had known her grandmother as a little girl knows an old woman. But I had met her as a teenager (though the word didn't exist then) no older than the various Megans.

"We were cleaning out the attic at Lake Geneva

last summer," Rob added, "or Geneva Lake as she properly called it. And we found the box with the letters, neatly tied up in a fancy red ribbon. She makes that world come alive better than anything I've read."

"Lake Geneva?"

Marian smiled. "Yes, Blackie, the same house where she and Grandpa enjoyed two seasons of summer love. The Cardins sold it when they bought their house in Eagle River. It changed hands several times until the Great Depression. Grandpa survived pretty well during those years with his limousine company and his car dealerships and especially his coal company. In 1932 he saw an ad for the house. On sale for practically nothing. He bet, as he always did, that times would be better. He presented it to her as a thirty-sixth wedding anniversary present. Typically she didn't argue, but just said thanks, like she did for the ribbons in her story."

"What do you think of her letters, Blackie?" Rob asked, cocking a cautious eyebrow in my direction.

"First-rate history," I replied. "It's a shame you held back the one letter, however."

Both of them were dead silent. I sipped my eggnog.

"No fooling you, is there, Blackie?" Marian said softly.

"I'm fooled often, Marian. But the lacuna was obvious."

"A hundred years ago this week, wasn't it?" Rob asked.

"Indeed."

Everyone else could subtract but Blackie Ryan.

"We debated a long time about that," Marian said. "We were afraid that it might have reflected on Gram, though I think it made her look even more wonderful."

"It was hard for us to make a judgment," Rob continued. "We couldn't tell what others might make of it."

"And we didn't want to embarrass the Cardins. It's kind of a gruesome story. We're going to release it eventually. . . ."

"I wonder if I might look at it," I asked very gently. "I won't tell anyone about its contents without your permission. I think that Clare has something important to say to me."

"How exciting!" Marian leaped to her feet. "Of course you can read it. Just a minute I'll bring it down."

"You have an interesting life, don't you, Blackie," Rob said, a shrewd glint in his eyes as we waited.

"Oh, yes. Clare Marie Raftery, however, is one of the most interesting people I have ever met."

"She's that vivid in the letters, isn't she? Too bad she had to die."

"Too bad any of us have to die, Rob."

"It would be intolerable if nothing remains of her, wouldn't it?"

"And unthinkable."

"Here she is, Blackie. Isn't she gorgeous."

Marian gave me a manila envelope and a stack of

photos of her grandmother. The first was a formal picture of herself and her first born, an appealing girl child whose name, I was informed, was Ellen Marie.

Clare was the woman I had imagined as I had read her letters—tall, beautiful with raven-black hair and a lovely figure. Her head was tilted defiantly, her arm cuddled the girl child protectively, and her eyes glowed with love and gentleness and laughter. With the years she aged as we all do (especially when we turn fifty!) but she never lost her grace or her charm or the glow in her eyes.

It would have been totally unthinkable that she was not still alive somewhere, still charming all who knew her.

"A grand woman," I said, putting the pictures aside. "You're sure I may read this?"

They both nodded solemnly.

January 4, 1896

Jesus and Mary be with those I love.
Dear Mary Ellen,
I can't believe all the terrible things that have happened since I wrote you, darling Little Sister, a couple of days ago.

I wasn't sure whether I should tell you about them. But I decided that it would be a good thing to have a record of our venture into the Levee and what we found. Someone in the future may want an explanation of the murder of our poor Mistress.

Last night after dark, my beloved Tony takes me aside and says, "Some lads I know say they've seen our phaeton in a yard behind one of the hotels on Dearborn Street near Van Buren."

"In the Levee?" I say, half shocked and half fascinated.

"Right down the street from Pat McCarthy's saloon. I asked one of the lads to check on who had brought it in."

"And?"

I was so excited that I was afraid I'd jump out of my skin.

"He said a strange couple who then checked into the hotel. Drunk most of the time. They're still there. Room 203."

"We know who they are, don't we?"

"Aye," he says. "Don't we now?"

"And the papers all saying that the Master killed the Mistress."

"The police aren't so sure anymore. His alibi is pretty good."

"Saved by the drink," I agree.

"I think I'm going down there and collect our phaeton and our horses."

"They must be terrible fools to take such a chance."

"Fools they are," he agrees.

"We should tell the police."

"Do you think they would listen to the likes of us?"

"You're right, love, they'd not pay any attention. Or might even accuse us of being in cahoots with the two in the hotel room."

We both waited before one of us said it.

"Well, Clare, I'll be going down there to collect the phaeton."

"And to make them tell the truth."

"Aye," he says, "I suppose I'll have to try to do that."

"Well, I'll tell you one thing Anthony Patrick O'Boyle, you'll not be going down there by yourself."

"Now, Clare," he begins patiently.

"Don't 'now, Clare' me. You know me well enough to realize that I won't let you take a chance like that unless I'm there to take it with you."

"But . . ."

"If you're going to marry me, you'd better be clear that I'm no weeping and fainting female who needs protection all the time."

He shrugs and then gives up. "Ah, sure, Clare Marie, don't I know that already!"

So we dress up in dark clothes and thick old boots, meself with a long black cloak that I borrow temporarily from the young Mistress, and we slip out of the house and into the cold winter night. It's not snowing, thank the Good Lord, but it is terrible cold and I'm shivering so bad that

Tony has to put his arm around me and draw me close to himself. Which I don't mind at all. I'm so frightened and so excited that I'm still shivering.

Now, Mary Ellen, you'll be thinking that both of us are awful young amadons and ourselves going to a dangerous place to confront dangerous people. And you'd be right.

We wait a long time at the corner of Indiana Avenue and Eighteenth Street for one of the omnibus things and I'm wondering if they've stopped running because of the weather. Then one comes along and we're the only ones in it. So we huddle by the tiny coal stove which isn't much help.

"What's the Levee like?" I ask my love.

"It's a terrible place, Clare. Suffering people who pretend they're having a grand time. Most everyone drunk. A lot of shouting and singing and laughing. Everyone playing cards or gambling some other way. Women who have been ruined and are now ruining themselves."

"Poor dear things."

"Aye, Clare, they truly are. We should thank God we're not part of it."

"Jesus, Mary and Joseph protect us," I says piously. Yet I'm still eager to see the Levee. Let me tell you, Mary Ellen Raftery, I don't ever want to see it again.

We get off the omnibus at Wabash and Van Buren. "Have a good night now," says the driver.

"What did he mean by that?" I ask Tony.

"He thinks that you're a . . . fallen woman and that I'm your procurer."

"Well, the nerve of him!" says I, ready to go back and fight with the man.

"It's a good disguise, Clare," he whispers. "And ourselves may be needing a disguise before the night is over."

How right and wise the good man was.

The Levee was a terrible disappointment, Little Sister. It wasn't splendid at all. Run-down hotels, cheap saloons, gambling dens, haunted people, the men determined to have a grand time and the women promising to offer it, some of them even younger than you are and themselves not wearing much in the way of clothes despite the cold.

We look inside a couple of places just so I could see what they're like.

"It reminds me of a drawing of hell," I says.

"It's the railroad stations and the cheap hotels that draw men here. And where there's footloose men, there'll be women and the drink and cardsharps and all kinds of sin."

"No one seems to be having a good time, they're all just pretending."

We are picking our way carefully through the slush and the mud and trying to avoid the drunks staggering down Van Buren Street.

"They're lonely, Clare."

"Aye," I agree, beginning to understand, "they truly are."

"I'm not sure a decent young woman should see the place."

"Don't be a dolt, Anthony Patrick O'Boyle. A decent young woman shouldn't be ignorant of what goes on in the world."

"I suppose you're right, Clare. Sure, aren't there places in Dublin just like this."

"Are there!" I says, shocked. "And Ireland a Catholic country."

"Catholic men feel lonely too," he says, hugging me even tighter.

In the gaslight the Levee looks tawdry, Little Sister; I'm sure that by daylight it would be nothing more than a rambling collection of wooden shacks. Above us is the new elevated railroad tracks which loop the heart of Chicago. It makes Van Buren Street seem even darker. I'm getting a little frightened. No, Mary Ellen, a whole lot frightened. Hell—and only a mile and a half from Prairie Avenue.

Then we turn on Dearborn Street which is the heart of the Levee. The elevated tracks are gone, but the noise is even worse. No one seems to notice the cold. I wouldn't mind a small jar myself, but I'd be afraid I'd die from it.

"That's McCarthy's," Tony says, waving his hand, "where the Master did most of his drinking and himself not wanting to do it at home."

I rush over to peer in the window and slipped and fall in the slush and the mud. I feel like I've been destroyed altogether.

My dear man helps me up. "Are you all right, darling?" he asks.

"I'm fine," I says. "Just fine."

I'm not telling the exact truth. I don't want him deciding to send me home to my snug little bed in the room with Delia.

"Drunk this early," says a man staggering along the street.

"Not as drunk as you are!" I shout after him.

Tony laughs. I hope he's not thinking that I belong on this street.

I peer in the frosted windows of Pat McCarthy's saloon. What a terrible place! All kinds of men, workers by the look of their clothes, drinking themselves into oblivion. A few of them playing cards, a few of them talking, most of them drinking or drunk.

"That empty table on the right is where the Master did his drinking. They've left it empty in his honor I suppose."

I think to myself that the Master could have slipped out of here and no one would notice, except maybe the man behind the bar.

"And yourself coming down here and bringing him home?"

"Sometimes. He'd tell me what hour he wanted me and he would never argue when I arrived. Other times he rode down in a cab. Then he would stay all night, like he did the night someone killed the Mistress."

"A horrid place. Why would the Master with so much money have his jars in here?"

"He said that he felt easy with the people."

I turned away from the window. Poor Master.

"That's Holmes Hotel," Tony says, taking my arm. "Just down the street."

"This close to McCarthy's?"

"Almost next door."

I figure that's important information, but I'm not sure why it's important.

We slip by the terrible place. I peek through the window. In the lobby men and women are drinking and fondling each other. No one sees us as we go around the back and enter the stable yard. There's no one guarding the yard. Sure enough, in the dim glow of the gaslight on the street we see our phaeton, banged up a bit but it still looks like it will run.

Our two horses are in the stable, looking cold and hungry and unhappy. My man pats them on their noses and they neigh, glad to see him.

"Just a moment, lads," he says, "and we'll have you out of here and home to your own snug little stable."

We both turn and look at Holmes Hotel from the back. There's rickety old stairs going up in the gloom. To the second floor, I figure. I don't want to climb it and neither does Tony. Still, we've come here to do a job and do it we must.

"I suppose we have to go up those stairs to get to the second floor," I says.

" 'Tis better to do it that way than to let the people in the lobby see us," my man agrees.

"Isn't it terrible dark?" I say with a sigh.

"Isn't it now?"

Still, we climb up slowly, clinging to each other lest we slip and fall on the ice. A couple of times I think we're both going to tumble down and break all our bones. Somehow we make it to a landing on the second floor. I'm exhausted and breathless and ready to go home.

My love pushes on the door into the hotel.

"It won't open," he says.

"Let me help."

We both push real hard and the door springs open. The two of us tumble forward into a corridor dimly lit at the other end by a single lamp. No electricity in Holmes Hotel, I think to meself.

We lay on the floor, panting for breath and afraid we'd made enough noise to wake the dead. But no one seems to notice. There's such a ruckus coming up from the lobby that the sound of two amadons falling flat on their faces means nothing.

"Are you all right?" Tony asks me.

"I am," I say, though I'm not at all sure.

"All right. Let's find room 203."

We feel our way along the corridor in the dim light and try to read the room numbers. I think that we should have brought a candle.

"Here it is," Tony says. "203."

Now it occurs to me that I have no idea what to say when we burst into the room where the two killers are. I hope that Tony does.

He pushed the door and it comes open.

I look in the room and I can't believe my eyes. It is the filthiest place I've ever seen in my life, filled with dirt and litter and broken bottles and the terrible smell of the drink and vomit. A single sputtering candle lights the room. Joe Carey is spread out on a couch in his underwear and trousers, a bottle in his hand. The old woman he sometimes brought with him is on the bed in her drawers and vest, she too holding a bottle.

"We've come for our phaeton," I says like I'm in charge.

You know what I'm like, Mary Ellen: speak first and think after.

Joe Carey leers at us. I'm surprised though I don't know who else to expect. What terrible fools they are to stay so near the murder and with our phaeton to give them away.

And what terrible fools we are to go blundering into their room.

"Would you look what we have here, Ma. Two innocents. Shall we do them too?"

The woman, his ma as he called her, opens her eyes and glares.

"Why not?" she says.

"This time I get to have my way with the girl before we kill her instead of after."

"Why not?" she says with a wicked laugh.

*"You're both intoxicated," I tell them, hiding
behind the fancy word. "We are going to take you
to the police and you'll confess you killed the
Mistress and the Master will go free."*

*I wonder to myself how we're going to do that.
Two oafs that we were, we'd never planned that
out.*

They both cackled like two dotty chickens.

*"Do you know who I am?" says the old
woman. "I'm Peg McGurn, your master's real
wife. He dumped me for that piece of yellow-
haired fluff back in '70 and myself being a good
wife to him for six long years when he was
making all his money selling rotten meat to the
army."*

"His wife!" I say in a gasp.

*"That's right, dearie," she says, cackling again.
"His common-law wife. But in this country that's
all that Catholics need to be married. I knew it. He
knew it. He's been living in adultery with that
woman for twenty-five years. She got what she
deserved. The lad is my son, Jack McGurn, or Jack
Cardin to give him his proper name."*

*"We've been waiting for years," Joe Carey
says, "to get even with them and we did it and
we're both as happy as two sows in the mud. Now
we're going to be rid of the both of you."*

All the pieces fit into place.

*"You saw the chance to kill the Mistress and
blame the Master on New Year's Eve when you
saw him drunk in McCarthy's," I say, trying to*

sound like the public prosecutor. "The saloon keeper saw you drinking with the Master often. So he didn't notice when you took the key from his pocket and came into the tower room from the back stairs. You killed the Mistress, messed up the room, and then sneaked out again. You think they'll hang the Master for killing her."

"Isn't she the clever one," Joe Carey sneered. "I'll have a grand time with her, won't I, Ma?"

"I brought along a pipe," his mother crowed, "and smashed her beauty with a single blow. Then I cut her up with a knife just for the fun of it. I'll do the same with you after Jack is finished."

"And now my Da is where he belongs—in jail. He'll swing for killing his wife, though he never did it. Isn't that clever of us!"

They laughed fiendishly. Later I might feel sorry for them. They were poor lost souls, blundering around in their own wickedness and stupidity.

"You made a lot of mistakes," I continued, though I was powerful terrified. "The worst one was being too smart by half and putting the key back in the Master's pocket and giving him a perfect alibi. He never left McCarthy's saloon and as far as anyone knows, he'll be out of jail tomorrow and the two of you will be in jail in his place."

"Come along now," Tony says to Joe Carey,

pulling him up off the couch. "Let's get this over with."

My man's sober and younger and stronger than Joe Carey or Jack McGurn, but McGurn fought like a demented man. Tony wrestles him to the floor and hits him in the jaw a couple of times. McGurn screams in pain, but rolls away and jumps to his feet with a pistol in his hand.

What happens next, Little Sister, probably took less than a half minute. Maybe even less than a quarter of a minute. But I'll remember it all for the rest of my life.

Tony grabs his hand and tries to pull the pistol away. The two of them wrestle, twisting and turning as they fight for the gun. I stand there like a complete fool wondering what I should do.

Peg McGurn thinks more quickly than I do. She jumps out of bed, a knife in her hand, sways a bit, and then closes in on himself.

Finally, my mind starts to work. I look for something to fight with, see a commode on the floor, pick it up, ignore the slop spilling from it, and hit her over the head with all my might.

She drops the knife and crumples to the floor, limp like a broken doll. I turn to hit Jack McGurn with the same weapon and see that Tony has twisted the gun around so that it was pointing at Jack's face instead of his own.

I hit him on the head too, not as hard, because he ducks a little. Then the gun explodes and Jack

McGurn's face turns to a mess of blood and other stuff.

"God have mercy on us," Tony cries. "We've murdered him."

"Before he could murder us," I say as I start to vomit.

Tony does the same thing. A fine pair of heroes we were.

"Is she dead too?" I gasp between heaves.

Tony rolls her over.

"There isn't any doubt. Blood is flowing from her nose and her mouth, just as like the Mistress' blood."

"God forgive me," I say, vomiting again.

"We were only defending ourselves," Tony says.

"'Tis true," I say.

"We'd better get the police," he says.

Now he's trembling something terrible. There's a cut on his poor face, and blood coming out of his nose.

I notice that I'm trembling too.

Then my mind starts to work again.

"Have they heard us downstairs?" I ask my battered man.

"Let me peek out in the corridor."

He opens the door very slowly and peers around outside.

"No one," he says. "The shot was muffled because we were so close together. Anyway, no one notices a shot or two here in the Levee."

How cheap life can be, I think.

*"Let's wait a moment before we do anything,"
I say.*

He nods.

*"No one saw us come in, Tony love. No one
recognized us on the street. Why don't we just
leave and go home?"*

"The police?" he asks, shocked at my cunning.

*"If we go to them, they'll blame us for killing
these two and they'll accuse us of being part of
the plot to kill the Mistress. That's what they'll
do, and you know it."*

*"Aye," he says sadly. "Woman, you're right.
That's exactly what they will do."*

*"So let's say a prayer for the repose of their
poor souls and go home."*

*So in that filthy room, now covered with blood
and slop and even more vomit, we say a Pater
and an Ave and a Requiem Aternum. No matter
what they did, God loves them. God loves everyone, as Ma used to say, even the worst of us.*

*Then we slip into the corridor, creep along to
the door, push it open—gently this time—and
then very cautiously climb down the slippery
stairs and slog through the mud to the stable.
Tony hitches the horses, who are delirious at the
touch of his hand. I climb into the phaeton. Tony
takes the reins in his hands and very carefully
drives us to Dearborn Street. We turn south and
leave the Levee behind. I never want to see it
again.*

I know we're taking a terrible risk. But it would be even worse if we trusted the police.

It seems like a lifetime before we're back on Prairie Avenue. Tony feeds the horses and they settle down for their sleep. Then we slip into the house. (I wasn't such an amadon as to forget to bring a key.) We're both still trembling. I think that maybe I won't stop trembling ever again. It's not every night that you kill two human beings.

I clean Tony's cuts and, borrowing some of the Master's Irish whiskey, pour us both a good strong jar to warm us up and maybe stop the trembling.

Then he goes to the coach house and I sneak up to my room and tiptoe in so as not to wake Delia.

I think that I won't be able to sleep a wink after what I've done and seen. But I go right to sleep and have terrible nightmares.

The young Mistress doesn't notice how shaky I am the next morning.

That was yesterday. At the end of the day, the Master came home, sober and sad. There's nothing in the papers about two deaths at Holmes Hotel. And only a small article about the police continuing their investigations into the Mistress's death.

I begin to breathe easier. But I'm still scared.

I feel guilty too, not much but a little. We didn't want to kill them. We didn't want to avenge the

Mistress's death. They would have done terrible things to us. Still, I think the world is a less dangerous place. I thank God that the young Master and the young Mistress are safe from them forever.

I'm sure the nightmares will stop eventually. Tony keeps comparing me to Grace O'Malley, which I don't like but I don't say so to him.

I've been working hard all day getting ready for the wake which begins tonight. If I keep busy and don't think I'm all right for a while. I tell myself that in time I'll forget that awful night in the Levee.

I don't believe that, however.

I'm sorry for such a long letter, darling Little Sister. Don't show it to anyone else. I hope it doesn't upset you too much. It makes me feel better just to be able to tell someone about it. Pray for me and my man. We love each other more than ever now, so maybe something good has come of this awful mess.

I'll be all right but pray real hard for both of us. And for all the dead.

May Jesus and Mary and Patrick be with those who love me.
Your loving sister,
Clare

There was an extra page added, in the same block letters but with a different color ink.

Later

In case someone ever reads these letters, which Mary Ellen, God bless her and keep her, brought over when she came to America, I must add a few more details.

There was never anything in the papers about the deaths of Peg and Jack McGurn. People die in the Levee all the time, I'm told, and the police barely notice unless they're someone important.

My husband and I look back on it and see what a pair of foolish children we were, risking our lives for no good purpose. We were trying to save the Master, so we meant well. But the charges against the Master would have been dropped anyway. I suppose in a way justice was done and the young Master and the young Mistress were protected from horror. We were not the proper instruments of justice. Yet we never intended to be.

The Master had used the McGurns cruelly. For that there was no excuse. But crazy drunken people that they were, their revenge was wrong too. I should not judge any of them.

Terry O'Mahoney told me much later that the police had informed the Master that they had discovered the killers of the Mistress but they were already dead, murdered in an apparent robbery.

Did the police think the Master had ordered their deaths? Did the Master know what hap-

*pened when he gave us the presents that meant so
much to us? Did he ever know the names of the
killers?*

*We'll never find the answers to those questions
in our present life. I think sometimes that the
answers to all of them were "yes."*

*It's long done now and mostly forgotten, like a
bad dream I had when I was a child. The
nightmares are infrequent. Often I think it never
happened.*

*As I look back on that turbulent and painful
time, I sometimes ask myself if I would ride down
to the Levee with my beloved, seeking to save the
Master, if I knew what was going to happen.*

The only answer is that of course I would.

*Sometimes I even look kindly on those two
young fools. They were loyal and resourceful and
brave and even a little bit intelligent. If they made
any mistakes it was not for lack of good inten-
tions or courage. I let myself feel proud that I
once knew them both.*

*May all the souls of the faithful departed rest
in peace.*

Amen.

Clare Marie Raftery O'Boyle

"Indeed," I said, closing the manila folder and
giving it back to Marian.

"Some woman, huh?" said Rob.

"Oh, yes. Some woman."

I felt like I had received a message from my friend Clare, sent in a certain fashion from beyond the grave. Only I couldn't quite figure out what the message was.

"You think we shouldn't have removed this letter from the file?" Marian asked.

"I understand why you withheld it for the time being," I said softly. "The story should be told, nonetheless. The whole story. Maybe even published as a book. Clare does not disgrace herself in that last letter. Quite the contrary."

They both nodded solemnly.

"The Cardins?"

"It was a hundred years ago. The name of Peg McGurn, Lord have mercy on her, was already associated with the founding patriarch. They would have no cause to be offended, though some of them might still be offended. Yet finally, the truth ought not to be hidden."

They nodded again.

"But," I sighed my west of Ireland sigh that one could interpret as a hint of a coming asthma attack, "there should be no rush in making that decision."

Yet again they nodded.

I glanced at the photographs again. Clare Raftery with her girl child would be the image I would always remember.

"If we do publish them all, would you write an introduction, Blackie."

"Oh, yes. I owe the young woman at least that much."

If I could only figure out what the message was that she was trying to send me over the years. It was somewhere in that scene in the Levee.

I did stop at my sibling's home for more eggnog. And fruit cake. And apricot muffins. We did not discuss the Cardins.

On my ride back to the Cathedral, I tried to review all that I knew about both puzzles. But, despite Clare Raftery's ingenuity, I could make no sense of the more recent of the two.

CHAPTER 11

THE NEXT MORNING after the Eucharist, over my second helping of waffles, I continued to be preoccupied by the astonishing venture of Clare Raftery and her love into the Levee in the name of loyalty and in search for justice. I was happy that in later years, Clare had come to realize that the two of them were not amadons. At least not merely amadons.

The angels and archangels, the seraphs and the cherubs, must have been working overtime that night.

I could not, however, see the link between a hundred years ago and the present, other than the alleged curse. And two women in jeopardy, though how much jeopardy was Chantal really in?

Try as I might I could not picture her indecisive husband as a cruel killer like Jack McGurn. Or Jack Cardin as he perhaps deserved to be called. Nor was there any equivalent of his vicious and vengeful mother. For all her verbal pyrotechnics, the Countess would not hit her daughter-in-law over the head with a pipe, then cut up the corpse's body and plunge a crucifix up her vagina.

And was there a locked room mystery in the present situation? Not as far as I could determine.

Then why had I pursued the Prairie Avenue story so avidly, other than because of its inherent interest? What light did it shed on the present mystery, if there was indeed a mystery? As far as I could see, none at all.

Yet my gut instincts said that within Clare's letters there was just the illumination I needed.

I had encountered little trouble in determining who the 1895 killers were or how they had arranged it. I had the distinct advantage over Clare that I knew about Peg McGurn from my reading of the article in *Chicago History*. Once she found out who Peg McGurn was, however, she solved the puzzle almost instantly.

Her "lost" letter only confirmed my suspicions—and provided a bloody answer to my question about what happened to the killers. I tended to agree completely with the affirmative answers she tentatively provided to the three questions about which she said that they would never know the answers in their present life.

Did Jack McGurn have any children? Might there be other claimants to the Cardin heritage, claimants who might have had some better right to the wealth long ago? Might there be more resentful descendants of the sinister branch of the Cardins?

It was possible, but not very likely.

The woman who wrote the article in *Chicago History*—why was she so interested in the Cardin curse? Where was she today?

Back in my room, I took a chance and called the Chicago Historical Society. Eileen Flynn was, after all, a dangerous-sounding name, was it not?

Not hardly.

"This is Bishop Ryan from the Cathedral," I said to the editor, invoking clout that works with conservative Catholics and agnostic intellectuals. "I've noticed some writings in your journal by a woman named Eileen Flynn. I wonder if you can tell me where I might reach her."

"That's easy, Bishop," said the New England voice. "She's one of yours."

"Patently."

"Yes, that too, but I mean she's a nun of the Order of St. Francis and teaches at Alverno College in Milwaukee. She has done a lot of very interesting work on Chicago. I think I have her phone number . . . yes, here it is. That rings directly in her office though she may be off on Christmas holiday."

Vacation, not holiday, in this country. But let it pass.

"Remarkable," I said.

He gave me the number. I dialed it promptly.

She answered on the second ring, "Eileen Flynn."

Clearly a new nun.

"Sister, this is Father Ryan from Chicago . . ."

"Bishop Ryan?"

"I suspect so, Sister."

"I've read your work on James Joyce. Very interesting indeed."

"Your name will certainly be written in the book of the elect, Sister."

She laughed cheerfully.

"What can I do for you, Bishop?"

"I recently had the occasion, Sister, to read your excellent article on Prairie Avenue."

"My turn to express my thanks, Bishop. I wrote that a long time ago. It's the hundredth anniversary of the wife's death, isn't it?"

"Indeed . . . what attracted you to that story, if I am not too bold to ask."

"That's easy. My grandmother, Mary Ellen Raftery Flynn, worked there for a time. She wasn't there at the time of the killing, came a few months afterward. Her sister Clare worked in the house at the time. Grandma had all kinds of interesting tales to tell. So I did a doctoral dissertation at the University about Prairie Avenue. Fascinating place. Vulgar and oppressively WASP. But kind of appealing in a gay nineties sort of way. Incidentally, Bishop, I don't really believe in the curse. I figure the Cardins have made their own misfortune."

"I tend to agree, Sister. Your grandmother had no theories about the murder."

"She always said it was Red Pete in a fit of jealous rage, but she wasn't there at the time, as I said. By the time I was working on my dissertation, she was dead and so was her sister who was there at the time. I would have loved to interview both of them. The sister I gather was a piece of work. Gram absolutely adored her."

So Mary Ellen had kept her sister's confidence, I thought. Then it came to me that I had stumbled on the perfect editor if the Raftery letters were ever to be published.

"Have you done any more work on the subject?"

"No, Bishop. No more data. I did note that Peter Cardin the Fifth died in a plane crash some years ago, keeping the string going."

"The Fourth," I said. "The Fifth is still alive and now there is a Peter the Sixth."

"Interesting . . ."

"Were you able to track down anything about Peg McGurn?"

"Heaven knows I've tried. Never could find a trace of her. Red Pete was not the kind of man to leave something like that to chance. As you may be aware, Bishop, the *Tametsi* was never proclaimed in the United States. So before the Code was reformed in 1919, if she was really a common-law wife, they were validly and sacramentally married."

"I know, Sister."

I did not add that Peg McGurn knew too and paid for her knowledge with her life, after having committed a terrible crime.

"Could I ask why you are so interested in the Cardins?"

"I'm afraid I can't answer that question quite yet. However, I promise to be back to you shortly.

Should I come up with more data, would you be interested in it?"

"You bet!"

"Excellent. I'll be in touch soon."

"Happy New Year, Bishop."

"And a festive Little Christmas to you, Sister."

She laughed, knowing the term the Irish have always used for what we now call, in an appeal to our Greek forebears, the Epiphany. Now a floating day, it no longer occurs necessarily on Twelfth Night. Which shows the mistake of leaving important things like festivals to the liturgists.

Well, as useful as the conversation might have been for my long-run plans, it was no help in resolving the immediate problem.

I felt confident that Jane Frances de Chantal Cardin was safe. As long as her husband knew that the police had his notes to her—or at least would soon have them—she was in no serious danger.

I'm sure that the reader who has perused this account of my behavior that morning will perceive how badly, I might almost say culpably, unperceptive I was.

I sat at my desk, drumming my fingers on Sister Flynn's article. Surely she did not know that it had been distributed to media outlets in Chicago.

The house phone buzzed. Since it was Christmas vacation time at St. Ignatius College Prep, we had a Megan on duty, Megan Kim this time.

"Bishop, a Mr. Cardin and a Mr. Reynolds would like to talk to you for a few minutes."

"Tell them I'll be down in a moment, Megan."

Well, another element in the family checking in. Their story might shed some light on the puzzles. As I remembered Ridley Becker's summary, Cardin was not interested in anything about the holdings except clipping coupons. Reynolds, Janie's brother, played a role like Terry O'Mahoney had played at one time, as had the unfortunate accountant who died in a plane crash off Nassau.

Once again I dressed in my clerical best, this time with the gold band (also with Brigid Cross) that served as my Episcopal ring.

"Gentlemen," Megan said with marvelous Asian-American formality as she conducted me into the room, "His Excellency, Bishop John B. Ryan."

"Thank you, Megan," I replied, trying my best to keep a straight face.

"Pat Reynolds, Bishop."

"Jack Cardin, Bishop."

Both men were content to shake hands.

For a moment the two men confused me.

Pat Reynolds was a compact man with piercing eyes and black hair and white skin like his sister's. He was, however, wearing a blazer and chino slacks, not serious enough to be the brains and the energy behind the Cardin Holdings. Jack Cardin, on the other hand, was big and blond, the Lennon genes still operating, and dressed in a somber, gray, three-piece business suit, too serious to be the fun-loving member of the clan.

Were they trying to confuse me?

I resolved to be genial in response, thus keeping them at a safe distance.

"Charming young woman." Jack nodded at the door from which the Megan had departed. "Korean-American?"

"Oh, yes. Typical Korean-American family. Mother a surgeon, father a physicist. Mostly an American teenager but with enough memories of Asian courtesy to go through the act when it amuses her."

"You called her Megan?" Jack Cardin said, lifting an eyebrow. "Isn't that an Irish name?"

"More a universal name now, like Brian and Kevin."

I explained the phenomenon of the four Megans, the obscurity of their scheduling procedures, and their confidence that they were really in charge of Holy Name Cathedral.

I told you I was being genial.

"You can imagine what we're here for," Pat Reynolds began.

"And we want to begin by apologizing for any, ah, clumsiness from other members of the family," Jack Cardin continued. "We are not here to threaten you or to persuade you to violate any confidentiality."

"I am happy to hear that."

Two polished, fit, well-tailored businessmen in their late thirties that you might encounter in the lobby of the Chicago Club—though never at a place as vulgar as the East Bank Club. They and their wives were doubtless in the Grand March at the opening night of the Lyric Opera, this year a march led by Dame Kiri herself.

"Rather," Reynolds said, sustaining the pas de deux, "we are here to determine whether you could, without violating any confidential commitments, act as a kind of mediator in our problem."

They were a smooth pair all right. Would Clare have considered them gombeen men?

Probably.

"Possibly," I said agreeably. "Would it not be better, however, to leave such a matter to lawyers?"

"I'm an attorney, Bishop," Reynolds said with a wave of his hand, dismissing the fraternity, "and I know the best advice an attorney can give to a client is to avoid litigation, indeed to avoid attorneys whenever possible."

"Arguably," I conceded.

"We would much rather propose a solution to my brother's marital problems, Bishop. He wants a reconciliation. Apparently his wife does not. Therefore we assume that there will be no reconciliation."

"Not at the present in any event," Reynolds added.

"Therefore we would propose an amicable settlement. A large sum of cash and substantial property to be vested in Chantal. . . . We're open to friendly negotiations on the precise amount. However, she would not need any money for the rest of her life."

"And we would not make this settlement dependent on whether she remarries."

"Moreover," Cardin went on, grinning amicably, "we would also propose a joint custody arrangement for the children, with the understanding that Chantal would really have charge of them. She would presumably want to keep them away from the influence of my mother and the Corpus Christi bunch."

"Indeed."

"We would like to accomplish this, uh, arrangement," Jack said, a salesman trying to close a deal, "with a minimum of publicity, a single morning in court and the matter would be settled."

"I see."

Oh, yes, they were a clever duo. Which one, I wondered, was Batman and which one Robin, the Boy Wonder.

Reynolds was Robin.

Jack Cardin filled the vacuum that I had deliberately created with my silence.

"My brother is a wonderful guy, Bishop. But he's trying to carry two heavy burdens which no man on earth could balance. He must carry on the family tradition of impeccable Catholic virtue and at the same time act as one of the most important businessmen in America."

"Not always impeccable," I whispered.

"Of course not, Bishop. It's nonetheless an image which the women in the family have tried to sustain for generations, in face of evidence that like everyone else the Cardins are far from perfect."

"My sister, to her credit be it said, simply doesn't

buy the tradition. She is, in many ways, a woman of
her own time and feels that such traditions are
absurd."

I would let them talk.

"In which respect, Bishop, she and my mother
are at constant odds. There was a time when Mom
didn't take the tradition of piety and conservative
Catholicism seriously. Then when my father died in
a plane crash, she turned to religion and to the
Corpus Christi Movement for consolation. The
quiet but intense religious faith of the Cardins is
what she lives for now."

As well as expensive clothes and even more
expensive jewelry.

"Would not there be some reason to hope that
your sister," I said, turning to Reynolds, "would in
time assume the same position?"

"Maybe, Bishop," he replied, "though I don't
think it very likely. Chantal—how should I say
this?—is a rather complex person. She is very
bright but in many ways very naive. My own
mother sent her to a, uh, very restrictive convent
boarding school. After her first semester at Bryn
Mawr, Mom withdrew her from the school and
arranged the marriage with Pete Cardin. As in
everything else in her life, Chantal obeyed dutifully,
not that she had a choice about it. As it turns out
resentment has built up through the years and has
now exploded."

"I see."

"I assume from what Pat has said, Bishop, you

can understand why she sees my mother as an extension of her own mother. The conflict is beyond resolution."

"Your brother then will choose his mother over his wife?"

They both stopped momentarily at that terrible swift sword of truth.

"I would rather say that my brother will choose peace over endless conflict. . . . You must understand, Bishop, the terrible blow my father's death was to the whole family. Peter was not yet prepared to take over the holdings, especially in the crisis which he found when he assumed command. At the same time, he was required to do all he could to restore whatever harm had been done to the family image by the nature of my father's death."

A lot of revelation in those couple of sentences.

"The alleged link with boys out on the West Side, I presume. But surely that did not become notorious."

"Hardly anyone was aware of that possibility. But my mother thought that everyone knew and that our reputation was in free-fall."

"The conflicting burdens, as he saw them," Reynolds took up the story, "have made life very difficult for Peter. He did manage to salvage the Holdings from the abyss and restore our fiscal soundness but by very cautious transactions—with constant demands and frictions at home."

"I understand. . . . I gather then, Mr. Cardin,

that your father's investments were not always sound."

"Hardly, Bishop, with all due respect to him. He was a gambler, but not a very clever one. He passed up opportunities to participate in the capitalization of Federal Express and Microsoft and chose rather to invest quite heavily in the chain of offshore casinos. . . ."

"Ah."

"This is not known publicly, Bishop, and I'd like to keep it confidential. . . ."

"Of course." I waved my hand in testimony to an agreement among gentlemen.

"It cost us an enormous amount of money to remove ourselves from the casino arrangement. The, ah, other parties, as you may understand, can be very demanding in their negotiations."

"So I am told."

"You must not misunderstand us, Bishop. Under the constraints he must tolerate, Jack's brother is a very able investor, perhaps a little too conservative for the taste of a younger generation, but sound, reliable, and intelligent. He has not taken full advantage of the prosperity of the last decade, but he has nonetheless done very well and at the same time protected the privacy and reputation of the family."

"At enormous personal costs," Jack Cardin added.

"I understand. . . . Are you active in the holdings, Mr. Cardin?"

I knew from the intelligence provided by Mike the Cop that he was not.

"Not really," he replied casually. "The tradition has it that only one Cardin son administers the holdings. My mother would not tolerate a second son actively involved in the day-to-day decisions. I would probably enjoy the game and I would certainly be a little more freewheeling than Pete—though God knows not as wild as poor Dad. However, I'm sensible enough to know that there are other things in life besides devouring every word in the *Wall Street Journal.*"

"I think Pete would much rather be a philanthropist than a businessman," Reynolds added. "And there's enough money now in the holdings, thanks in great part to his determination, to be able to retire and play that role. I think Jack agrees with me that his mother would not tolerate such a change."

"Absolutely. . . . Mom does not control the administration of the holdings, but she's a powerful moral force in the family, too powerful for either of us to take on. And, Bishop, as I'm sure you noted, she's in excellent health."

All right, he wasn't quite Batman after all.

"You must understand, Bishop, that while I love my sister, I must be candid in these circumstances. I think she needs to be free from Peter, for a time certainly and perhaps permanently," Reynolds said.

"Ah."

"The strains she has lived through, quite bravely, I must say, for the last twenty years, have had a strong impact on her, ah, mental health. There is no threat of violence to her. None whatever. The Countess may talk sternly, but she would never do physical harm to anyone."

And the emotional harm didn't count?

"I am happy to hear that."

"I can understand my sister's alarm. But she really has nothing to fear. Not to put too fine an edge on it, Bishop, she tends just now to be a little paranoid. I'm sure that will clear up when she has had a little more freedom for several months or even several years."

What would happen to the cool demeanor of these two smooth-talking gombeen men when the laser-printed notes with Peter Cardin's signature on them fell into the hands of the scandal-hungry Chicago media, especially with Sister Flynn's article already on the news directors' desks?

"Again I'm happy to hear that."

"We haven't said it explicitly, Bishop," Jack Cardin said, moving in for the deal, "but we're here speaking for Peter with his full knowledge and consent. If there is to be a public airing of the family's somewhat meager dirty linen, then he is prepared to accept it as a part of the vagaries of life. But he would like to spare his mother, his wife, and naturally himself from such a situation."

I bet he would.

"I understand."

What was this all about? Did they hope to forestall the release of his letters? If she were a trifle paranoid, he was off the wall crazy to write such letters.

Long silence. They had already told me a lot, but yet they had told me nothing at all. Except that both of them thought that they could do a better job with the holdings than Peter Cardin V.

"Peter then wishes to be separated from his wife?"

Jack Cardin gulped at that question and then tried to essay an answer.

"He is ambivalent about it, Bishop. He claims that he still loves her. I think he believes that. Yet he has neglected her for so long because of the demands of the holdings that he realizes his chances are thin of effecting a reconciliation. He has always put off Chantal and the family until another day, a day when there are fewer pressures. I don't think he realizes yet that such a day will never come."

"At the moment, Bishop," Reynolds continued, "he looks on the arrangement we have proposed as a temporary solution. He feels that in a year or two he will be free to win her back. I need hardly say that I believe such a hope is wishful thinking."

"Arguably."

More silence. Time for another terrible swift sword.

"Mr. Reynolds has suggested that the strain of the years has affected his sister's mental health. I wonder, Mr. Cardin, what your opinion is about your brother's mental health?"

"Well . . . to be perfectly candid, Bishop, he shows the strain at times. He wants to be a perfect husband, a perfect son, a perfect father, a perfect businessman, and a perfect Catholic. Small wonder that these cross pressures would depress him on occasion and that he would, well, ah, be less a paragon of mental health than we would like him to be or that he himself would want to be."

"Indeed."

"Candidly," Reynolds said, "and quite off-the-record, we both have suggested on occasion that he might seek professional, ah, counseling. Perhaps he and Chantal together."

"Mom of course would not stand for that."

Naturally. You're forty-five years old and a very rich man, but you cannot seek psychiatric help without your mother's permission.

"What are the prospects for continuing the tradition of a Peter Paul Cardin presiding over the holdings?"

A leading question, but I had learned all I needed to know from these two and was preparing to send them on their way.

"You mean young Petey?" Jack Cardin said with a laugh. "Oh, I'd say not a chance in the world. He refuses to take my mother seriously. Charms her and ignores her. No, the tradition, for what it is worth, ends with my brother. I don't know what the kid will do with his life, but it won't be at 310 North Michigan."

"It may not be a bad thing either, Bishop," Pat

Reynolds said wearily. "Too much agony has gone into sustaining a tradition which is mostly a pretty fiction."

And sometimes not so pretty.

"Speaking of traditions and fictions, are either of you aware that this New Year's Eve will be the hundredth anniversary of the death of the wife of the first Peter Paul Cardin, indeed of her murder by person or persons still unknown?"

As far as was on the public record.

They both seemed surprised and even mystified.

"You mean that curse thing, Bishop?" Jack asked. "You surely don't take it seriously?"

"Not as a doom imposed by a dying Confederate officer, but as paradigm that subsumes much of your family's history. There is indeed a record of men and women, especially men, dying rather early in life."

"Of natural causes, Bishop. Except for my father. And, what was her name, Rose Cardin."

"And your grandfather at Bastogne."

"You know a lot about the Cardins, don't you, Bishop?" Reynolds said, a suspicious frown replacing the genial mask he had worn until this point in our conversation.

"Not much actually."

"The question, Bishop," Jack Cardin said, trying to slip away from questions of curses, "is whether you are willing to act as an intermediary for us in this matter."

"Oh, yes. I will be happy to. As an intermediary, not as an agent, however."

"What do you mean by that?"

"I mean simply that I am willing to transmit your proposal to Ms. Cardin in approximately the terms you have used to describe it to me. I will even present it sympathetically, with as much understanding as I can muster of your position. However, I will not urge her to accept it. That decision necessarily will be up to her."

"You will not urge her not to accept it?" Reynolds said uneasily.

"Certainly not."

They both sighed with relief.

"I'm sure we can live with that," Jack Cardin said.

Then as an afterthought, he asked, "What do you personally think of it?"

I put on my Buddha face.

"It seems not unreasonable. I regret the suffering both parties have endured. Of course, the Church normally advocates attempts at reconciliation, but since the ordinary course of reconciliation procedures seems to have been foreclosed by the Countess, this may well be the best way out."

They both nodded solemnly.

"So long as," I added lightly, "there is no violence against Chantal Cardin."

"There won't be," her brother said.

"You can count on that," Jack Cardin agreed.

Surely you know about the letters, I thought to myself.

I conducted them politely to the door, shook hands with them cordially, and added that I would pray for a happy outcome of the matter in which we were involved.

They left, satisfied with the success of their mission, though not completely satisfied.

"You'll get in touch with me, Bishop?" Jack Cardin said at the door. "Here's my card. All the personal numbers are on it. Even the one in my car."

I took the card and nodded.

I went back to my study on the second floor of the Cathedral Rectory, sank into my easy chair, wondered how long it was to lunch, glanced at my watch and noted that it was still an hour, and began to reflect on the discussion.

What was it all about?

They seemed to have been utterly candid, according to their own lights. What they proposed made perfect sense under the circumstances. It would have been completely acceptable if they had mentioned Peter Cardin's threats to his wife and, in effect, withdrew them. However, they had said not a word about them directly. They merely had asserted that there were no dangers to Chantal's life. But did they expect me to be won over by such discreet references to outrageous threats? They certainly must have known that they would have to explain the twisted mentality that put such words on paper. They had not tried to do that. They admitted some strain and some depression in Peter Paul Cardin's life, but nothing more.

How could they expect Chantal to accept a compromise with threats of violent death hanging over her head?

The only solution I could think of was that they *didn't* know about the threats.

If that was true, if Peter Cardin had sent his emissaries on a peace mission without filling them in on the details of his estrangement from his wife, then he was even crazier than I had thought he was.

Or maybe he was keeping it all to himself, waiting for the ax to fall. Maybe he tolerated the emissaries' visit to me but was not seriously involved in it. Maybe they were working on an agenda of their own, an agenda of easing Peter out of control of the holdings, so they could take over.

The house phone buzzed and the Megan informed me that Ms. Cardin was on the phone.

"Father Ryan."

"Chantal, Bishop, or Janie to use my real name. I'm at our co-op on the Drive. I don't want to see any of them. I'm checking in to let you know that I'm still hanging tough."

"Capital," I said.

"I talked to my divorce lawyer this morning. He is preparing the papers which we will serve bright and early on January 2. He has already handed over copies of the notes to some friends in the police department. He can't understand why my husband would be so stupid to put such things in writing."

"Can you?"

"Not completely. He can be very dense, but those threats must mean he's completely crazy. If he is, that woman has driven him to it."

"Arguably." I stirred uneasily. Something was wrong, wrong, wrong.

"Petey thinks we should compromise but he'll go along with whatever I want to do."

"I had a visit from two of your husband's emissaries this morning."

"Who?"

"Your brother and John Mark Cardin."

"What did they want?" she asked in a neutral tone of voice.

"They proposed a compromise."

"Did they?"

"With your husband's consent."

"Really."

"I agreed to transmit it to you without an endorsement."

"What was it?"

"You can have just about anything you want in the way of settlement. They may haggle a bit but they won't fight. They suggested joint custody of the children, but hinted that you could have full custody if you demanded it."

"In exchange for?"

"A minimization of public conflict. A day in court and it's all over. Not unusual in the case of the divorce of celebrities."

"And Peter's threats on my life?"

"Were not mentioned."

"Not mentioned? How could they not mention them?"

"It occurs to me that they may not be aware of them."

"How could they not be aware of them?"

"What if your husband had not told them?"

"He might have done that all right. He has the ability to deny lots of things he has done and said, particularly when his mother is involved. But what is to be gained? He knows that the threats will be public in a couple of days."

"Maybe he denies that situation too."

"Then he really is out of touch with reality, Bishop. Completely crazy."

"Arguably."

"Do you think I should accept their suggestions?"

"What do you think?"

"I don't want to humiliate anyone, especially my children. It would be a sensible procedure if it wasn't for the letters . . ."

"Given those letters?"

"Well, he'd have to admit that he sent them and apologize . . . wouldn't he?"

"Arguably."

"Tell them that condition."

"I will indeed."

"It's all crazy, Bishop, isn't it?"

"Arguably. . . . Janie, I did have a thought. Might it be possible that the Countess could have written the letters and constrained your husband to sign them?"

"Regina? Bishop, that woman is semiliterate. She can hardly put a word on paper. Certainly not some of those words. I doubt that she even knows them."

"Indeed."

"So tell them I'm interested in the compromise but only if I can add one more condition to it. All right?"

"Certainly."

"I'm not afraid of them anymore, Bishop. I'm really not."

"I'm glad to hear that. I will call Jack Cardin tomorrow and relay your response."

"Thank you, Bishop. . . . By the way, I met Petey's date last night. I gather she works at the rectory there."

"One of the Megans."

"Lovely young woman. She wouldn't permit anyone to push her around the way I have let them push me around."

"I think you can bank on that, Jane. . . . One more question: do you think either your brother-in-law or your brother would like to become president of the holdings?"

She pondered. "Both of them would, I'm sure, Bishop. They'd have a lot more fun if they were in control. Probably do a better job. I think Peter lets Pat do a lot of things on his own now. But he could never give up final control. His mother wouldn't let him.

"Besides, Jack has too many other interests. He'd like to dabble in the mornings and then go off to the Bob-o-link for golf at noon. Or Pebble Beach. My brother wants to be the power-behind-the-throne, the cool, quiet operator, the man of mystery. He's almost that now, but not quite."

"They both would enjoy it, however, if your husband agreed to reign but not rule."

"You got it, Bishop. If he would do that—and withdraw his crazy threats—and agree to therapy, I'd be willing to risk a reconciliation."

"Do you want me to add that to my response?"

She thought about it. "Under those circumstances I would be willing to discuss reconciliation."

"I shall relay the message."

It would be interesting to hear their reaction.

The man did not deserve it as far as I could see. Yet Chantal Cardin, despite her anger and her fear, still loved him. So he couldn't be all bad. Just a little crazy.

No, a lot crazy.

It was only a half hour to lunchtime.

We had a visiting curial cardinal at the rectory who attempted to explain to Sean Cronin the problems of Catholicism in Chicago—without ever having been in our fair city (Richard M. Daley, mayor) before. We shredded him in the discussion but he was too dumb to realize it. The younger members of my staff sat around the lunch table hardly able to restrain their laughter. When the visitor thanked me effusively for the meal and for the "sparkling—that is the right word, isn't it?—conversation," some of them did snicker.

They did not realize that your typical curial cardinal is almost always charming under such conditions.

All the better to stick the curial knife into your back.

CHAPTER 12

THE NEXT MORNING, Mike Casey was on the
phone at eight thirty.

"Blackie, an addendum on the Feds and the
Cardins."

"Ah?"

"I hear from utterly confidential but very high-
level sources that they're closing in again. This time
they think they have all they need to put someone,
Peter Cardin probably, behind bars for a long time
and bring the whole operation to its knees."

"Indeed!"

"It's all very hush-hush. My sometime colleagues
at the CPD know nothing about it. Neither does
your good friend, the State's Attorney."

"Doubtless both will be furious."

"They sure will."

"When will it go down?"

"Soon . . . they still need to get approval from
Washington. But if the Department of Justice delays
too long, they'll leak the stuff to the media. They
can't see, however, what the Attorney General has

to gain by declining to indict. They're all Republicans anyway."

"Yes, I've heard there are some such people in our nation. Not, however, in Chicago."

"I think what they're going after is some kind of technical violation. The sort of thing they wouldn't bother about if it were someone else. Not an actual injustice."

"What would happen to our country, Michael, if the various United States Attorneys abandoned technical charges against famous people, particularly of the opposite party?"

"Well, they wouldn't get their pictures on television, they wouldn't have the opportunity to declaim righteously against evil. They might even have to spend some of their time on drug cases."

"God forbid!"

"I'll let you know, Blackie, if I pick up anything else. I'd thought you'd want to know."

"Oh, yes."

I put down the phone and tried to think again. The plot thickened. Peter Cardin's house of cards was collapsing all around him. Maybe he was losing control of his words and actions.

All of this caused by his slavish devotion to the Countess.

A pretty heavy price to pay for mother love.

I waited till ten o'clock to phone Jack Cardin. He was at home. Naturally.

"Yes, Bishop. Did you have any success?"

"That is for you to judge, Mr. Cardin."

"What did she say?"

"She asked me to tell you that she too is sensible to the problems of publicity and would like to avoid conflict which would fascinate the media but would harm all concerned."

"That's good."

"She also believes that discussions might be possible about the general outline of the settlement you proposed."

"Wonderful!"

"With one proviso. Your brother must apologize for the threats he has made and withdraw them."

"There have been no threats, Bishop. You can believe that."

"That is as may be, Mr. Cardin. The point is that your brother's wife believes that threats have been made. You and your family must accept that as a given and deal if not with the factuality of the threats at least the factuality of her convictions."

"I understand. At least I think I do."

"There must at least be some reasonable discussion of the content of those threats."

"I'll talk to Peter about it, Bishop. But let me assure you that he is harmless. He wouldn't hurt a fly. I can't imagine why Chantal would be afraid of him."

"You or someone else might want to discuss that with her and her attorney."

"I'll see what Peter wants to do. . . . No hope for a reconciliation, I suppose?"

"Oddly enough, Mr. Cardin, there still is. In

addition to the one condition that I have already described, Ms. Cardin is willing to talk reconciliation if her husband is willing to step down as operating head of the holdings and enter into therapy. The nature of that therapy was not specified and might be subject to some negotiation."

There was silence on the line for a moment.

"Dear God, Bishop, that would be the best thing in the world for him. I think they could make a go of it under those circumstances. He'd be a hell of a lot happier if he could get rid of the millstone round his neck."

"Arguably."

"He'll never do either. Our mother would not tolerate it."

"Once more he is given a choice between his mother and his wife."

"He won't see it that way, but you're right."

"You will not pass on these conditions to him?"

"Oh, sure I will. He'll agonize and then say that he'd like to but he just can't."

"Ah."

"I'm surprised that Chantal is still willing to try again."

"There is no accounting for love."

"He has never done violence to her, Bishop, neither physically nor verbal. You've got to believe that."

"Her beliefs on these subjects are what is relevant, not mine."

"Agreed. . . . I'll talk to Pat and see what we

can do. Damn it, Bishop. There's light at the end of the tunnel, but how will we ever get there?"

"You won't unless your brother accepts her conditions. I think you can take my word for that."

"Yes, Bishop, I do. Thank you for being so helpful. We appreciate it very much. I'll try to get back to you after the first of the year."

"Capital."

I held my hand suspended over the phone. I was missing something. I still did not grasp the importance of the message from Clare Raftery. What was it? Who was doing the obfuscation?

It was not absolutely impossible that Janie had forged the notes from her husband, but it did not seem to me that it was very likely that she had. But who knows what she might have done, and even come to believe, under the enormous pressures of her life both at home before the marriage and then after she became Mrs. Peter Paul Cardin.

Yet Jack Cardin sounded absolutely convincing too. And had not the diffident, anxious, sad man I had encountered on Michigan Avenue before Christmas seemed quite incapable of sending his wife to Dante's hell in as painful a manner as possible?

Well, soon his threats would be a matter of public record. His lawyers would probably charge that they were forgeries. But, besides the allegedly semiliterate Countess, who else would forge them and why?

I was missing something. No doubt about that.

So to protect against my own failures of insight, I dialed the Reilly Gallery again.

"Mike, do you think any of your colleagues would be willing to forego a New Year's Eve party?"

"Double time, but why not?"

"Capital. I want two of the very best to shadow Chantal Cardin until 1996 arrives."

"Sure. Where is she now?"

"At their co-op on Lake Shore Drive."

"No problem. . . . Twenty-four hours?"

"Absolutely."

"Any reason?"

"Threats have been made on her life and it will be the hundredth anniversary of the murder of the wife of the first Peter Cardin."

"That's kind of thin, Blackie. Still, better to be safe than sorry. I'll take care of it."

"The very best, Mike."

"The very, very best. . . . Are we going to see you at Mary Kate's party."

"This year I think not."

I have an aversion to such parties and normally fall asleep before they have fairly begun—and not because of too many "jars" either. This year I deemed it wise to stay close to the phone

The aforementioned sibling called shortly thereafter and, after something of an argument, accepted my plea that something very important might happen and I had to say close to the Cathedral.

"Life and death important?"

"Oh, yes. Very much so."

"OK, but you'll come the Sunday after New Year's?"

"I don't know why not."

By Sunday the anniversary of the death of Rose Cardin would have passed.

I told myself that I was too deeply involved emotionally in the case to have any perspective. Maybe after the immediate threat was over I could see things more clearly.

At least Janie was safe, guarded by Mike's very, very best.

The snow came back as December wound down, a roaring blizzard. Just as well that I had begged off from the drive out to Beverly.

On the morning of New Year's Eve, Jack Cardin dropped in at the rectory.

"Only take a minute, Bishop," he said. "Pat and I talked to one another. We intend to corner Peter on January second. Mom will be on her way to one of her shopping expeditions in Paris. We think it just possible that in her absence, he may agree with Chantal's terms."

"Possible?"

"Possible, but not likely."

"I understand."

"As to the threats, I guess we'll have to sit down with her attorney and find out what they are. I think my brother would be willing to do that."

"When?"

"January second if possible. At least we will urge him to do so."

"I see."

"You will pass this on to her?"

"Naturally."

"I'm trying hard, Bishop."

He certainly seemed to be.

After he had left, Megan Anne cornered me.

"Is that Pete's father, Bishop Blackie?"

"His uncle."

"He seems to be a nice man."

"So he does."

"I've met his mother, but not his father."

"Rapid progress."

"Pete doesn't talk much about his father, but I think there's something wrong. He sounds like, you know, kind of postal."

The little witch was fishing for information. As Pete had said, she was transparent and didn't care who knew it.

"Indeed."

"Do you know his mother, Bishop Blackie?"

"I have met her."

"Any man who wouldn't love a woman as sweet and as beautiful as she is has to be a dweeb."

"Arguably."

She nodded, having gained all the information she needed on that subject.

"I don't have a date with him tonight."

"A disaster!"

"Not really," she said with a giggle. "I have lot of parties to go to."

"I do not doubt it."

"He's like I have to go to a party with my parents at the Casino. . . . What's the Casino, Bishop? Do they gamble there?"

"Not hardly. . . . Do you know that ground-hugging building whose stones are painted dark green which kind of huddles beneath the spiral driveway up to the Hancock Center parking lot?"

"Sure. I'm like it's a warehouse or something."

"That is the Casino Club, the most exclusive place in Chicago."

"Really!"

"Really. I was permitted in there once and it is indeed gorgeous."

"Do you think he was ashamed to bring me there?"

"Absolutely no way, Megan. Bank that."

"Uh-huh . . . then he has to be ashamed of his family, doesn't he?"

"Could he not think that they are simply BORING!"

"Yeah!" she said, brightening considerably. "That's it. . . . Is the Casino Club like totally boring?"

"Totally."

"Great. . . . Thank you, Bishop."

I returned to my lair on the second floor. Wise decision on Petey's part. You didn't want to expose your new date to the Countess' prying questions about her family and their origins, especially when said new date was altogether likely to jab right back with her own deadly wit.

The Casino, huh? Well, that was in my parish too.
Under my canonical jurisdiction even if most of the
"swells" (to use Clare's admirable noun) didn't
know that.

Janie would hardly be there under the circumstances.

Only a few more hours and it would be 1996 and
we would have frustrated Colonel Pettigrew's curse.
I hoped that the issue of the threatening missives
could be cleared up quickly on January second, the
day after tomorrow before the media broke the
story.

After lunch, Mike the Cop called me.

"Not resting your eyes, Blackie?"

"Certainly not."

In fact my eyes were partially closed.

"I'm reporting on Ms. Cardin."

"Indeed?"

"My colleagues report she is an easy tail. No
problems following her and no one else tailing her."

"Does she know someone is watching her."

"They don't think so. Any instructions?"

I thought about it. "Tonight might be a critical
time."

"I'll warn them to be careful."

"Capital."

I hung up vaguely troubled, not sure what it was
that made me uneasy.

How could anyone harm Chantal when she was
safe in her co-op and all the usual suspects were at
the Casino with everyone watching them?

Like everyone was watching Red Pete in Pat McCarthy's saloon a hundred years ago.

Something clicked in head. An image rose and quickly faded.

Such pictures cannot be pushed like I was trying to push this one. When it comes, it comes. And that's that. I volunteered to take the phone calls that night, out of due turn and, as I assured the staff, because I didn't want to ruin anyone's celebration of a new Year of the Lord.

"Common era," one of my more intellectual colleagues ventured.

"I am not unaware of that. However, as you know, both terms can be used depending on the context."

Laughter. They were grateful for the night off.

I wanted, however, to be sure I got any incoming calls.

This could be the critical evening.

The ten o'clock news informed me as I was preparing for bed that it would be the coldest day of the year in Chicago, between ten and fifteen below with a windchill of thirty-five below. Strong northeast winds off the lake and a winter storm watch by morning. Between six and eight inches of snow expected.

Protect all who are mad enough, I requested of the Deity, to venture forth on this frigid night, even though they should be prudent and stay in their snug beds like I am. Please take care of Jane Frances de

Chantal Cardin. Protect her from my own ineptitude. I realize You have assigned me to protect her and I seemed to have failed.

You could of course give me a few more hints.

CHAPTER 13

I WOKE UP at midnight from a deep sleep with a clear and horrible picture in my head.

I couldn't remember the picture. What had awakened me? The noise celebrating the coming of a new year?

Yes, but there was another noise. What was it?

The phone, yes, the phone.

I rolled over and punched a button for the main line into the Cathedral. Phone kept ringing.

"Mike Casey, Blackie. I have bad news."

"Yes?"

"My people lost her!"

"What!"

This was obviously a nightmare. I was still asleep. Soon I would wake up.

"She slipped out in some kind of disguise. They got suspicious when only one light remained on in the apartment. They managed to, ah, get in. They found a note from her husband, a letter of, well, passionate love. He proposed a tryst in their house in Park Lane tonight, to begin a new year and a new

life. He apologized profusely for whatever he had
done in the past and said he would accept all her
conditions for a reconciliation."

"Oh."

"Sorry, Blackie . . . he warned her that there
might be people watching her and urged her to
sneak out."

"He's at the Casino Club. Or was supposed to be
there."

"I'll check and call you back."

I tried to think. No dice. Nothing. The case was
getting more weird. I could not imagine Peter
Cardin writing such a note.

I called Mike back.

Busy. He was checking with the Casino at the
foot of the Hancock Center where he lived. Of
course Mike knew the doorman. He knew all the
doormen in Chicago.

I pushed the redial button.

"Casey's," said Annie Casey.

"Annie, Blackie."

"Right! Here's himself!"

"He's still there."

Dear God, how had I messed up so badly.

"You have contacts with the cops in Forest
Lane?"

"They talk to us occasionally."

"Call them and tell them that it's a matter of life
and death that immediately, repeat immediately,
one of their squads go to the Cardin compound. I
believe a murder is in progress."

"Will do."

I slept fitfully for two hours. The phone rang. Three o'clock.

What had happened.

"You scare the hell out of me, Blackie."

It was Mike the Cop.

"Arguably."

"The Forest Lane squad found Ms. Chantal Cardin tied to a tree near the lakeshore. She had been beaten, raped, and covered with water. She's unconscious and suffering from hypothermia and other injuries. Apparently she put up a hell of a fight. Her bedroom is covered with blood that would appear to be that of the attackers. They're flying her down to Northwestern Memorial on a helicopter. The hypothermia unit there is a donation of the Cardins. Condition extremely critical."

"But still alive."

"Still alive."

Patently to anyone but a fool, the attack would come independently of possible release of the notes.

I dressed hurriedly and as I left my suite I pointed a warning finger at the ivory medieval Madonna that is alleged to resemble my mother when she was a young woman.

"It's Your job," I informed that worthy, "to see that she doesn't die."

Make up for my mistakes.

I awaited the helicopter with the oils of the Sacrament of the Sick as it groped in the snow and the wind for Northwestern Hospital heliport.

On the first try it missed and rose sharply again, lest it crash into the walls of the hospital.

It tried again, very carefully, and skidded off the roof. The pilot quickly pulled it up.

The third time the helicopter landed, only just barely. It swayed in the wind. I was afraid that it would be swept off the roof. The pilot jumped out in the thundering wind and tied a cable to the front of the craft. Two techs from the hospital dashed in the storm and tied down the rear. The copter fought desperately against the ropes, trying to hurl itself to the ground below.

The medical team dashed out with a gurney. They took her off the helicopter as quickly as they could with the wind tearing at their bodies and the snow blinding their eyes. I discovered that I had run out with them.

I dabbed the sacred oil on her forehead and began the prayers for the dying as I followed the team into the emergency room of the Cardin Pavilion. Only then did I notice that I had forgot to put on an overcoat.

"No heartbeat!" someone shouted as we fought our way out of the snow and the wind and the bitter cold. "We've lost her!"

"Not yet," a black woman resident shouted back. "Not yet."

"Touch and go, Father," said the young woman. "We won't let her die. What kind of monsters do these things?"

"Family," I said.

In the emergency room they had the equipment
ready. The resident punched a hole in her groin
artery, injected a tube, and flipped a switch. The
Extra-Corporal circulation unit, the resident explained to me, would heat her blood and return it to
her body. Another young woman opened two small
holes in her chest, inserted test tubes, and poured
warm fluid into them. Someone else slipped a
nasogastric mechanism into her nose and began
pumping warm fluid into her stomach. Nurses
wrapped electric blankets around her. Others pushed
intravenous tubes into her arms. Monitors began to
blink.

"We still have brain waves!"

"No blood pressure!"

"No discernible heartbeat!"

Dr. Dale Kauffman, the head of the unit, rushed
into the room, looked around, nodded his approval,
and felt for a pulse.

"Who is she, Father?"

"Chantal Cardin."

"Dear God, I would not have recognized her."

A monitor blinked and blipped.

"We have a heartbeat!"

After a few hesitant blinks and beeps, the line on
the monitor went flat. Then it began again, hesitantly and slowly. But it didn't stop.

"We have a sustained heartbeat!"

"We have blood pressure rising!"

"Let's see what we can do for her extremities!"

"The immediate danger is over, Father," Dr.

Kauffman whispered to me. "She's extremely critical and we may still lose her, but now there's at least
a chance. I don't know how much of the damage
will be permanent. I'll call you if she begins to slip
or if she shows signs of reviving . . . I know the
Cathedral number."

I had done all that I could.

I called Mike Casey as soon as I was in the
Cathedral. "Sorry to disturb you, Mike."

"No chance of our sleeping. What's happening?"

"She's still alive, though only barely. They think
she has a chance of making it."

"Thank God."

"It might be wise to dispatch some of your people
to guard her. The hospital might do it but we don't
want to take any more risks."

"We certainly don't," he sighed.

"Do you have the note her husband allegedly sent
her?"

"Naturally."

"Laser printed?"

"Right, on his personal stationary and with his
signature."

"Indeed. You must see that your friend John
Culhane at Area Six gets it immediately. Is he on
duty tonight?"

"He sure is. He loves a night like this."

"Good."

Then a long delayed light went on.

"Mike, your wife, the virtuous Annie, works with

computers. Would you give her the letter and put
her on the line."

"Yes, Blackie," Annie said. "What a bastard this
guy must be."

"Arguably. . . . You can tell the difference between various kinds of DPI on a laser?"

"Certainly. Let me get a magnifying glass."

I waited.

"OK, Blackie, it is unquestionably printed in
three hundred dots per inch. A Hewlitt Packard
Laser III or some equivalent."

"Good. Tell Mike I'll be in touch."

Certain things were becoming clear.

Then I saw what Clare Raftery had been trying to
tell me.

Of course! How stupid can one be!

The pieces of the puzzle began to fit together.

I tried to sleep, but could not do so. I struggled
out of bed at five o'clock. One radio all-news
station, on the basis of the report of no heartbeat,
said she had already died. The other station reported
that she was extremely critical.

I wasn't going to take any chances that the first
one might be right. Putting on an overcoat, a
woolen cap, earmuffs, a scarf, and gloves—none of
which matched one another—I slogged through the
snowdrifts, bent my head against the wind, and
hurried back to the hospital.

The wind was so strong that sometimes I could
make no progress against it.

The African-American woman resident, whose

name I discovered from peering at the tag on her surgical gown was Melanie Jefferson, M.D., her eyes weary, told me that the news radio stations both had it wrong. Chantal had been upgraded to "extremely critical but stable."

"We could lose her any moment, Bishop. The traumas to her organisms are horrific. Still, our chances are improving. Come have a look at her. Give her your blessing."

Chantal, with even more appurtenances projecting from her battered body, did not seem to be breathing. Yet beeps on the various monitors pinged away with hopeful regularity.

"Blood pressure moving up to normal, Dr. Jefferson," said one of the three nurses presiding over Chantal.

"It gets a little better each passing minute, Bishop," Dr. Jefferson whispered to me. "I think we're moving slowly toward fifty-fifty . . . I'll call Dr. Kauffman and tell him. He's resting down the corridor. I made him take off for a half hour. We'll need him at full strength as time goes on."

"Indeed."

"He's never lost one with a regular heartbeat, Bishop. Though there's always a first time."

A woman's voice bellowed, "What is going on here?"

"Who's that?" the resident asked.

"That is her mother-in-law, the Countess Cardin. She is a blatant racist, Doctor. You have my permission to rebuke her if she becomes difficult."

The doctor smiled. "I'm so worn out, Bishop, that I might just do that."

The Countess barged into the room, resplendent in a maroon evening gown and a sable cape.

"I demand an explanation. I am the Countess Cardin. I bought this treatment center. What has this foolish woman done to us now?"

"You may not enter this room, ma'am," Dr. Jefferson said mildly enough. "Our patient's life is in jeopardy."

"Nonsense! Get out of my way."

Dr. Jefferson restrained her and pushed back.

"Who are you?" the Countess demanded haughtily.

"I'm Dr. Jefferson. I'm the resident in this unit."

"Nonsense! Peter Paul, get rid of this person and get us a real doctor. The very idea of a woman like this treating a member of our family!"

"Look, you white racist bitch," Dr. Jefferson exploded. "Stop endangering my patient's life and get out of here."

She pushed hard. The Countess spun through the doorway.

"I'll have your job," she bellowed as she fell into her elder son's arms. "Now let me back in."

"Nurse," Dr. Jefferson ordered, "call security and have them remove this woman. Tell them to charge her with disorderly conduct."

A man and woman elbowed their way through the Cardin clan—dressed in their elaborate white tie party finery—that was massed in the corridor.

"We're security, Doctor."

Mike's people. Here before hospital security, probably long before.

"Restrain her please."

They appeared to be only too happy to do just that.

"Is this necessary, Doctor?" Peter Cardin asked.

Not "How is my wife doing?"

What an asshole!

"Are you the husband?"

"Yes, Doctor," he said apologetically.

"What is more important to you, sir—your wife's life or this woman's whims?"

"My wife."

He was a haggard, haunted man, distraught, confused, not quite certain that he was not in a nightmare. I knew the feeling.

"Good. Then keep her out of that room. We are battling to save Ms. Cardin's life. We must focus every moment of attention on her. We cannot risk distractions."

"My mother."

"I don't care whether she's Queen Bathsheba. Keep her the hell out of that room and shut her up or I'll have security remove her and lock her in a room. You keep her quiet for a while and maybe, just maybe, I'll let you see your wife."

"Yes, Doctor."

"I demand to see Dr. Kauffman," the Countess shouted. "Immediately."

"Nurse," Dr. Jefferson said to the floor nurse who

was hovering uncertainly in the background. "Call Dr. Kauffman and tell him the Countess Cardin is creating a disturbance in the corridor outside her daughter-in-law's room."

She turned on her heel and strode back into the emergency room.

"What happened, Father?" Jack Cardin asked. "'Cuse me, Bishop. We heard about it on the radio just as we were leaving the Casino."

Like the others in the corridor, he seemed troubled, confused, unbelieving. Petey was slumped in a chair, his head buried in his hands. Red-haired Lisa looked like she was about to become an erupting volcano.

What a bunch of jerks.

"I'm glad someone cares enough to ask, Mr. Cardin. Your sister-in-law was attacked, beaten, and raped in her Forest Lane home. She was then tied to a tree outside the house and sprinkled with water from a hose. Fortunately the Forest Lane police, acting on a tip, arrived in time to free her and Med-Evac'ed her down here. I met the copter on the roof and anointed her and said the prayers for the dying. There was no discernible heartbeat at first. But Dr. Jefferson revived her and Dr. Kauffman arrived shortly thereafter and has supervised the treatment. It is my understanding that her chances of survival now approach fifty-fifty."

"Dear God," Jack said, his face turning pale. "How terrible!"

"She'll be nothing but a vegetable!" the Countess

sneered. "How dare that woman do this to our family."

"Mother, please," Peter begged.

"Madam," I said firmly, "your behavior here disgraces your family more than anything else. Please restrain your hatred."

Well, it made me feel good to say that.

"Bishop Ryan is right, Mother," Peter said. "Your behavior is utterly inappropriate."

"What kind of son are you?"

"A son whose wife may be dying."

"Where is Dr. Kauffman?"

"I'm right here, Mrs. Cardin."

"Countess Cardin."

"Very well, Countess Cardin. I cannot tolerate disruption of my staff under these circumstances. . . ."

"I bought this unit. I am entitled to some consideration."

"Indeed you are, but that does not mean that you are entitled to threaten the life of one of our patients. Mr. Cardin, with your permission, I am going to ask the security people here to remove your mother, to take her to another part of the hospital and sedate her. Clearly this terrible event has caused her to behave hysterically."

The woman cop glanced at me. I nodded briskly.

Peter took a deep breath.

"Of course, Doctor, do whatever you think is necessary."

His mother sobbed at such a blatant betrayal.

"I'll go along with her, Peter," Cordelia, Jack Cardin's wife, volunteered.

"Thank you, Delia." Peter nodded gratefully.

When his mother had disappeared down the corridor, Peter turned to Dr. Kauffman. "I'm sorry, Doctor, my mother is deeply troubled by this terrible event. . . . Will Chantal live?"

"Possibly."

"Will there be any permanent damage?"

"Maybe. Maybe not. It's too early to tell. She is in excellent physical condition which means something."

"I see. Thank you, Doctor."

"Why don't you and your family go down to the waiting room at the end of the corridor? Bishop Ryan, will you show them the way?"

"Yes."

"Can we see her, Doctor?" Lisa asked.

The young woman was weeping, her eyes were red with tears. She had apparently switched sides as teenagers do.

"I'll have to see how she's doing."

Lisa turned and joined Petey, still slumped in his chair. She put her arms around his shoulders.

"She'll be all right, Petey," she said. "I just know she will."

"Why don't we walk down to the waiting room?" I said. "And get some coffee."

Silently they trudged along behind me.

"We were at a formal dance at the Casino when

we heard the news," Pat Reynolds explained. "Storm or no storm we came right over."

I busied myself with the pouring of coffee, a heated pot of which awaited us.

Dr. Kauffman joined us again.

"Brain waves are good," he began. "And getting better. Apparently no serious damage there. We have to get her temperature up and make sure there's no internal injuries. God only knows about the psychic damage."

Shock and disbelief and grief had drawn all the faces tight. Only the two weeping teenagers displayed stronger emotions. Private and reserved to the bitter end. Well, their privacy wouldn't last the day. Even if she died, Chantal would reach out from the grave to destroy this viper's tangle.

"Dr. Joseph Murphy will be available as soon as she regains consciousness," the doctor added. "He is the best psychiatrist in Chicago, the best male psychiatrist, that is."

"Our family does not accept psychiatry," Peter Paul Cardin V said automatically.

Dr. Kauffman stared at him as though he were a creature from outer space.

"We'll let the patient decide that."

"Yes, of course, Doctor. We will accept whatever treatment you suggest."

Dr. Kauffman nodded curtly and turned away. Dr. Melanie Jefferson joined us a few minutes later.

"Dr. Kauffman is with her now. Her body temperature is rising. Not as rapidly as we would like, but still at an acceptable rate."

"I'm glad to hear that," Peter Cardin said. "We'll wait for you to approve of a brief visit."

"Let us say a prayer," I invited them and by way of compromise with their version of the heritage said a whole rosary. The nurses and the residents joined us. Papists everywhere.

The Countess returned during the rosary, Mike's off-duty cops watching her closely. Her eyes were glazed and she walked unsteadily as the Valium took effect.

"She promised to be good," Cordelia whispered.

"What kind of monsters do this sort of thing to a woman?" the resident, now almost asleep on her feet, repeated her question of the previous night after we had finished the rosary.

"It's God's punishment on an adulterous woman," Regina Cardin proclaimed. "The depths of hell are frozen ice."

"Mother!" a number of voices exclaimed.

I'd had it with the whole crowd.

"You're quite correct, Countess Cardin," I said. "In Dante's hell, the deepest regions are ice. However, and you might profitably meditate on this fact: the ice is not for the lustful but the proud."

"I hate you, Grandmother." Lisa leaped from her chair and waved a finger in the Countess's face. "You are a vicious, evil, arrogant old woman. I'll never forgive you for what you've done to my mother and father."

"Lisa," her father said gently.

"It's true, Daddy," she raged. "And you're a wimp for letting her do it."

Petey put his arm around his sister and led her back to her chair. The Countess, now quite out of it, sank into another chair, Cordelia still in gentle attendance.

I poured more coffee.

An hour passed. Lisa and Pete were no longer weeping. I rejoiced inwardly that Megan Anne had not been at the Casino Club.

Dr. Jefferson returned.

"I think you may see her now, Mr. Cardin," she said.

"Thank you, Doctor."

"Would you accompany him, Bishop?"

"Oh, yes."

Chantal Cardin's breathing was stronger. The heartbeat seemed vigorous. Despite the black and blue marks on her face and the bandage on her head, her beauty seemed to have returned and with it a certain kind of serenity.

The two nurses in attendance stood next to the bed, one on either side, like the seraphs guarding the entrance to Paradise.

"Her temperature is almost normal," Dr. Jefferson whispered. "We're pleased with her progress."

Great, silent tears were pouring down Peter Paul Cardin's handsome face.

"Will she regain consciousness, Doctor," he asked softly.

"No guarantees, Mr. Cardin, but we think it not unlikely."

He nodded. "Thank you, Doctor."

We tiptoed out of the room.

"Perhaps the two young people," I said to Dr. Melanie Jefferson. "They're her children."

"All right, but they must be quiet."

"I'll warn them."

Petey and Lisa, arms protectively around one another, stood with me at their mother's bedside. Like their father, they wept quietly. Neither of them said a word.

"She's doing better than we expected," the doctor said. "We're being quite hopeful."

The young people inclined their heads solemnly. We left the room.

"Do you have an early Mass, Bishop?" Dr. Jefferson asked me.

"Yes, as a matter of fact, I believe I have been scheduled for the eight o'clock Eucharist."

"It's seven-thirty now. You can go back to the Cathedral. Off the record, she's going to make it, but don't quote me. I'll stay in touch with you."

"Capital."

I told the Cardins that I had to go back to the Cathedral to say Mass, but that I would return later in the day.

"Pray for all of us," Pat Reynolds murmured.

"Certainly."

"Bishop, wait a minute. Can I talk to you?"

Peter Cardin, his face still immobile, stopped me on the way to the elevator.

"I suppose so. Out in the lounge?"

We found a private place in the corner. The snow outside was so thick that one could not see Lake Michigan.

"My brother John Mark," he got down to business immediately, "says I'm obsessive and possessive."

"Indeed."

"He insists that I am Othello and my mother and brother-in-law and daughter are Iago. He and Cordelia, his wife, dismiss my suspicions about Chantal as neurotic jealousy."

"Your daughter seems to have changed sides."

He nodded. "Now she blames me . . . how perceptive of you to notice."

He took a deep breath and continued. "An event like this shatters everything. I believe Lisa and John Mark may be right."

"Arguably."

"Does one get second chances?"

A most important religious question, maybe the most important of all.

"Peter Paul Cardin, God gives us N order chances. The problem is that we rarely seize them because of the habits we have acquired."

"Can a man," he hesitated, "can a man stop being obsessive? And possessive? And a wimp in the face of his mother's rage."

"Most likely not."

His shoulders slumped.

"Why not?"

"The costs are too steep."

"Such as?"

"Therapy for the rest of one's life."

He drew a deep breath. "Our family has always avoided that, as you doubtless heard just now."

"Precisely."

I stood up. He was still worried about family privacy. Too late. Before the day was over the vicious and obscene notes to Chantal would be on the five o'clock news and he'd be in jail. Then all his power and wealth would not prevent him from falling into the human condition that his family had managed to avoid for at least a century.

He rose with me. "I hope they catch him soon."

"Who?"

"The man who did these terrible things to her."

"Two of them."

"The man we thought, wrongly perhaps, was her lover and another?"

"No way. The police have checked on him. He's in San Francisco for the holidays, celebrating with friends. And, by the way, Peter Paul Cardin, he was surely not her lover. He's gay."

I punched the elevator button. The door opened immediately and I entered. As usual the people on the elevator did not notice me.

I still didn't like what was happening. Did Peter Cardin really intend to deceive me? Could he have imagined that his wife did not show me the notes he had written? How could he be so innocently unprepared for what was about to happen?

On the way back to the Cathdral, I saw the whole picture. Finally. I examined it carefully, checking each little detail.

Chantal Cardin had been attacked from three sides, each attacker with a different goal, each one with their own responsibility. But only one attacker had been responsible for the physical violence done to her. How could I prove that?

I went over the possibilities. It should not be too difficult.

Everything fit.

I offered profound thanks at the New Year's morning Eucharist. I had figured it out very late. But, in Herself's Providence, not too late.

CHAPTER **14**

MILORD CRONIN, A sweater over his fatigue
uniform of shirt without a collar but with French
cuffs and loafers without a tassel, awaited me in the
dining room after Mass, disposing of his small daily
ration of Raisin Bran and skim milk.

"Just come from the hospital?"

"Just came from presiding over the eight o'clock
Eucharistic community, five perfectly sober members of the People of God, the youngest of whom
might not have been quite eighty."

"You were at the hospital before that?"

"Naturally."

"What happened? What's going to happen?"

I provided him with a detailed outline of the story
thus far and forecast what would happen for the rest
of the day and on the morrow.

He put down his spoon, folded his arms, and
listened intently.

"Will the woman survive?" he asked somberly.

"There seems to be little doubt that she will live

and eventually come out of the coma. I gather it is not very deep."

"And emotionally?"

"Perhaps."

He remained silent for a few moments.

"You're sure about all this other stuff."

"Oh, yes. We need to collect a few more supporting details."

"Blackwood, you scare the hell out of me!"

"Possibly."

Before I made a concerted effort to regain some of my lost sleeping time, I called Mike the Cop.

"Yeah, Blackie."

"I have a small request."

I made the request.

"So that's the way the wind is blowing. You sure?"

"Sure I'm sure."

I told him some of my reasons for being sure.

"It figures," Mike agreed. "You'll have a hard time selling it to the Forest Lane cops."

"If your inquiry reveals what I think it will reveal, we can give them the tip."

"They'll like that."

"When will the arrest of Peter Paul Cardin go down?"

"This afternoon, in time for the four o'clock news."

"Naturally."

As I expected, Peter Paul Cardin was unprepared for what happened to him. The four o'clock news

showed him being fingerprinted and charged at the
Chicago Avenue Police Station, a big, handsome,
powerful man, still in his dinner jacket, being
dragged down to earth—violated, confused, frightened. He was to be arraigned the next day, because
holiday court was already closed.

Both local and network news carried the story of
the arrest and the letters, denials of a love affair
from the trainer, comments by therapists and lawyers, discussion by financial experts of the holdings
and by historians of the Cardin family history.
There were ample references to the murder of the
first Mrs. Cardin a hundred years ago and copious
quotes from Sister Flynn's article. Two of the
channels offered half-hour specials after the ten
o'clock news, both entitled "The Rise and Fall of
the House of Cardin."

They knew nothing of Clare Raftery's letters.
Moreover it would require them more time than it
had taken me to understand their implications.
Nonetheless the Cardin story was a treasure trove
for news directors on a night when there is almost
no news.

In due course, I now expected, the Raftery letters,
including the missing one, would be made public.
By then they would be a sensation.

The reporters and anchorpersons made not even a
passing reference to Chantal's condition that now
was, according to Lisa who had chosen me as
someone to call at ten P.M., "critical but with strong
and stable vital signs."

"Your father?"

"Poor daddy. They won't let us see him. His lawyers are trying to get him out on bail."

"I see."

"And Bishop . . ."

"Yes."

"This Megan person has been with me and Petey all day."

"Indeed!"

"She's so great! She even makes us laugh."

"Ah."

"I want to go to her school."

"That might be advisable."

I had not anticipated that development, though patently I should have. Unless I moved quickly, that Megan person would lay out her solution to the crime and demand that I follow her advice.

There were a number of plausible paths we could follow. All they would do would be to release Chantal's husband from the county jail where he was being held without bail. Yet if the cops and the cement-head State's Attorney were persuaded that Peter had not paid a pair of thugs to attack his wife and that someone else had a reasonable motive, they might seek out evidence that could be easy to find.

First thing the next morning I visited Chantal in the Cardin Pavilion. Only her two older children were in attendance. The men in the family were busy trying to get Peter Paul out of jail.

"She's a little better, Father Blackie," Lisa said.

"I think she recognizes me. She even smiled once. I think."

Dr. Melanie Jefferson nodded. "Somewhat better. I think she smiled too. We'll take her off critical later this morning."

"She's going to be fine," Petey insisted. "Now we have to get poor Dad out of jail. I know he didn't do it."

"Arguably."

I offered no promises.

Then I stopped at the Casey apartment in the Hancock Center, consumed my customary cup of orange mango herbal tea and four oatmeal raisin cookies with Annie and Mike Casey. They were both in robes, awakening leisurely from a night of sleep undisturbed by my frantic calls. The Gallery would not open till the morrow.

I explained my solution to them.

"Dear God in heaven!" Annie exclaimed.

"I believe that She is indeed involved, though this time Her crooked lines are a bit too crooked for my taste. Not that She has consulted me on the matter."

"It all makes sense." Mike rubbed his chin slowly. "Perfect sense. What do we do with it?"

"We proceed logically and forcefully, understanding as we do how the interaction between police and media operate."

"Yeah," he said, somewhat more dubiously than I thought appropriate.

I was thereupon offered a cup of eggnog (without rum) and some apricot Christmas cake made from my sister Mary Kate's famous recipe. Then I called Kevin Maher, the husband of my niece Caitlin and an expert on computers. He agreed with my supposition. Then Mike the Cop called a friend at the Office of the United States Attorney for the Northern District of Illinois who confirmed most reluctantly what I suspected. But only when Mike told him that we already knew who the Feds were hunting.

"Don't ask how I know, Jeff," Mike said. "You know better than that."

The squawks at the other end of the line indicated deep pain. We were spoiling their eventual press conference announcing the investigation and indictment and the leak before they could.

"Jeff, I understand that it's top secret," Mike explained patiently. "But you can't expect to keep it quiet with this attempted murder charge going down."

More squawks of protest.

"It won't wash, Jeff. You guys had better be prepared for the locals to lean on you. You won't lose your press conference, but you've got to do it tomorrow. There might be even more coverage because of the tie-in."

No more squawks. Jeff had calmed down at the prospect of a tie-in.

"We have to know how much. . . . No, Jeff, I'm not going to tell anyone how much until you do, but you'll be doing it before the day is over. . . . Uh, huh . . . that much!"

Mike murmured some more reassuring words, ended the conversation, and hung up the phone.

"At least three hundred million dollars," he said. "More than enough, though only if you are a little crazy."

"Patently."

"Well, Blackie, you've got your case."

"Precisely . . . now how shall we play it? John Culhane at Area Six detectives or the State's Attorney?"

"John of course. You make the call. He owes you."

"Arguably."

I encountered no difficulty in getting through to the commander of Area Six detectives.

"Mike was certainly right about that terrible mess up in Forest Lane," he began. "I don't know how you do it. Probably saved that poor woman's life, from what I hear."

As I assumed, he had heard from his colleagues from Forest Lane about the call.

"Perhaps . . . am I correct in my expectation that you have in your possession either the originals or prime copies of the alleged letters from Peter Paul Cardin V to his wife?"

"Prime copies, sure."

"Have one of your own technicians look at the notes and tell you whether all of them are six hundred DPI. Believe me, they are not."

"So?"

"Then sort the notes by DPI. You will find that

none of those with six hundred DPI are threatening and all of those with three hundred DPI are threatening. Does that suggest anything to you?"

He considered. "Yeah, sure. One set are forgeries."

"Right. Then put your handwriting people on the signatures. They'll find that the signatures sort by DPI too."

I had no absolute proof of this fact, but I also had no doubt about it.

"All right, I'll do that. I can see his lawyers making a big deal out of it in a trial, but I'm not sure it will play before a jury that hates rich people, like all juries do."

I then relayed information about the Federal case. I did not tell him how much money was involved.

"How much?" he promptly asked.

"Enough."

"Uh-huh. State's Attorney won't like this."

"Obviously."

"We'll need more to go on."

"That more should be available soon. . . . Are you going to give the accused a lie detector test?"

"His guys are pushing for it. Our mutual friend over at the County Building is dragging his feet. We can do it anyway."

"Do it."

I then explained my theory.

John listened carefully. "You sure of that Fed stuff, Bishop?"

"Have one of your bosses call his boss and

suggest that if they don't confirm it they are obstructing justice."

"Yeah, that will be a pleasure."

"I hope to have more proof before the day is out."

"Your good friend the Mayor should hire you full-time."

"The Cardinal would never agree."

"We'll give Cardin the lie detector test. If he passes we won't arraign him. We'll have to let him out tomorrow morning. At the latest. Watch the brave prosecutor do an elaborate dance. Well, the Cardins are Republicans, aren't they?"

"So I am given to understand."

"OK, I'll see what goes down. Be back to you."

"Excellent. Then start looking for more evidence."

"I can tell by the sound of your voice, Bishop, that you know where to look."

"Arguably. I may be back to you with some hints."

"Fair enough."

I hung up and said to Mike the Cop, "John will love every bit of it. Clever detective work clears the innocent and convicts the guilty."

"If John were not such a smart cop, he'd never believe you," Mike observed. "It's wild. Wild enough to be true."

"Patently."

Then, like the true caring angel that she is, Annie observed that I probably needed a salami sandwich since lunchtime was drawing near and I had eaten only my usual meager breakfast.

I called heaven's blessings down on her.

The phone rang while I was disposing of the sandwich. Hard salami of course—the only kind.

"Casey. Yeah. Really. Isn't that amazing. Bad records both of them, huh? How did we know? We just did, that's all. Not sure you want to shake them yet? Wait till after the arraignment? Suit yourself, but I hear there may not be an arraignment. Yeah. Hey, you know better than to ask about my sources. Yeah, I know they're pretty damn good. I work only with the best. Yeah, be back to me."

"You know what they found out, I suppose, Cousin Blackie?"

Mike always calls me "Cousin Blackie" when he thinks I am lucky on a guess. I smiled smugly as I always do when a lucky long shot comes home.

"I had better call John Culhane again."

"Culhane."

"I have something more for you, John."

"I was expecting that. By the way, the lie detector test is going down in a half hour. Our mutual friend is already cautioning me not to rush to judgment."

I told him where to look for more evidence.

"You're sure of that?"

"John, would I be telling you that unless I were? As I said, Forest Lane has already checked them out."

"And don't want to move on it?"

"Right."

"Figures."

"Your colleagues can also check it out and then tell Forest Lane to start shaking them."

"It blows my mind."

"Ingenious to the point of being diabolical. But also clumsy. Clearly a mad scheme."

"A good morning's work," Mike observed, after I hung up. "That should tie it all together."

"Perhaps. . . . Might I therefore earn a second salami sandwich?"

"Arguably," Annie said as she began to cut the precious sausage. "It'll ruin your lunch, though."

"That is most improbable."

Rarely does something ruin my lunch. I defend myself for my morning and noon consumption of food on the grounds that I need the energy and that anyway I never put on weight.

I returned to the Cathedral. The snow had stopped and the temperature seemed to be rising. More slush and then frozen streets. Why did anyone live in middle-western America? Or more pointedly, why did they not build Chicago somewhere else?

Upon entering the rectory I encountered immediately Megan Anne who was waiting for me.

"Bishop Blackie," she began breathlessly.

"I did not know you were the Megan on duty today, Megan!"

"I'm totally NOT on duty. Megan Flower is. I'm here to talk to you about the *crime*."

"Indeed!"

"I know who did it, Bishop Blackie, it's so totally clear."

"Ah!"

"And you've got to get Mr. Cardin out of jail, he's like totally *innocent*, even if he's a little postal. He didn't beat up poor Ms. Cardin."

"And who did?"

She told me her suspicion. She was right.

"How do you know that?"

"I just like totally *know*. I mean the person is like totally a Monet, you know?"

"A Monet?"

"Yeah, like the French painter, you know?"

"Ah?"

"Looks good from a distance, but up close, you know, like fuzzy and mixed up and confused."

The quality of slang was obviously improving dramatically.

"Do you know these things often, Megan Anne?"

"Sometimes. I go like I'm kind of fey, you know?"

"Have you told anyone else?"

"Course not. I can keep a secret."

"Megan, if I promise you that Mr. Cardin will be out of jail by the end of the day tomorrow will you promise me that you won't mention this to anyone else."

"I totally won't. Like, it'd be dangerous for any of the other Cardins to let on they know. I'm not *totally stupid*, Bishop Blackie!"

"I would never suggest that you were, Megan Anne. But promise?"

"Cross my heart and hope to die," she said mechanically and crossed her heart several times.

"Fine. We can talk more about this in a day or two . . . I gather you were quite a consolation to Lisa and Pete."

"Huh? . . . Oh, yeah, I went over there and, like, made them, you know, laugh. I don't think the nurses wanted to let me in, but they did."

My solution did not appear on the nightly news. The law enforcement mechanism was grinding carefully and slowly. It was said, however, that the arraignment of Peter Paul Cardin had been "postponed" because "the investigation is continuing."

The State's Attorney cautioned the reporter that they should not rush to judgment. When asked whether the investigation was continuing because Mr. Cardin was a major contributor to the State's Attorney's last campaign, he lost his temper as he often did and said that everyone was innocent until proven guilty.

An irrelevancy it seemed to me, but he had proven before that he was coated in pure Teflon.

At least he had held up prosecution until there was more evidence.

One of my young associates came into the breakfast room where after Mass I was eating my usual modest breakfast of waffles, Raisin Bran with berries, orange juice, melon, raisin cinnamon toast, and Irish Breakfast tea.

"Commander Culhane for you, Boss." He handed me the phone. "Looks like another triumph for the bishop-detective!"

"Arguably."

"He'll walk at ten. The State's Attorney is agreeing to bail. But he won't even be arraigned. Clearly he didn't do it. We're keeping an eye on the guys you suggested. It's looking good there too. We don't want to move till Mrs. Cardin regains consciousness. She may be able to describe them for us."

"Fair enough."

I pushed the button disconnecting the phone. It rang. I pushed the button again.

"Father Ryan."

"It's Lisa, Bishop. My mom is better. They say she's only serious now. She's even regaining consciousness."

"Great, Lisa. I'll be over in a half hour or so."

I put down the phone and returned to my waffles.

Then, for the first time in this case, I used, as my mother would have said, the intelligence God gave me. I dropped the fork with the waffle, jumped from my chair, and headed for the dining-room door.

"Call Mick Casey," I told my astonished associate as I dashed out of the room, "and tell him to get over to Northwestern immediately."

If Janie truly regained consciousness and if it looked like the charges against Peter were being dropped, then her life would be in grave danger.

I thought about driving to the Cardin Pavilion as I raced down the steps to the door of the rectory.

Too slow in the morning rush. I would have to run, behavior that would shock those who erroneously believed that when Bishop Blackie was tempted to exercise he took a nap.

On the way out the door, I grabbed one of the portable phones we keep there just in case. As I stopped traffic on Wabash Avenue and sloshed through the melting snow and ice, I punched in a number on the phone. The person I hoped was already at the hospital was not there. I left a message on his voice mail.

"Joe Murphy, go immediately to Chantal Cardin's room."

I demanded that my friend Sophie stop traffic on Michigan Avenue, which she did without question.

"Go get 'em, Bishop," she yelled after me. It didn't matter to her who "'em" might be.

Breathing far too heavily for my episcopal dignity, I charged into an elevator at the hospital, ordered everyone else off it, and rose to the eighth floor.

Lisa was in the lounge across from the elevator bank with a paper coffee cup. Dear God, child, you shouldn't have left her alone.

"Where's your coat, Father Blackie? You'll catch cold! . . . Mom's looking great!" she called after me as I plunged by her, knocked over an innocent Pakistani resident, and hurtled into Chantal's room. The one who I was afraid might be there was indeed there.

So too, God bless him, was a handsome man with

white hair, a warm smile, and an incurably Irish face—Joseph Murphy, M.D., according to my sister Mary Kathleen Ryan Murphy the second-best psychiatrist in Cook County (herself of course being first).

"Good morning, Bishop," he said genially.

I collapsed into a chair.

"I may need an inhalator."

"Good morning, Bishop," Mike Casey entered the room. The North Wabash Avenue Irregulars were converging.

"Good morning, Bishop," Chantal Cardin said, opening her eyes. "So good of you to come."

While we celebrated the other person drifted out of the room. The drift would not go very far.

An hour later, Joe Murphy, Mike Casey, Lisa, and I were joined by Peter Cardin and young Pete.

"Chantal," her husband shouted happily and grabbed her hand.

She shrunk from him in fear and pulled her hand free. His remained on the bed, listless and rejected.

"He didn't write the letters," I yelled.

She looked at me, nodded, and extended her hand slowly toward her husband. Their fingertips touched. She eased her fingers over his.

Lisa, then Petey, hugged them both.

Family unity restored, albeit in a preliminary step.

An hour later, despite Dr. Melanie Jefferson's strenuous protest, Chantal gave the police artist a detailed description of her two assailants.

"I'm fine, Melanie dear," she said. "I'll feel even better when those evil men are in jail."

Commander John Culhane nodded as the faces emerged on the drawing paper.

"Exactly the ones you predicted, Bishop," he whispered.

In time for the five o'clock news, the Forest Lane police had arrested two grooms at Patrick Reynolds's stable whom they had been watching since yesterday. The scratches on their faces and arms showed how fierce Chantal's defense had been. In time for the ten o'clock news they had admitted that Patrick Reynolds had paid them ten thousand dollars each to kill his sister in the precise way he had prescribed.

He tried to escape to Canada, but being fundamentally inept, he was arrested two days later at International Falls, Minnesota, traditionally the coldest place in our republic.

CHAPTER 15

SEVERAL DAYS LATER I explained to the other members of the family the development of Pat Reynolds's brilliant, twisted, and demented scheme. We were sitting in the lounge outside the Northwestern trauma unit. Janie was with us, happy to be out of bed and able to walk. She was bright and cheerful, as would be a woman who had come partway back from hell and was confident she would come the rest of the way.

She had traded her hospital gown for an old-fashioned pink nightdress and matching robe. She was thin and pale, her face was back to its normal size but almost every inch of it was black and blue. The robe covered the dark marks on her arms from the IV tubes. Yet she had survived with all her limbs and all her fingers and toes and her mental and emotional abilities apparently intact, however damaged they might be. She was a violated woman but a resilient and lovely violated woman.

"The insight came from a letter written by a young maid of all work shortly after Rose Cardin's death in 1895. I became interested in that story because someone had anonymously sent copies of a 1967 article from *Chicago History* about the Cardin family curse to a number of Chicago people, including the Cardinal who, concerned about curses in which he does not believe, turned it over to me.

"The article asserted that suspicion had always leaned in the direction of her husband, Peter Paul Cardin I, but that the police were unable to explain how he could have committed the crime when scores of people had seen him elsewhere when the murder happened."

"I know the article," Peter Cardin said. "I don't believe in curses, but . . ."

"There may be a curse in too much obsession with money," I said. "That is much worse than the dying words of a sick and crazed Confederate officer."

"I believe that," he replied. "And I intend to end that curse now."

"It may have looked like a shrewd media ploy to distribute that article but it was excessive and unnecessary and potentially dangerous. In fact, as it turned out, very dangerous."

"He always liked the spectacular move," Janie said sadly. "The clever trick which won everyone's admiration."

"He played the derivatives game with the same flair of the spectacular," Peter Cardin agreed. "He bragged of his successes and hid his failures. He should have known they would catch him, but he thought he could outsmart them."

"They did and he didn't," I said, steering the conversation back to my story. "However, this young woman, who reported what was happening in a series of vivid letters to her sister back in Ireland, had other ideas."

"Can we read the letters?" young Pete asked.

"Yes indeed. All of them and soon. I hope you agree that they should be published."

"I'm sure we will." Peter Cardin gave his prompt approval. "It seems we owe this young woman a good deal."

"You do indeed. She had the ingenious idea that the murder of the wife was an indirect way of killing the husband. She and her young man, whom she subsequently married, set out to find the real killers. They did indeed find them in a dramatic confrontation about which you will read shortly. Your ancestor rewarded them both appropriately. But the story, while in this private journal as we may call it, never became public."

"How old was she?" Pete asked.

"About your age."

"Seriously! Do you have pictures of her?"

"Oh, yes. . . . Whoever sent the article around did not have access to the letters, so he presumed that the curse and its history would apply to a situation in which a husband killed his wife. But in fact someone else had killed the wife to implicate the husband in a murder charge that would lead to his hanging. The plot failed because the plotters were clumsy and stupid and drunk much of the

time. That alerted me to the possibility that someone was trying to do the same thing in the current
generation."

"It was me that Pat wanted to ruin?" Peter Cardin
asked incredulously. "Why?"

I was not quite ready to answer that question
because it interfered with the flow of the story.

"I was baffled by the fact you simply did not
seem to be the kind of man who would write those
letters. Moreover I noticed but only casually that
two different kinds of laser printers had been used.
That raised the possibility that there might be
someone else who was in fact forging the messages
to implicate you."

It had taken me a long time to think this out, but
there was no point in the present narrative in
blaming myself for my own tardiness. Rarely did
anyone believe how slow and inept I can be; it is
useless for me to try to argue this point.

"I did remember that Patrick Reynolds was an
active member of the Chicago Historical Society
where he had probably come across the article. It
ought to have been clear at the very beginning that
he was likely to be the one and the only one who
would benefit from your death, Jane. I suspected
that there was some arrangement in your father's
will which left money to you and then, upon your
death, to him. You told me during your recovery
here that your father had left most of the family
wealth to you, possibly because he had some
reservations about your brother's financial acumen.

While that wealth was not as great as that of the Cardins and not so extensively invested or, as it turned out, so heavily leveraged, it would have enabled him to continue to live the good life and play the financial game, even if he were dismissed from Cardin Holdings when Peter discovered the huge loss that resulted from Patrick's speculations in derivatives. Presumably Peter would not have revealed the losses to the public and in those particular adventures there was no violation of the laws."

"He certainly was hard-pressed on all sides." Peter Cardin nodded. "I should have watched him more closely."

"You were too busy expanding the holdings to notice a couple of hundred million dollars," Chantal added.

It was not a hostile comment, but a statement of fact. Chantal was recovering rapidly and had assumed once more her cool and aloof demeanor. She and her husband were more distant than in the earlier days of her recovery, but not antagonistic.

"The holdings are taking a beating now as the vultures swarm around," he said sadly. "Probably a good thing for all of us. Jack seems to be protecting most of them."

"With dignity and grace," his wife agreed. "And not a little flair."

"Yes," Peter Cardin said. "It turns out he likes the game."

"But to kill his own sister . . ." Lisa, striving to be a bridge between her parents, exclaimed.

"He always resented me, dear. I was the favorite, the bright one, the tough one. Besides not everything those men did to me was his idea."

Of that I was not so sure.

"It seemed obvious," I continued, "that if he were behind the attempt on your life, he must have felt he desperately needed money. Hence I asked about possible Federal investigation of his investment behavior, which the Feds would have kept to themselves if they could have gotten away with it since they wanted even more evidence against him on other matters. When it turned out that he was in deep, deep trouble, the finger of suspicion pointed at him. Like the killers a century ago, he had good reason to want to be rid of you, Janie, and, as he saw it, better reason to want to be rid of you at the same time, Peter. He knew that if the Feds came to you, you would cooperate in their investigation because of your renowned integrity. He was patently guilty of forgery as they had expected. He thought he had time to destroy your credibility and thus destroy their case."

"Why did he forge those crazy notes from me?"

"He's an opportunist, as you well know from working with him. He saw your mother attacking your marriage . . ."

"With my help," Lisa said sadly.

"That's finished, child." Her mother reached for Lisa's hand and held it tightly.

Pete put his arms around his sister. "Totally."

"He saw you in a paroxysm of jealous rage

sending foolish notes to your wife . . . about school grades and such trivial things."

"I was out of my mind," Peter said, bowing his head.

"Arguably."

"Neither of us cherished her enough, Daddy," Lisa said.

"I know that now."

"Well," said Petey. "Now's a good time to start. Mom is special."

"Fersure," his sister agreed.

"He thought he saw a wonderful opportunity to get rid of the two of you. Not only would his sister die, but his brother-in-law would be accused of her murder and perhaps convicted. He assumed that Janie would save the notes and that the police would find them after her death. He obtained some of your stationery, produced the notes, and forged your name, which he had been doing in the office for a long time. A servant slipped them under Chantal's door just as you had slipped your own foolish communications."

"I'm sorry," he murmured.

"We know you are, Daddy."

Chantal remained silent, but she watched her husband intently. Was she calculating the changes for the future or remembering the moments of tender and respectful passion? Or both.

"The threats and the death had to be gruesome to establish that you were a raving madman as well as a jealous husband. In my two encounters with you,

you certainly were not the former. I concluded that you were the primary target, especially when I had established that the notes came from different laser jet printers, and reasoned that Janie was to be the victim basically so that you could be destroyed."

"I'll be fine, Bishop Blackie. As good as new."

"I'm sure you will be. Arguably better. . . . Patrick is an ingenious and resourceful man, as well as a criminally insane psychopath, but, as we now know from the revelation about his mishandling of the derivative financial instruments, careless and even sloppy. Eventually the police or defense technicians would have looked at the notes and discovered that while the typefaces were the same, the DPI were different and one set of signatures had been forged. You would have been cleared. Then they would have looked for someone else as the possible killer. Subconsciously I had noted the DPI difference the first time I looked at the notes, but I missed the implications of forgery."

"You thought I was capable of those threats?" Peter turned to his wife.

"I would never have thought you would suspect me of infidelity." She shrugged. "Once you were so crazy as to believe that, I felt that you were capable of anything."

"I'm sorry."

"I know that."

A hint of forgiveness? More likely a hint of its possibility.

"The two grooms?" young Pete asked.

"A lucky guess on my part which your mother's subsequent description of them made unnecessary. I knew your uncle had a stable with his own racing horses. I assumed that there were men watching the stable and the horses. I knew that in the profession there were some men of dubious background who might do anything for a bit of extra cash."

"Astonishing, Bishop," Petey said enthusiastically. "You make it sound so simple."

That's what they all say.

"Basically it was indeed simple. Elementary as another and better detective would have said. Once all these matters were clear it was merely a matter of getting the proper evidence in the hands of the proper police officials and the rest was easy."

"Mike Casey and John Culhane," Peter Cardin said. "Good men."

"Oh, yes," I agreed. "Anyway, to continue, Patrick got the idea to send that last note to Janie from the conversation about her conditions for reconciliation.

"You see, your move into the city, Janie, had knocked his plans out of kilter. It would be hard to dispose of you in a way that would fit with the threats as long as you were in your co-op. He might have spotted a car around the corner and thought that you had guards, which in fact you did. He played on your desire for a reconciliation."

"Crazy bastard," said Lisa. She then blushed, furiously.

Young Pete smiled at his sister. "Crazy but clever in a sick sort of way."

"An ingenious improviser and manipulator," I commented, "so caught, however, in his own creativity that he could see only the details and not the big picture. Maybe that's the nature of his kind of madness."

"Do you still want a reconciliation, Mom?" Petey asked, perhaps the only one in the whole family who could get away with it.

Janie pursed her lips thoughtfully and then nodded briefly.

"Sure."

"Hooray," his sister added.

Peter Cardin said nothing. However, his face, still gaunt from the strains of recent times, flushed.

"And, Bishop Blackie, you thought that Uncle Pat was going to kill Mom that morning you came rushing into the room?" Lisa asked.

"He was an opportunist, as I have said. When you left, Lisa, to obtain a cup of coffee, he had approached the life support mechanisms just as the good Dr. Murphy entered the room. He backed off."

"You saved my life, Bishop Blackie. Twice."

"Arguably."

"I will use it well."

"Of that I have no doubt."

"That's an incredible analysis, Bishop," Peter Cardin said. "Just amazing."

"Arguably. However, I should tell you that the day last week when I had finished tying it all together, I returned to the Cathedral Rectory to discover that our mutual friend, Megan Anne, had arrived at the same solution by methods of her own and without any of my clues or my sources of information. I swore her to secrecy, and she kept her promise."

"She is like totally neat," Lisa said. "Totally."

"I'd like to get to know her better," Janie said.

"No easy task that," her son said, shaking his head. "She's transparent and opaque at the same time."

"That's what makes a woman attractive," his father observed.

His wife colored faintly.

Well, he would get another chance all right. He'd better not blow it.

I reflected that I had already discovered the truth only a couple of days before Janie's description of her assailants had solved the mystery. However, if I had not resolved the puzzle when I did, Jane might not have lived to identify them.

There is not much else to tell. Six months after the event Patrick Reynolds is still engaged in plea bargain negotiations with both the Feds and the locals. Lisa Cardin has left the Pines and enrolled at St. Ignatius. Jane Frances de Chantal Reynolds Cardin is the director of the new Cardin Foundation to which large sums of money from the holdings are being dedicated. Peter Paul Cardin V has turned the holdings over to his brother John Mark so that he can devote more time to his family and to public service. He is the chairman of the board of the new foundation. "I'm being obsessive about not being obsessive," he tells me with a laugh. Regina Countess Cardin has been in Paris and London and Milan for a prolonged shopping expedition. The Corpus people have vanished from the field of battle. It does not follow that they will not, like the proverbial bad penny, return.

Peter Paul Cardin VI and Megan Anne date occasionally but not intensively. As she says, "Like, Bishop, I go Cleveland, Ohio, is a long way off and I'm, you know, a senior. But he is taking me to my senior prom. Isn't that neat?"

"Righteous," I say.

Peter Cardin and his wife are not fully reconciled. He moved into an apartment and left her in charge of both homes. She sold the house in Forest Lane and moved into the Gold Coast co-op. She and Peter are not, however, antagonistic. She certainly is not pressing for divorce. They work together, amicably enough one gathers, in the Cardin Foundation offices. Both are in touch with appropriate sources of psychological and spiritual help. They have lunch together frequently and apparently are "dating" one another. It has been reported to me that they have spent time together at their condo in Florida. To judge by their complacent smiles when they show up at the Cathedral for weekday morning Mass, they on occasion sleep together. On those mornings she is more beautiful than ever.

In fact, she asked me for "permission" to sleep

with her husband while not yet moving back in with him. She wanted, in fact, not permission but to make a progress report to me. "I'm not sure yet that we're ready to live with one another. But, in the same office and all, erotic tension does become distracting, especially when you have slept with a man before."

If it were not for erotic attraction, most reconciliations would flounder. I assured her that it was none of the Church's business nor mine how she plotted her strategies. She found that remark hilarious.

"She absolutely adores you, Blackie," the good Ridley Becker tells me.

"Arguably," I reply with a sigh as I silently thank Herself for canceling out my stupidity.

Finally, Sister Flynn is working on an annotated edition (with pictures) of *Clare: Prairie Avenue Letters of an Irish Maid of All Work.* I have finished my introduction to the work.

I have a copy of the photo of Clare Raftery O'Boyle and her firstborn on the wall of my study, between the medieval Madonna and the posters of the three Johns of my youth—Pope, President, and quarterback of the (then) Baltimore Colts.

Perhaps because she is a good friend. Perhaps to remind me of the ever-present male obligation to listen more closely to what a woman is saying.

Perhaps both.